Following Ophelia

SOPHIA BENNETT

Stripes

In an Artist's Studio

One face looks out from all his canvasses,
One selfsame figure sits or walks or leans;
We found her hidden just behind those screens,
That mirror gave back all her loveliness.
A queen in opal or in ruby dress,
A nameless girl in freshest summer greens,
A saint, an angel; – every canvass means
The same one meaning, neither more nor less.
He feeds upon her face by day and night,
And she with true kind eyes looks back on him
Fair as the moon and joyful as the light;
Not wan with waiting, not with sorrow dim;
Not as she is, but was when hope shone bright;
Not as she is, but as she fills his dream.

Christina Rossetti
1856

PART I

THE PEACOCK DRESS

Chapter One

An uncommonly dangerous young woman. She has to go.

The words echoed around Mary Adams's head to the rhythm of the paddle steamer that bore her down the River Thames.

She has to go. She has to go. She has to go.

Standing on deck, Mary drew the ribbons of her bonnet more tightly under her chin and hugged her crimson wool shawl around her shoulders. Even so, the winter wind whipped her face and stray tendrils of long copper hair caught in her eyes. Ahead, the shapes of buildings, tall and ominous, loomed out of the mist. The *Queen of the Thames* was getting closer to London now, leaving everything Mary had ever known in its churning wake.

It wasn't supposed to be like this.

It's the girl, I tell you. No good will come of her.

Thrown out of the job she loved. Beaten by her pa in a drunken rage. Sent to work as a drudge for a family she'd never met. She didn't know when she'd see home again.

Mary glanced around the deck. There were hardly any passengers outside, and the few willing to brave the cold were huddled at the stern of the boat.

Checking that nobody was watching, she leaned over the rail as far as she could stretch, until she could see only the dark, endless waters beneath her. The wind whipped the waves into pounding jets that stung her skin. Under the crest of each wave the water was a thousand shades of green and grey. The colour of her own eyes. Mary thought of the darkness waiting to claim her. How easy it would be to lean further … further … and be gone from this world forever: a mermaid, a skeleton, a ghost.

She breathed in sharply. Gasping, she felt her lungs contract with the shock of the ice-cold air.

Yes! Her skin tingled. Mary laughed at the freezing water. *This is how to feel alive.*

Wet hair clung to her face and rivulets of water ran inside her shawl, down her neck, and into her blue-green bodice. She caught sight of the ringlets trailing untidily from under her bonnet, turned a river of ruddy clay by the spray. Half-closing her eyes against the bitter wind, she peered at the unknown city emerging from the fog.

"Watch me, Pa! Watch me!" she shouted, throwing out her arms and leaning into the spray.

She was terrified – of the city, the new life, the work and all those strangers. But fear was part of what made Mary cling to life so tightly. And life was ice-cold today, and bitter, and strong as the iron rail. It was sharp on her tongue and stinging in her eyes. It made the blood throb in her veins.

"Look out, miss!"

A voice pierced through the wind behind her. Then came the sound of running feet and a strong hand on her elbow. She looked round to see the anxious face of a young man as he pulled her back from the rail. His coal black eyes met hers.

"You awright?"

Mary shook her arm free of his grip and tried to seem dignified.

"Of course I am … sir." It seemed odd to address this slight young person so formally, but she didn't know what else to say. Back in Westbrook, she knew everyone by name.

"It's just … over the rail. You looked…"

"I'm perfectly well, thank you."

His face clouded. "But the waters…" He glanced down, embarrassed. "You gave me a fright."

"I'm sorry if I startled you," Mary said, lifting her chin. "I was merely admiring the view. I'm quite safe, thank you." She tried to sound like Miss Elsie Helpman, the teacher at the village school who was always a picture of ladylike composure, and not like a sixteen-year-old girl, cold and wet, leaving home for the first time and forever.

The young man raised his eyes again, and they travelled from her face to her blue-green skirts and back again. Mary noticed with a spark of amusement how long his gaze rested on her very pale skin with its dusting of light freckles, seeming to take in every detail.

"Well then. If you're safe, I'll take my leave. Sorry to have troubled you."

She stood still as a ship's figurehead, whipped by the wind in her bonnet ribbons, while he backed away, never taking his eyes from hers.

"Mary Adams," she said to herself with a smile,

"I do believe that if this were Westbrook, you might have found yourself a beau."

She thought of Mrs Foster, the bitter crone who had called her dangerous and wanted rid of her, and laughed again. *I'm going. And never coming back.*

By now the city – the biggest in the world – was very near. Tall chimneys spewed smoke into the leaden sky. The fog had a sulphurous tinge and there was an acrid smell in the air. Fresh from the country, with its green and brown and earthiness, Mary's senses were overloaded with this strange new world. It was much as she had heard hell described from the pulpit at St Michael's every Sunday.

The steamer moved relentlessly towards the heart of it.

Chapter Two

At the pier, a tall girl in a black woollen dress waited patiently for the passengers to disembark. Anyone watching might have been surprised to see this calm and sober creature greet the vibrant and rather wild one with such joy and tenderness. But looking closely, they might have noticed the same rosiness in the cheeks illuminating the girls' freckled skin, and the same copper note in their hair, although one had hers tucked neatly in a coil under her bonnet while the other let hers fly free.

"Harriet!" Mary said, hugging her cousin to her. "Two years and look at you! You're a lady now."

"I'm no such thing," the tall girl scolded with a smile. "I'm a servant and so are you – and don't you forget it."

"As if I could," Mary groaned. "Yes, ma'am, no, ma'am. I've been practising."

"Try to say it without looking *quite* so disgusted. They're not so bad as you think. And the house will be warm, with food on the table and…"

Her cousin trailed off, but Mary could tell from the troubled, tender look that flitted across her face what she was thinking. *And no Pa to beat you.* Well, that was true. But would living in another man's house be any better? A stranger's house indeed? She would have to keep her wits about her.

Mary didn't want to think about that now. "Talking of food on the table," she said, "I'm starving. Shall we eat? I have some pennies saved. That man is selling cockles, look. Shall we get some?"

"No indeed," Harriet said sharply. "I have only the morning free, and that was a special dispensation to come and fetch you. We must hurry to the Aitkens' or I'll be late."

Trust Harriet: the older cousin and always the sensible one. She was the girl who had helped Mary with her letters in the schoolhouse and told her off for scrumping apples with the boys at harvest time.

"If you say so," Mary sighed.

"Wait here while I find us a ride."

"Can't we walk? My trunk isn't heavy."

'Trunk' was a rather grand word for the wicker basket at Mary's feet. It was made to carry picnics, really. Beautifully made, by her father. Pa was good with his hands in many ways – some more beneficial than others.

Harriet looked at the basket doubtfully. "Is that all you have?"

Mary nodded. It contained everything she possessed that was worth carrying: two night shifts; her spare dress, tightly folded; petticoats and underclothes; her sewing box; some ribbons for her hair; bible, soap, pumice stone; and Little Miss Mouse, all raggedy and chewed, whom Mary would never leave. She picked up the basket, ready to walk to her new place of employment, wherever it might be.

Harriet laughed. "Put that back down. If you try and carry it to where we're going, we'll be walking till nightfall."

"What do you mean?"

"London's not like Westbrook. It's fifty villages all together. More, even. Only a carriage will do for our journey."

Mary blushed, feeling like a country bumpkin.

While she waited for Harriet to negotiate a ride, she cheered herself up by defiantly spending a penny on two folds of cockles. They were fresh and salty and delicious. She and Harriet ate them as they travelled, sitting on empty beer barrels on a dray heading west from the docks. The horses looked heavy and slow, but with a light load they could trot along at quite a pace when traffic allowed.

Traffic. Mary had never seen so many horses, carriages and people. All criss-crossing the roads in the most dangerous manner. London was *full* of people. And noise. Grinding wheels, clopping hooves and ceaseless shouting. Everywhere she looked, there was someone leaning out of a window, rushing out of a doorway, leaping out of a carriage or running to catch up with one. Harriet, in her letters home, had made London sound like a smoky, dangerous place, but she had never said it was so *busy*. Every street contained a building site. Ancient, tumbledown inns jostled for space with stone counting houses. Carts were piled high with goods from the docks. Mary felt their vibrations run through her as they rattled by with inches to spare.

Beside her, Harriet finished her cockles and chattered on about Mary's new life.

"You'll like the streets of Pimlico, they're very smart and new. The Aitkens are a good family – not so rich as my Harringtons, but respectable. Professor Aitken is Mr Harrington's great friend from Oxford. All the gentlemen in London have been to college. The professor teaches at London University. It's not as prestigious as Oxford, Mr Harrington says, but it will do. Your mistress is about five and thirty, I would guess. She is younger than Mrs Harrington, but not as pretty…"

Mary knew she should be paying attention. After all, the professor and his wife were as close as she had to a family now. But she was distracted by Harriet herself. There was something odd about her cousin today. She had always sounded homesick in her letters, but the more she talked, the more Mary noticed a certain flush in her cheek and a sparkle in her eye.

"London suits you," she said, causing Harriet to blush even deeper. "Tell me, what's its secret?"

"It's, um … nothing. London is exactly as I described. Can you not see?" They clung to each other as the dray bumped sharply over a pothole in the road. "It's grimy and much too big. My skin's always black with coal dust. Mrs Harrington must have a fire in every grate…"

She prattled on again and Mary was left to wonder what she was hiding under the talk of dirt and grime.

Eventually the streets became quieter, with space for trees in elegant garden squares. The dray dropped the girls on a wide road lined with shops. From here they would walk, but it was not so far, Harriet said. Mary didn't mind, in spite of the mud from recent rain. At every corner there was something to see: a builder's yard; a shop window filled with jars of enticing sweets; another with leather-bound books, and – was there? – yes! – another with bright-coloured satin ribbons.

Mary loved shops as much as any sixteen-year-old, and knew more about them than many a country girl. For a moment, she was nostalgic. In the little Kent village of Westbrook where she'd lived all her life, she had been lucky enough to work in the smart haberdashery shop, owned by kindly Mr Foster. It was the talk of all the local villages. Mary had encountered Mr Foster at school, where he came sometimes to teach drawing: the only lesson that wasn't a physical agony to sit through. He had noticed something in her. What? Her hair?

Her face? Her talent with a pencil or a needle? Her dresses were always prettier and finer than her friends' clothes, she reflected, because she worked on them long into the night, until the guttering candle had finally burned itself out. No matter what he'd seen in Mary, what mattered was that as soon as she was released from the clutches of the village school, Mr Foster had invited her to come and work for him.

While her cousin slaved away in London, Mary had loved nothing more than to be surrounded by satin ribbons and cotton lace, bolts of thick tweed from Scotland and colourful chintz from India. Ladies came from miles around to choose fabric for their frocks and trimmings for their hats. Gentlemen, too, Mary found, who stood around admiring the stock and smiling, and would buy a yard of green ribbon for no reason at all. Until Mr Foster's God-fearing mother had come to stay, clad in black from head to toe. Her husband dead, her cottage sold, Mrs Foster inhabited the shop and the rooms above it like a brooding Cochin hen. If anyone smiled at her, she scowled. And God forbid anyone should smile at Mary. Especially any young gentleman buying ribbon. *Especially* if he happened to be the son of the squire and happened to remark on how well the green satin would sit in Mary's flame-red hair.

That hair. It had been the bane of her life. All through her childhood, she had been 'Coppernob' and 'Carrot Top'. Her mother and siblings had the same affliction. Some people said they were changelings, others that it was a sign of sorcery. But since coming home from university, the squire's son had started to see it differently, it seemed.

She has to go. She has to go.

And so Mr Foster, who was forty-one years old, did exactly as his mother told him. Mary was sent home that very day in disgrace. She still remembered the look of thunder on Pa's face when he came home that night after hearing the news.

She remembered, too, the look Mr Foster gave her as he presented her with a pretty sewing box as a parting gift. Thinking now of the heartfelt pain in his eyes as he had said goodbye made Mary suddenly wonder whether it was only the gentlemen callers his mother had worried about.

She shook herself out of her reverie as Harriet announced, "Well, here we are. St George's Square."

Stepping quickly across the road to avoid a hackney carriage, they approached a row of tall white houses with swags above the windows, and steps and pillars leading up to the smart front doors. "Mind your skirts on that puddle, Mary. Why you wore your best dress to travel in, I shall never understand. Maids are *understated* girls, you know."

Mary considered this comment as she hooked up the rich peacock blue sateen of the skirt she had recently finished making. *Understated.*

It is not a word I recognize, she thought. *If anything, I want to be overstated.* She laughed aloud at the idea, shaking her head so her curls swung about her shoulders, causing Harriet to frown in concern.

"And that's another thing. Your hair. You must wear it up. In a cap, to keep it out of the way. I'm sure they'll give you one."

She was peering at Mary in an odd way, pursing her lips and frowning.

Is she jealous of me? Mary wondered in surprise. *And a little afraid? Of her country cousin, who knows nothing at all?*

She laughed again, nervous and excited, and held out

her hand to her cousin. "Of course, Hattie. Lead me onwards. I begin to wonder if I shall like it here."

Chapter Three

The house where Harriet stopped looked to Mary like a wedding cake with a black front door. It was several storeys tall and sugar-white, like its neighbours, though the London soot was already starting to cling to the edges, sharpening them with thin black lines.

A smart flight of steps led up to a black-and-white tiled threshold, where the front door boasted a gleaming gold knocker in the shape of a lion's head. It was framed by a portico, above which four floors of shining windows seemed to stretch towards the sky.

"Is this really the place?" Mary asked, looking up and up. It was even taller than the manor house at home. And every other house on the square was like it.

Harriet laughed. "Does it seem so unusual? For Pimlico, it's quite ordinary. Wait till you see where the Harringtons live."

Ignoring the front entrance, she turned right and led the way down some steep concrete steps to a smaller tradesman's door in the dingy basement, where a scrap of a girl with sallow skin and dull brown eyes answered her knock.

"Yes?" the girl said cautiously.

"I have brought Mary Adams, the new maid," Harriet announced, with the calm, slightly superior confidence of someone who worked for a better family.

The girl peered past Harriet in silence, taking in Mary's vivid blue-green skirts, trailing bonnet ribbons and unkempt hair. Mary stared back at the girl's ill-fitting black dress and dirty apron, and the old-fashioned mob cap on her head.

Is this how I must look, too, now? she wondered. *Like a half-starved waif?* But she squared her shoulders and smiled.

"How d'you do? I'm Mary."

The girl kept staring. "Annie," she muttered in a low voice. "You'd better come in."

She led them through a short corridor into a kitchen that was dark, plain and immaculately clean. Its simple furniture reminded Mary a little of the cottage in

Westbrook. But at home there was always the sound of chickens in the yard, cats and dogs to pet, and the smell of Ma's baking. Here there was only a ticking clock and the acrid smell of coal. Mary bit her lip and told herself not to be homesick. There was nothing for her there. She kept her smile plastered on and tried not to cling to Harriet too tightly when her cousin hugged her goodbye.

"I'll see you soon. We're lucky to be so close."

"Yes." *Lucky*. Mary tried to believe it.

❧⟡❧

There was silence in the kitchen for a moment, except for the ticking clock. *This is it*, Mary thought. *My new life. My new world.* Annie, the maid, stared at her intensely. Then she put her red hands on her bony hips and laughed.

"Will you just take a look? In her satin dress with her slattern hair. Why, she looks like an actress or worse!"

The lilting Irish accent reminded Mary of the labourers who came to Kent to mend the roads or pick fruit in the summer. The voice was soft but the words felt like a slap. Mary took a breath and tried not to let the other girl get the better of her.

"It's not satin, it's *sateen*," she retorted, smoothing out the lustrous cotton of her skirts. It wasn't silk or anything 'fancy' but it was as good as she could afford at the shop. And why shouldn't a girl make the most of herself?

"Oh, I see. *Sateen*. *Sateen*, she says. Well, that's all right, then. And will you be happy to kneel on this floor and polish it to a shine in your fine *sateen*?"

Mary reluctantly admitted that she wouldn't be.

At that moment, the kitchen calm was shattered by the sudden clamour of a brass bell. Annie glanced at a rack of them above the inner door and set off at a run. Unsure what to do, Mary followed her.

She ran up two flights of narrow back stairs, which led to the main living quarters of the house. Here, ceilings were high and the floor was thickly carpeted. Without glancing back, Annie went through an open door at the far end of a light-filled landing. Mary hovered a few feet from the doorway, taking in the large room beyond.

She had never seen anything quite like it. The light was muted by heavy red swagged curtains at the windows. Chairs were padded and stuffed, walls were painted indigo blue and patchworked with drawings in narrow black frames. Between the windows, giant plants in pots made it seem as if the jungle had come to Pimlico. Mary marvelled at the multitude of china ornaments and little silver boxes on every surface, of rugs and embroidered cushions. She wondered nervously who did all the dusting.

In the middle of the room stood a short, plump woman, her hand hovering near the bell pull. This must be Eliza Aitken, her new mistress. She looked padded and stuffed, too, in a high-necked silk dress the colour of mushrooms, with red velvet trimmings and a deep white lace collar. The colours worked oddly together, Mary thought. She tried not to look at it.

"Annie, I need you to get my— Who's that behind you?"

The maid whipped round and scowled to see Mary standing there.

"The scullery maid, ma'am. I'm sorry – she's just arrived."

"The new girl? I must see her. Bring her in."

Mary stepped slowly forwards while the mistress gawped at her like a curiosity. Pale grey eyes examined her from a round face framed by two loops of neatly plaited light brown hair. *My hair would never consent to sit in such a style*, Mary thought. She dropped a deep curtsey and decided to break the silence. "Good morning, ma'am. I'm Mary."

She had dared to hope for a welcoming smile. According to Harriet, the family were desperate for a new maid. But instead, the mistress narrowed her eyes. "Mmmm," she said, through pursed lips. "In this house servants speak when spoken to."

There was another silence.

"Yes, ma'am," Mary muttered.

Mrs Aitken sighed. "Your cousin spoke highly of you to my friend, Mrs Harrington, but I wonder. You'll need to change out of those extraordinary clothes. I don't know what they wear in Kent. Our servants are plain, honest girls."

"Yes, ma'am," Mary said, bobbing again to be on the safe side. How often should a girl bob? She didn't know. She could almost feel Annie sniggering behind her.

"We certainly need another pair of hands. Annie's rushed off her feet, what with the children and my husband..." Mrs Aitken flourished her wrist vaguely, as if to suggest an exhausting, difficult family.

"He's an academic, you know. A professor of Classics at the university. You know what a university is?"

"Yes, ma'am." What kind of country animal did Mrs Aitken think she was? A goose? She happened to know the squire's son had gone to Trinity College, Oxford. And the rector had been to Cambridge.

"Well … good. The professor is a very serious gentleman. Strict, but fair. You will do well with him as long as you do exactly as you're told. You're never to interrupt him when he is working in his study, or interfere with his work or his papers, do you understand?"

"Yes, ma'am."

"Don't even tidy there without his express permission. Don't annoy him with minor household matters. If anything arises, come to me."

"Yes, ma'am."

"Good … well … that is all. I'm feeling rather tired. Annie, bring me my shawl and my lemon drink. And my sewing basket. Alice has a party tomorrow and I must fashion a fairy costume out of something."

"I could help," Mary offered. She felt encouraged for the first time since arriving here. She could think of nothing nicer than to spend an hour or so working with netting and wire. However, at the sight of Mrs Aitken's stony gaze, she faltered. "I-if you wanted. I like to sew."

Eliza's lips formed a thin, tight line. "I am quite capable of making my daughter's costume. I'm sure you will be busy enough with your duties."

Flushing, Mary bobbed a last, quick curtsey and left the room. Annie followed and threw her a look of quiet triumph on the landing.

"Wait here while I get the sewing basket. Then it's time to change out of those fancy skirts," she whispered nastily. "You'll be working hard today. *Sewing!* Ha!"

Chapter Four

Once Mary had collected her trunk from the basement Annie led her up to a room at the very top of the house. This was the bedroom they would share – her home for the next few years.

"Are ye pleased with your grand hotel?" the Irish girl asked, in her mocking voice.

Mary took it in slowly. The room was long and narrow, tucked inside the eaves, with whitewashed walls and pine boards on the floor. There were two beds, not far apart, a chair, a painted pine chest and a washstand. The ceiling sloped so sharply that the girls could only stand upright on one side. That was Annie's domain. Mary's was the lower one, under a little skylight that looked out on to dark tiled roofs, an army of chimney pots and a dove grey sky. There was no green at all in the view, Mary realized – only shades of grey.

"Well…" Annie prompted.

Mary nodded. It was dry at least – and warm. But she didn't know yet if she loved or hated it. She hardly knew what to think at all.

Annie opened the painted chest and rummaged around. She emerged with a pile of dark fabric that turned out to be the bodice and skirt of a much-worn black wool dress.

"This'll be yours for now. We mustn't dirty the fine *sateen*."

"I have a black dress," Mary said quickly, opening her trunk and retrieving it. Harriet had told her to bring one. Annie frowned as Mary held up the skirt. "Look at the braid, that will never do. Wear this one." Mary stared in horror. She had sat up for hours sewing on those yards of braid. The dress Annie was holding was in even worse conditon than the raggedy scrap she was wearing. The black material was fading to brown and it was frayed along most of its seams.

"It was. In my younger days. Now hurry. We've a lot to be getting on with."

As she changed out of her lovely skirt and bodice, Mary felt as if she was taking off the last of her old self.

She felt lost and unmoored – a ship drifting out to sea. She adjusted her chemise to hide the worst of the bruises from the beating Pa had given her. The new self then had to scrimp and squeeze to get into the thin, shabby clothes. She could only just hook the bodice to the skirt by breathing in tightly. Looking down, her heart sank – the hem ended several inches above the floor. Shame flooded through her. She hadn't worn short skirts since she was a little girl.

"Is… Isn't there anything else?" she asked.

Annie rolled her eyes. "Oh yes, we've a whole fine wardrobe. Just ask for my ermine cloak, why don't you?"

"What about … one of the other maids?"

"Listen to the girl!" Annie said, with a high, forced laugh. "She thinks she's come to Buckingham Palace, so she does!"

Mary felt tears forming and willed them away. She would not cry. Harriet's letters had mentioned several servants where she worked. The one thing she had been looking forward to was the company of the servants' hall. It took a moment to find her voice and breathe so it wouldn't wobble. "So it's just you and me?"

Annie tipped her head to one side. "If you count Mrs

Green there's three of us, but she sleeps downstairs near the silver. She won't be lending you her wardrobe. Ha!" And off she went again, laughing until she wheezed.

"Who's Mrs Green?"

"The cook. She's after finding a new butcher. The old one was serving rancid meat." Mary's stomach turned. "But when she comes back, you're not to speak until spoken to, understand? A girl like you must know her place." Annie's pinched, pale face was lit up with a strange sort of challenging look.

A girl like me? Mary wondered. What kind of girl did she mean?

"D'you understand?" Annie asked sharply.

Mary nodded.

"You say 'yes'. 'Yes, Annie.' Say it."

Mary swallowed. "Yes, Annie."

"That's better. Now, put on this cap and apron, and follow me."

When Mrs Green came bustling into the kitchen half an hour later, Mary knew better than to greet her. She waited until spoken to and Annie watched her sharply to make sure she did.

But the cook was not made of the same stuff as the housemaid. Mrs Green had a broad, friendly face, hands shiny with work, dark blue woollen skirts under a big white apron and a look of kindly wisdom about her. She was from a village not twenty miles from Westbrook, though Mary had never been there. But she had lived in London most of her life and welcomed Mary to the city as if she owned it.

"Work hard and you'll be happy here. A girl can do anything in London if she works enough for it. Isn't that true, Annie?"

Annie didn't reply. She was busy listing Mary's new duties around the house.

"You'll start at dawn with the grates. Then get the kitchen fire going. Then do the slops for everyone in the household. Wake Cook with a cup of tea. Then clean the kitchen floor…"

The list went on and on. Mary would be responsible for cleaning and polishing everything in the house, it seemed, as well as helping to prepare the food and serve it, and a myriad of other tasks. The wedding-cake house was huge! Lovely, if you were to live in it at your leisure.

Not so if it was your responsibility to swab down every floor twice daily. Mary struggled to hide her dismay. Annie smiled at her with grim satisfaction.

"You'll have to learn fast, as I did. I'll be much too busy to help you out, you know. I have my own duties – dressing the mistress and the children, and fetching and carrying. Show me your hands."

Reluctantly Mary held them out. Once they had been rough but after a year of working in the shop she was proud of her soft skin and neat nails. Annie took them in her bony fingers and laughed.

"We'll have those red-raw soon enough. When I first started, mine bled every day."

Mary blinked away the new tears that formed before Annie could see them.

What have you let me in for, Harriet?

⁓

Having been so closely examined at first, Mary quickly came to feel almost invisible. Cook kept herself to the kitchen, which was sweet-smelling and welcoming, and Annie seemed to enjoy helping her in its steamy warmth. But Mary's tasks kept her upstairs when they were down, or outside when they were in. Even downstairs, washing and scrubbing, she was relegated to the dark, airless scullery, whose cold, dripping tap provided her only companionship.

She was not introduced to the children but merely caught sight of them going up to their nursery after sharing lessons with the children next door. They were a girl and a boy, Alice and Henry. She saw them through the half-open door to the parlour, where she was busy lighting the fire. Her first impression was of petticoats and ringlets, red cheeks and stained white trousers. These worried her a little, as Annie had made it plain that she would be the one to wash them. The children, if they saw her, made no sign of it. She wondered whether they would notice the difference between her and the last scullery maid. One smut-faced girl, covered in coal dust and silently working, must look very like the next.

It was the same when the master arrived home from work. Mary only met him at all because he needed his coat brushed and Annie was busy with the children. As Mary went to find him in the hall, her heart was pounding. If he was anything like her father, she had much to be afraid of. She stopped at the top of the back stairs when she saw him. He gave the impression of a wall: tall, dark, wide and made somehow thicker still by an impressive beard. It took him a while to see her and when he did, he merely beckoned her forwards to hand her the coat.

"Thank you, sir," she said, bobbing.

Only then did he look long enough to notice her face at all.

"Ah. You're the new girl."

"Yes, sir. Mary, sir."

"Good, good." With that, he strode upstairs and left her.

Strangely though, she breathed a little easier after he passed. She still felt almost invisible, but safer. She knew the lurking menace in a man who meant you harm. There was none of that in Philip Aitken. Stern, possibly, and somewhat godlike in his bearded magnificence. But not unkind. It made Annie's next scolding easier to bear.

<hr />

Annie was the exception to the invisibility rule. She noticed everything Mary did and nothing, it seemed, was right. Life in London soon came to feel like a constant scolding.

"Do it again!", "Do it faster!", "Scrub it harder!", "Make it cleaner!"

It didn't help that she was bad at her duties. They were boring and hard, which was no surprise, and she couldn't keep her mind from wandering to other, better places. The fields around Westbrook on a warm summer's day. Or the yard, collecting fresh eggs with her brother and sister… And the next thing she knew, an hour had passed and she had only cleaned two grates, and Annie was back in a fury.

The grates were the worst. There were eight of them in the house and each one seemed to gobble up coal like a little monster. Black coal dust got in Mary's eyes, in her nose, under her nails, all over her clothes. It had to be shovelled, scraped, brushed, carried and bagged. Each morning at dawn she cleaned and relaid the fires. By lunchtime half of them needed to be laid again and in the evening every one of them mocked her with its filthy, smouldering ashes. Meanwhile, smoke dust settled in dark, sticky freckles on every surface and had to be polished away. Eliza Aitken liked to run a gloved finger along the mantelpiece in the drawing room on returning from her outings and if she found dirt on the fingertip she blamed Annie, who in turn berated Mary.

But how was she supposed to dust every minute, when there were rugs to be beaten and vegetables to be peeled and scraped? In addition, Mary had the laundry to wash, rinse and put through the mangle. And the washing-up to do before and after every meal. She spent hours up to her elbows in water, either too hot or too cold. Her skin was soon rubbed raw, as Annie had promised, her back ached and she was usually hungry. But though the work was hard, the hardest thing was the loneliness. There was no one to share a joke with, or bargain with, or dream with, for hour after endless hour. She thought she would go mad with it.

She had never been so dog tired, either and hadn't known it was possible. At home, when the sun went down they all went to bed. Here there was gaslight in the streets and endless candlesticks and oil lamps round the house. Two nights in a row she was kept up until midnight working. Cook found her next day in the kitchen after dinner, with her cheek on the table and her hair in the soup.

But at least that soup was good. Mrs Green's talent with food was the one thing that kept Mary going. Eliza Aitken had a taste for French cuisine and Cook was constantly experimenting with new recipes to impress her dinner guests. Any new dish that didn't quite work or that wasn't eaten by the family was eagerly consumed below stairs. At first, Mary didn't understand how Annie could eat so much at every meal, steal bread whenever she was able and still remain skinny as a pipe cleaner. But she soon learned that running up and down five flights of stairs several times a day wore off all the scraps of meat and vegetables that any girl could consume. Before long Mary's cast-off uniform, at first so tight, would be falling off her, without any need to let out the seams.

Cook had her moments of kindness, too. Five days after Mary's arrival, Annie was asked to reclean the front steps after Mary had done them badly. She polished them to a shine, then slapped Mary across the face so hard that Mary saw stars. Cook noticed the red mark on her cheek. It was impossible to hide it.

"Have a bun," Cook said, sliding a fresh, sugar-topped pastry towards her. Mary ate it ravenously before Annie could catch her at it. "And don't think of her too unkindly."

To this, Mary said nothing. How could she think of Annie any other way?

Cook sighed. "She had this job before you. And the last housemaid treated her cruelly. She'll settle, I'm sure, in time."

She might, Mary thought. *Though I wonder if I'll live to see it.* Cook's explanation didn't help much. She still thought of Annie as her new, unwanted enemy. But she was grateful for the bun.

Chapter Five

Early on the first Sunday morning, after the fires were laid, Annie summoned Mary back upstairs to their little room. She proceeded to undress to her chemise and indicated a clean bodice and skirt, which she had laid out on the bed.

"You can help lace my stays today. You might as well make yourself useful."

"Are you going somewhere?" Mary asked.

"Going somewhere? Of course I am. And so are you. What are you, a heathen?"

"No," Mary said, stung.

"Well, then, we're off to church. You'll need to get a move on – when you've done my stays. I've never seen a girl take so long to do a grate. If you're not ready, we'll be off without you."

"I'd have been ready ten minutes ago if only you'd

told me," Mary muttered under her breath, as she busied herself with lacing the older girl tightly into her bodice. Annie liked to behave as if the family's routines were carved in stone, but how was she supposed to know if nobody told her? By the time Annie was satisfied with the fit of her dress, Mrs Aitken was already calling the girls downstairs. Mary had to slip into her peacock dress at record speed, hooking it together anyhow, with no time to brush her hair.

"Mary Adams, you look a fright," the mistress announced with a horrified stare as she raced, breathless, into the hall. "I'm quite ashamed."

They descended the outdoor steps in a little crocodile, with Professor Aitken going last so he could lock the great front door behind them. Mary followed in the family's wake towards the nearby steeple of St Gabriel's – a silver spike against the pale grey clouds of a cold spring morning.

Annie nudged Mary as they turned out of the square.

"This is where I leave you."

"Why?"

"My church is that way."

She indicated a street off to the left and headed

quickly down it. Alice Aitken, looking back, noticed Mary staring after her.

"She's Catholic," she explained simply. "She doesn't understand about true religion the way we do."

Mary smiled, grateful for the explanation – and also for Annie's absence, which made the walk so much more enjoyable. This was the first chance she'd had to collect her thoughts since starting work – although she was too tired to have many thoughts at all. Sitting at the back of the church with the other servants, she hardly noticed the service go by. Familiar words and phrases floated over her head. She joined in the responses without thinking.

Her gaze fell on the jewelled stained-glass windows, not as big or beautiful as those in St Michael's at home, and all she could think about was Ma and Bessy and Jonah, who had always been by her side at church on Sundays. Pa was often still too drunk to make it. "The devil can find me here," he would mutter from his bed, turning his face to the wall. Mary used to spend her time keeping her little brother amused with games and stories. How she used to scold him when he talked too loudly. How she missed him now.

Following the service, the great and the good of the parish gathered in front of the church steps to greet each other and exchange pleasantries. The professor hailed an old friend and the family followed him to say hello. Mrs Aitken was soon deep in conversation with his pretty, elegant wife. Mary hung back, patiently waiting. After her loneliness in church she was shocked beyond measure to hear her name.

"Mary! Mary Adams! Mary!"

She spun round to find Harriet rushing towards her, beaming. The cousins held each other tightly. Mary closed her eyes and breathed in the fresh, familiar smell of Hattie's skin. At first she couldn't talk. She could feel Hattie's heart beating against hers through all the layers of cotton and whalebone and wool. It was impossible to hold her close enough.

"Hey, hey!" Hattie laughed, pulling back at last. "It's not like you to hug so tight. It's hardly a week since I saw you last."

"You're here with the Harringtons?" Mary asked.

"Of course. That's them with your professor. Mrs Harrington looks very fine in her new bonnet, does she not? The blue silk suits her well. It's the latest style from Paris. Soon Mrs Aitken will be wearing one, too, no doubt. She always copies, always a step behind."

"Hark at you!" Mary said with a grin. "So pleased with your fine family. La-di-da!"

She had begun to think she would never be happy again and yet here she was, a cork bobbing on the ocean. And Harriet was clearly just as pleased to see her, too. Indeed, there was a glow of happiness about her cousin, like the halos on the saints in church. Mary remembered her pinched look back in Westbrook and the serious set to her jaw. Working hard in a big house should have bowed Harriet down by now – and yet she looked more cheerful than she ever had at home. Not at all the way she had sounded in her letters.

Mary glanced across at the magnificent Mrs Harrington and her husband, now deep in conversation with the Aitkens while Henry and Alice played chase among the remaining churchgoers. She felt a faint pang of jealousy. Mrs Harrington was indeed taller, prettier and more fashionable than her own mistress, with large blue eyes, a long straight nose, and an air of carrying herself that suggested she was quite aware of her superiority. Mr Harrington, similarly, wore a shinier top hat, elegantly tailored fawn trousers and better polished boots than his friend the professor. However, the way the men laughed together told of an easy friendship, not marred by matters of dress. It was not their looks that made Mary jealous, but the impression they gave of being at ease with the world. Harriet seemed to have caught it from them.

Beyond them, three young men stood together, nodding courteously to the people who passed them on their way from the church. They caught Mary's eye because of the similarity in their looks. Though one was taller than the others, all had the same wheat-blond hair, the same striking jawline and florid cheeks. They had a natural way of smiling, too, that caught Mary's heart for a moment and lifted her spirits just to look at them. She quickly recognized where they got their straight noses from and their cheerful demeanour.

"Those are the Harrington boys?" she asked.

"Yes," Harriet nodded. "Harry, Joe and Edmond."

"How angelic they look."

"Do they?" Harriet laughed. "It depends which one you mean. Harry is quite angelic, I suppose. He's due to be married soon. He's a lawyer, like his father. Joe's the black sheep. He's training to become an engineer and Mr Harrington says he'll make the family famous one day but, in the meantime, he's always having to be rescued from rich, unruly friends and bad company. Edmond… Oh! I must go."

Mrs Harrington had glanced across at the two girls and given Harriet a short, sharp nod. It was enough for obedient Hattie – she ran to join her mistress.

Mary watched them prepare to leave, and saw the envious glances they received from some of their fellow churchgoers. She admired the beautiful golden profiles of the three Harrington boys and fell to dreaming. To think of spending one's days with such a family. She wondered briefly what Harriet had been about to say. She had dipped her head as if it had been something important. But by now she had joined the other Harrington servants and the opportunity to ask her was gone.

⁂

That afternoon Cook was busy with her accounts and Annie was away on an errand. Mrs Aitken went upstairs with a headache and the professor went out, muttering about being home for dinner. The house should have been quiet but it wasn't. Alice and Henry were at home with no one but Mary to look after them, and Alice seemed determined to take advantage of her freedom.

Little Henry, aged six, was shy, preferring to spend time with his toy soldiers, recreating great battles from Wellington's campaigns. But Alice was a whirlwind in the shape of a nine-year-old girl. At the beginning of each day she descended from the nursery like a model child, her light blond hair held in place with a satin ribbon carefully chosen by her mother to match her clothes. The impression lasted until her father left for work, at which point all hell broke loose. She ripped her skirts regularly, running around the house when she wasn't supposed to, climbing furniture, listening in to conversations, picking things up and breaking them.

When Alice was bored, which was often, she would wheedle Henry into following her and get him into trouble, too. Mrs Aitken despaired. Only Annie had any patience with her – which struck Mary as odd. Wilful Alice brought out a tenderness in Annie that was quite different from her normal temper, though often she was sorely tried. She managed Alice by threatening unknown horrors if she were ever to upset her father.

That Sunday, Alice's sense of mischief was worse than usual and Mary was nervous.

"Give him *back*!" Henry demanded, amid gleeful shouts from his sister. "Give him back or I'll *kill* you."

Mary watched the children race around the house while she gathered carpets to beat in the garden later, when it was safe to leave them alone.

"He's mine now!" Alice crowed, running past Mary on the second-floor landing.

"No he's *not*. He's my general! My Napoleon! I *need* him!"

Alice caught Mary's eye and beamed. She was holding the little wooden soldier aloft while Henry panted to keep up with her. Faster and faster she ran, down the landing corridor.

"No! Not there!" Mary called. The professor's study door stood open at the end, because she had just been inside to fetch the rug. Alice ran at full pelt towards it but when she realized where she was heading, she tried to slow down. The study was absolutely out of bounds. Even Alice did what Father said. Nobody knew what would happen if they disobeyed him, because nobody had ever tried.

But Henry didn't notice where he was going.

"It's *mine*!" He ran helter-skelter down the polished floor and crashed into his sister, sending her cannoning into the room ahead. With no carpets and rugs to slow their progress, the two of them skidded across the floor, arms outstretched to save themselves, hitting tables and bookcases as they went. Finally they smashed into Father's mahogany desk, which rocked under their combined momentum. They landed in a heap and watched in horror as pile after untidy pile of books and papers slowly shifted, slipped and slid towards the floor.

It was like an earthquake in slow motion. First one pile, then another, then another. Thump, thump, thud. A fluttering of papers. The children were covered in them.

They sat up slowly as the shock subsided. Henry sent up a penitent wail.

Mary took a deep breath and cautiously went to join them.

"Are you all right?" she asked Henry, noticing a swelling red patch on his knee.

"Noooooo!" he sobbed. But it wasn't his knee he was

worried about. Next to him, Alice had gone white as her pinafore.

"Help us!" she mouthed to Mary. The sheer dismay on her face melted Mary's heart.

Mary looked around the room. It was as if Napoleon and his invading armies had just marched through. However, at least Annie wasn't here to scold them.

"H-how can we make it better?" whispered Alice.

Surveying the heaped volumes and scattered pages on the floor, Mary realized it wasn't quite as bad as it looked.

"We can work out where each pile came from. See? That one's near the bookcase that wobbled, so the books must come from there. These are from the desk. Henry, you put those thick books back in the bookcase like a good boy. Can you do that?"

Henry nodded, sniffing and rubbing his knee.

"Good. Alice, you make that table look nice. I'll have a go at the desk. We'll have it looking right in no time. You'll still have to explain and apologize, mind, when your father's home, but at least it won't be so…" She indicated the battlefield. The children gratefully got on with their tasks.

Mary picked up the first book near her feet and opened

it. The pages were covered in tiny print, in a language she couldn't understand. She thought it might be Latin because some of the words looked like those carved in stone in St Michael's church at home. Another, sprawled open on the floor beside her, was written in an alphabet she had never seen before. How clever the professor must be to read it. Perhaps this was why his family were so scared of him. Mary scanned the words, looking for any she might recognize, but there were none.

"Come on, Mary!" Alice chided, noticing her standing still.

Mary grinned. "Sorry!"

She picked up another book, as big as a tea tray, bound in green leather. Awkward to hold, it fell open in her arms, and she saw that it contained reproductions of old paintings – paintings of women nude (Mary quickly turned those pages, for fear Alice might see), and others in grand, exotic dress, with their hair caught up in pearls and distant mountains fading to blue in the background behind them. Old men, mad-eyed and wrinkled, scowled. Young men with beards and ruffs looked ready to rule the world. The colours were viridian and magenta and azure. Mary knew them well because of Mr Foster's drawing classes at school and from working in the shop. She knew them as paints and ribbons, but not as these stunning pictures. She could hardly drag her eyes away.

In one, a woman sat in a crimson velvet gown that pooled round her waist. She held a hand to her chest, covering one breast but revealing the other, while she examined her face in a mirror held up by a winged little boy. Mary wanted to turn the page – she *needed* to, Alice could look across again any minute – but she couldn't help staring: at the naked, perfect breast; at the luminous skin of the body and the folds of fabric; at the flushed, rosy face and bright, golden hair held up with gemstones. At the little boy wearing only a sash, with birds' wings oddly attached to his shoulders. *He could never fly*, Mary thought. But her mind was soaring. She had never seen such beauty.

A label underneath said: '*Venus with a Mirror* by Titian'. Mary closed the book reluctantly and looked down at her own neat apron, her dark skirts, falling to the floor. Now that she had altered them there was no hint of an ankle, never mind a…

"Henry! Alice! Off you go," she said sharply.

"But we haven't finished yet!" Alice anxiously surveyed the room, where scattered books still littered the desk and tables.

"I'll finish it for you. You don't want your father to catch you here, do you? Now, go!"

The children didn't need to be told twice. They ran out of the study almost as fast as they had careered into it, crowing with relief. Mary breathed in the peace of the room for a moment and opened the book again. She found the page with Titian's *Venus with a Mirror* and admired it at her leisure. The glowing flesh tones, pink on pink … the pooling fabric … the smooth, curving back and oh-so-naked breast.

She thought she heard Annie calling her name, back from her errand, and ignored her.

Her eyes feasted on the crimson and gold, the luxury and jewels, and the delicate, milky skin. To think a real woman had once sat for this picture and a man had painted her … like this. Mary felt her neck flush rosy, like the Venus's cheek, as she imagined it.

Annie called again, more urgently. Mary glanced up and gasped. If it had been a warning, it was too late. A tall figure stood in the doorway, his wide coat silhouetted by the light from the corridor. Oh Lord, the master! And here she was in his study! Looking at his books!

In her shock, she dropped the heavy volume, which landed on her foot, causing her to cry out in pain. But as the figure stepped towards her, she realized it wasn't Philip Aitken at all. This gentleman was much younger. He had sandy hair, swept to one side in neat waves, and a slightly buffoonish expression – so different from the learned seriousness of the professor.

Mary suppressed a groan of fear and dropped into a curtsey.

"I'm sorry, sir. I shouldn't be here."

"No matter. I like … watching you. Let me help you."

He picked up the book she'd dropped and handed it to her. The eyes underneath his bushy eyebrows were hazel and seemingly unblinking. They were fixed on Mary's face. She flushed again at the thought of the page she'd been looking at. She didn't know what to say.

"Who are you?" he asked.

"I'm Mary. The new maid, sir."

"And a reader?"

"Not really, sir. I mean, I can read, but I was looking

at the… I'm so sorry, sir. I was just tidying the room. I'll leave you in peace."

"No! Please, stay. I only came to borrow something."

Mary glanced in panic around the study. "I'm not supposed to—"

"You looked incandescent, with the light coming through your hair."

She stared at him. "What does 'incandescent' mean?" she asked. If he was going to watch her so shamelessly, she wanted to know what he was talking about.

"*Incandescent*," he repeated. "It describes something that emits light as a result of being heated. It means passionate, too. Oh, I'm sorry, I've made you blush." But he kept staring and made her blush more. He didn't seem sorry at all. "Just look at you. That mane of hair. That glory. You remind me of my favourite muse, Mary … what's your other name?"

"Adams, sir," she said. She bobbed a quick curtsey and headed past him for the door. The way he stared at her made her want to be anywhere but there. "Excuse me. I'll come back later."

To finish tidying, she meant, when the room was empty.

"I'll wait," he said fervently. "I'm Rupert, by the way. Rupert Thornton. Pleased to meet you, Mary!"

She ran at full pelt down the stairs to safety, nearly tripping over the rug pile on the landing as she went.

Chapter Six

Mary saw Master Rupert Thornton a few times in the days that followed. Several of Professor Aitken's students visited the house to borrow books or talk in low voices behind his study door, but Rupert was the only one invited to stay to dinner. He was livelier than the others and richer, too, Mary guessed, from his fine silk waistcoats and scented pomade.

Cook, who made it her business to know everyone else's, confirmed her suspicions. "That Master Thornton would be quite a catch," she ruminated to Annie, having been told to change the dinner menu from five to seven courses that evening in his honour.

"Why so?" Annie asked. "I don't like the look of him. Those eyebrows…"

"You wouldn't let the eyebrows get in your way if you were a lady, Annie O'Bryan. His uncle owns a good portion of Lincolnshire. His father's richer still."

"Richer how?" Annie asked, curious.

"Ships," Cook said, nodding wisely.

"What's the shipping business to me?"

Cook sighed. "Learn your history, girl. This is Great Britain. We rule the waves. This muslin bag? Those tea leaves? Half the things in this room came in ships like Mr Thornton's. The father, that is. The son owns nothing. But Mr Thornton Senior gives him money to keep good horses and a house, and wear fine clothes and study ancient history."

Annie sighed wistfully. "I'd forgive the eyebrows for a life like that. Except for the ancient history."

"I'd forgive much worse. Now help me with this piping. I've three layers of cake to do and it must be perfect if Master Thornton's coming."

Mary had been listening from the scullery corridor, as much for the fun of hearing Cook speak as for curiosity about Rupert Thornton. Now she pictured her journey upriver on the *Queen of the Thames* and all the other boats they'd passed, heading for the docks. Many were fat, ugly beasts but one or two had been slim, fast clippers with tall masts and billowing sails.

She imagined one of them now, heading from China to England across choppy waves, carrying its precious cargo. Nothing, she thought, could be more romantic.

As for Rupert Thornton himself, she still wasn't sure what she thought about him. She found it hard to agree with Mrs Green about forgiving the eyebrows. As well as these – and his habit of blatantly staring at her – his lips had a disconcerting sheen to them, Mary thought. His table manners were impeccable, though, and from what she heard he usually made the most interesting conversation of any of the guests.

Occasionally the professor would invite him alone to stay on after supper, to smoke cigars and drink port with him in his study. If he did so, he would call for a jug of fresh water. "I'm not going up there," Annie would mutter from the kitchen. "Nasty, smelly smoke, lingering in your clothes however hard you wash them. You take it, Mary."

Mary felt self-conscious entering the smoky room. But the professor was always gruffly courteous. He'd heard the story of Alice and Henry in the study, of course – the whole house knew about it – and though he had punished them with a talking-to that had made

Alice weep for hours, he didn't seem to blame Mary for what they'd done. In fact, he had asked her to tidy the study twice since then. Sometimes he was too deep in conversation with his student to do more than nod in her direction when she came in, but at least his nod was kindly. Rupert was different, though. When she entered he always faltered, losing his train of thought. She was aware of him watching her every move, in silence, as if she was a ship full of treasure and he was waiting for her to come home.

❦

Three weeks after the disaster in the study, Eliza Aitken rang for Mary in the drawing room. She was sitting at her desk, which, though small, was adorned with three Staffordshire shepherdesses and half a dozen miniatures in velvet frames. In her hand was a letter.

"Ah, Mary," she said, looking up. Mary bobbed. "I have news for you."

"From Westbrook?" Mary asked, alarmed. Had someone died? Pray not Ma or Bessy or Jonah. If it was Pa, she could bear it. But then what would Ma do? Mary felt the blood rush to her head and her heart start to thud. How could the mistress look so calm?

"No, not from Kent. From Tottenham, a few miles north of here. A friend of mine is holding a ball next week and requires extra staff. Someone suggested your name. I'm not sure why." Eliza peered at the letter again, as if to check she'd read it properly. "However, she has very specifically asked for you. I said you would of course help however you could."

"Yes, ma'am."

"A carriage will be sent for you. You're to be on your very best behaviour, because you represent the family. Do you understand?"

"Yes, ma'am," Mary said. But it wasn't true. She understood nothing. Which friend? What ball? How could anyone possibly ask for her by name when she hardly knew anyone in London? Was it something to do with Harriet? But none of these questions could be asked aloud. The mistress wouldn't stand for it.

"Good," said Eliza, nodding absently and looking almost as perplexed as Mary felt. "Don't let me down, Mary. That is all."

It was Annie who explained what the favour was all about. Annie who listened at doorways and knew everything.

"So, you'll be working for a Mr Windus," she said, showing off her information, as the girls climbed into bed that night.

"Who's he?" Mary asked.

"A coach builder, so the mistress told her friends this afternoon. And his wife is dead, so a lady called Mrs Canterbury has taken on the task of arranging the ball for him."

"But how did Mrs Canterbury know about me? I've never met her," Mary said.

"The mistress didn't know, either. It's a proper mystery. She's only met the lady once or twice, though she'd like to *think* they were friendly. This Mrs Canterbury obviously hasn't seen your work."

Mary ignored the slight, which she secretly admitted to herself was well deserved. She was hardly the most efficient maid in London. What surprised her – apart from the mysterious Mrs Canterbury asking for her by name – was that Annie didn't seem cross or jealous at all. "Don't you want to go?"

"Not me!" Annie scoffed. "Traipsing all the way across London? To Tottenham? Working my feet off all night and what for? Lords and ladies dancing? For a coach builder showing off like the king of England? No, thank you."

"Oh…" Mary hardly knew what to say. Suddenly, she had discovered two new Annies. Annie the snob, who cared where the money came from, even though she herself had no more than two shillings to rub together. And Annie the party-hater. That was a shock. Mary simply couldn't imagine hating a party.

❦

Mary discovered a third, unexpected Annie early the next day. She had emptied the slops and cleaned out most of the grates, working faster than usual so she would have plenty of time at the end of the day to get ready for the party. Even servant girls should look their best at a ball, she thought. When she got to the final grate in the parlour, she didn't have quite enough coal to relay it and ran down to fetch some more. To her amazement, she heard voices in the kitchen. Was Annie up already? And who could she be talking to?

Cook was never awake at this time. She relied on the maids to get everything ready for her. Besides, one of the voices belonged to a man. Mary hovered in the corridor, peering through the gap in the hinges of the kitchen door. Two dark figures stood in the open tradesman's doorway, framed by pale yellow daylight. Mary could now make out Annie's familiar silhouette. The taller figure wore an overcoat and an oversized tweed cap. Their heads were close and they talked quietly – Mary couldn't make out what they said. As the man turned to go, Annie held him back, ran to the dresser and took up a small package she must have left there. She handed it to him, embraced him briefly and sent him on his way.

Mary stayed where she was and said nothing. When she heard Annie's fleet footsteps on the kitchen floor, she melted into the shadows behind the door. The other girl didn't notice her as she ran back upstairs.

How often, Mary wondered, did she come down here and meet this man while the rest of the household were sleeping? She'd been giving him food, Mary was sure of it. Bread and cheese often went missing, and sometimes a slice of pie. They were always old, mouldy things that Cook was about to throw out anyway. Cook wasn't one to rock the boat for the sake of some mouldy cheese and nor was Mary. But who was this man? Why was Annie hiding him?

A few minutes later, Annie came downstairs yawning theatrically, as if just roused from her bed. Mary said nothing. Why waste her breath on accusations that would only be denied? She decided to wait and see what happened. Even maidservants could have secrets, it seemed.

Chapter Seven

If I come back in a future life, Mary decided, *I shall do so as a man who builds coaches.*

She stared out of the window of the hired carriage, provided by Mr Windus himself, as it pulled up in the circular drive in front of the biggest house Mary had ever set eyes on. According to Cook, Mr Windus provided carriages to half of London. Coach-building might not be 'noble' in the eyes of a girl like Annie, but it was profitable.

A liveried footman came out to meet her, but when he saw the drab black of Mary's servant's uniform he quickly withdrew his hand and left her to descend by herself. Mary didn't mind. She was too busy admiring the grand brick façade of the house behind him, with its arched windows that flooded the drive with golden light.

Her duties tonight were simple. She was to take coats

and wraps from the footmen who collected them from the guests, to pin a number to them so they could easily be identified and retrieved later, and to take them from the hallway to a darkened library to be stored. This involved standing discreetly in the vestibule, which was only the hallway to the rest of the house, but was the most magnificent room Mary had ever seen in her life. It was three storeys tall – more like a church or a temple than an entrance – with archways lined in purple stone leading up to a great glass dome. The floor was tiled in multi-coloured marble.

She felt as if she was in another country, in another time. Money could buy not only silks and comfort, she discovered, but also exotic desires. And to think that Annie would rather be at home in the kitchen, clearing up the soup.

The guests arrived in dribs and drabs at first, and then in a flood. Mary was soon busy with silks and furs and wool, bobbing to great ladies in gowns with low decolletées, sparkling with diamonds. Hair was piled high and adorned with jewels and feathers. Waists were tight and skirts were large, coming in every colour under the sun. Men arrived in tight trousers and high collars with rich, embroidered waistcoats that made them, too, look like exotic birds. Champagne flowed, the band struck up; she spotted the ladies and gentlemen in distant rooms, talking and dancing. Her head spun with the splendour of it all.

"Mary, Mary!" A loud voice rang out across the hall. Mary paid no attention at first, assuming one guest was hailing another, but the cries got closer. "Mary!" She looked up. It was Rupert Thornton, heading right for her. He had a coupe of champagne in his hand and, from his flushed and happy face, Mary guessed it wasn't his first.

She curtseyed. "Master Thornton."

"Oh, 'Mary, Mary, Quite Contrary', call me Rupert, just for tonight. Isn't it a lovely party?"

"It is, sir."

"I told Rosamond Canterbury she would like you. She only hires the most *fascinating* servants for Mr Windus, have you noticed? He likes beautiful things on his walls and also around the house."

Rupert was beaming. He was very drunk. But happy-drunk, at least. So *he* was the one responsible for her being here tonight?

"I must thank you, for thinking of me."

"Oh!" He flourished his champagne coupe. "The pleasure's mine. There's something I need you to see."

Mary shook her head. "I must get back to my duties, sir."

"Stop calling me sir and start calling me Rupert," he insisted. "A girl like you should never call anyone sir." He was staring intently at her now. And longingly. "Anyway, what duties? I've been watching you. You've been collecting coats and now everyone is here. No more coats."

Mary couldn't help but smile. "What if someone leaves and needs one returned?"

"Won't be for ages. It's a marvellous party. Come and join me."

He moved as if to take her hand and lead her away.

She swayed but kept her feet planted. "I can't!"

"Yes, you can. Be a devil. No one will miss you here. But *I* will if you don't come. And you really have to see what I've got to show you. It's why I wanted you to come." He held out his hand to her.

Mary laughed and shook her head. What would a drunk young man want to show her in a house like this, with rooms all over the place, empty and unguarded?

She was flattered but she wasn't a fool.

As if he could read her mind, he bowed extravagantly. "I promise you, my honourables are intentions. I mean my intentionables are honours... You know what I mean! It's a painting, Mary. Come."

Oh – a *painting*. Mary felt her heart beat faster as she remembered Titian's *Venus*. If it was a painting, she longed to see it. And Rupert's eyes gleamed with the excitement of an art lover, not a dangerous seducer.

"All right then, show me."

Laughing, he took her hand and led her down a series of corridors, away from the main party rooms.

"Mr Windus is famous throughout London for his art," Rupert said.

"As well as his coaches?"

"More so. The coaches are merely the means to an end. He has the finest paintings in the city."

"He paints, too?" she asked.

"No, he collects. The biggest and the best. Look."

Rupert guided Mary into a large, square room, brightly lit by several crystal gas lamps. The walls were lined with emerald green silk, but they were mostly obscured by dozens of paintings, large and small, hung from wainscot to ceiling. She gaped at the effect. So much art in once place. It was nothing at all like the modest etchings, framed in narrow black and gold, displayed at the Aitkens' house. These paintings were as tall as a man, some of them, and mounted in extravagant gold frames. There were dreamlike scenes of far-off countries with high mountains and wide deserts, and English fields that could so easily be the treasured land around Westbrook. But what Mary noticed most of all was weather: dark, glowering skies and clouds chased by the wind; a towering summer's day; the sun setting in a golden glow through evening fog.

"Turner," Rupert murmured reverently.

Mary had heard the professor speak of William Turner as: 'The greatest of his generation. Perhaps the greatest of all.' Now she understood why. She was back at home again, staring up at the endless skies, mesmerized, just like she used to be as a child. She had thought them ever-changing and impossible to capture with a brush or pencil, but this man had done it, over and over again. Mary felt a strange tingle run up her spine.

Several guests in glamorous party clothes came in to admire the canvases and she felt their eyes turn to her. Mary glanced at the floor self-consciously. She must have been staring like a lunatic, caught between homesickness and happiness, when she should be serving them wine or sticking to the shadows. She wanted to stay and soak in the paintings but Rupert was tugging at her elbow. "This isn't the room. I wanted you to see the Turners because they're famous, but the real treasure is down here." He pulled her away and down the corridor. "Now, close your eyes."

They were standing in the doorway of another room, much like the first, but lined in red this time. It was near the back of the house, large and airy, and much emptier of people than the rest. Mary closed her eyes unwillingly. She felt something tugging at her scalp and put a hand up, to discover her cap had gone. Liberated waves of hair tumbled loose to her waist.

"Rupert! What are you doing?" In her shock, she had used his Christian name.

He giggled. "Trust me. I'll guide you."

He took her elbow with a mixture of firmness and gentleness, leading her across the marble floor, until finally he stopped with a sigh.

"Ah. Here we are. You can open your eyes now, Mary."

She did.

Her gasp echoed around the room. This was not like before. No mountains and deserts here. Her first reaction was to feel afraid.

Right in front of her, inside a pale gold frame with a curved upper edge, an almost life-size girl floated in a stream, buoyed up by the billowing skirts of her gold and silver dress. Her arms were outstretched beside her and in her right hand she held a trail of wild flowers. Her eyes were open and her lips, too, as if she wanted to groan or speak. Her cheeks were flushed, but the rest of her skin was deathly pale. Her hair fanned out into the cold, dark water and all around her were banks of plants and trees and moss, so vividly depicted it was possible to imagine you were standing right beside her, watching, but unable to reach her as she slowly drifted...

Mary felt the blood drain from her face. She swayed for a moment.

"Mary!" Rupert put a hand at her elbow to steady her.

Breathing deeply, she recovered herself. "Who is she?"

"Isn't she wonderful?" Rupert said. "Millais' masterpiece. Does she remind you of anyone?"

Reluctantly Mary looked again, though it pained her

to see the poor, half-dead girl.

"Well?" Rupert asked impatiently.

Mary shook her head.

"Aha!" came a booming voice from behind them. "I see it!" Mary spun round. A portly gentleman, older than Rupert, beamed at them both and came over. "You have a fine eye, Mr Thornton! Are they related?"

"Not that I know of," Rupert said. "Mary, you're not kin to Lizzie Siddal, are you?"

"Who's she?"

"Why, she's you!" the older man laughed. He grinned at her and Mary found herself staring back. He didn't dress in sharp, tight clothes like most of the men here tonight. Instead he wore a loose velvet jacket with a floppy cream silk neck tie. His pale brown hair was dressed in long, flowing curls that reminded Mary somewhat of her sister Bessy. His buttonhole boasted a perfect white camellia.

"This is William Hunt," Rupert said. "He paints. Rather well, sometimes." The other man laughed again. Rupert turned to Mary. "And this is—"

"An angel sent from fiery heaven," Hunt interrupted, bowing low, catching her hand in his and brushing the back of it with the tips of his lips. Mary blushed to her core. He glanced back across the room, where a younger man watched them with amused detachment. "Come and look, Felix. A perfect stunner!"

The young man declined to come over. "You're embarrassing the poor girl, William. Can't you see?"

"Not at all. Such a beauty is above embarrassment. Aren't you, my gorgeous?"

Hunt grinned at her confidently, looking for an answer. Mary was not above embarrassment at all. She tried to change the subject by going back to her original question.

"Who is the lady?"

"In the painting? Ah!" Hunt put a hand to his heart. "That's Ophelia." He looked at her blank face in astonishment. "You don't know *Hamlet*? What do they teach young girls these days? *There is a willow grows aslant a brook...*?"

She shook her head.

"*Hamlet* is Shakespeare's finest tragedy. What can I tell you? He is the Prince of Denmark and Ophelia's in love with him. She becomes a victim of his madness. He kills her father – it's very complicated – and she loses her mind with grief. Oh, the pity of it! She goes about picking herbs and muttering nonsense until finally she's discovered floating in the river. Hamlet's mother tells the tale. Though it's off stage I always find her death the most tragic:

'Her clothes spread wide;
And, mermaid-like, awhile they bore her up:
Which time she chanted snatches of old tunes;
As one incapable of her own distress'."

Though slightly drunk, or perhaps because of it, Hunt orated beautifully, letting his voice boom out around the room. Mary stared at the picture, seeing it in a new light. Not a girl today, but a prince's would-be bride from a play. It made her feel better, somehow.

"Until, at last, she's dragged down to her muddy death," Hunt concluded, in a matter-of-fact tone. "John spent weeks at the riverbank, capturing the scene. Then he had to capture Lizzie."

"The model?"

"Yes," Rupert butted in, keen not to be left too long in Hunt's shadow. "Lizzie Siddal – the original stunner. She was discovered in a hat shop, you know. Of course, she's Gabriel's girl really, not John's. But this is her triumph."

A hat shop? So Lizzie was an ordinary girl like her. Mary looked at the painting again. Now, knowing the story, she was spellbound by the hallucinatory quality of Lizzie's face, the dreamlike effect of Ophelia's dress in the water, the sheer, sad beauty of the riverbank.

As one incapable of her own distress...

"It was nearly a disaster," Rupert went on excitedly. "Millais painted her in his studio, in a bathtub full of water. He lit a candle underneath to keep it warm. A candle! Needless to say, she caught a cold and nearly died."

"It was the talk of London!" Hunt grinned. "Though she recovered, glad to say. Her father nearly had John whipped for it. D'you remember, Felix?" He turned to the other young man, who still hadn't joined them. He was watching and clearly listening to their conversation, but he simply nodded and stayed in his place. "Ignore him," Hunt grumbled to Mary. "Felix Dawson. Another painter. A would-be member of the Brotherhood."

Mary stole another look at the younger man. Like Hunt, he was dressed in velvet, with a silk neckerchief loosely tied. Though he made no attempt to introduce himself, he was studying Mary in a way she didn't remember ever being studied before. It wasn't cruel, like some of the boys at school, or wantonly appreciative, like Rupert. Instead it was a lingering, critical, unwavering gaze.

She turned away and looked once more at the drowning girl. The red hair, turned rust brown by the water, reminded her of her own that day on the *Queen of the Thames*.

"Oh!"

This time, at last, she finally saw what Rupert wanted her to see. As well as the hair, she saw the pale skin, the large eyes and strong nose... Mary had never liked her own. She realized why she had felt so shocked when she had seen the girl so close to death. It was like watching herself drowning.

But still. What had Hunt called Mary when he spoke to that other artist? *A perfect stunner*. He and Rupert were staring at her again now. She felt a flush bloom on her neck.

"I thought from the moment I saw her..." Rupert murmured to Hunt.

"Stupendous."

"An ethereal ideal."

"You're remarkably percipient."

"Most kind."

"My dear," Hunt said, addressing Mary, "if you ever decide to pose for a painting, young Master Thornton here knows where to find me." He lifted her hand to his lips again and she felt his breath on her fingertips. Then he bowed and left them.

In the silence that followed, Rupert laughed.

"Ha! I certainly didn't think… Well, well! The famed William Hunt, no less. Would you like to pose for him, Mary?"

"I … I don't know," Mary said. The thought of nearly dying in a bathtub of cold water did not appeal. But being 'a perfect stunner'…

"Rupert! There you are! I've been looking for you all evening!"

A grand lady swept into the room in a flurry of hoops and petticoats, gold silk skirts swirling around her as she moved.

"Mother! This is… I'm sorry. I was distracted."

Before he could make his introduction, Mary bobbed a curtsey and moved as fast as she could for the far exit without actually breaking into a run. Rupert wasn't thinking. No gentleman could introduce a maid to his mother. She shouldn't have been talking to him at all.

Moving quickly, down one corridor and then another, she headed in the direction she thought she had come from until she reached a pillar where she could quickly hide and replace her cap. As she paused, she heard running footsteps on the tiles behind her. *No!* Had the mother sent someone to find her? The footsteps paused, too, then started up again. She peeked out to see who was following and to her surprise, there was William Hunt's quiet friend heading directly for her. Before she could do or say anything, he came right up to her and put his hands on her shoulders.

"Pose for me!"

"I … I beg your pardon?"

"Pose for me! Nobody but me. I know I can capture you the way no one else can. Not Hunt, he's much too grand these days. Not Gabriel, you'll hate him. For me."

Mary stared. This was the man who had all but ignored her a moment ago. Yet now she had never seen such intensity as there was in his dark eyes. There was something compelling, too, about his high cheekbones, the lips soft as berries and the coffee brown curls that fell in waves down to his collar. He reminded her of a portrait of the poet Byron that Miss Elsie Helpman had shown them in the schoolhouse. Like Byron, he looked dangerous and sounded it, too. Mary found it thrilling.

But what he was asking was ridiculous.

"I couldn't possibly!" she said, fighting a smile and pulling away at last.

"Of course you could. Come to my studio. Here's the address." In his right hand he held a small visiting card. He gave it to her. "Come on Wednesday. I'll be alone then. I promise I won't stick you in a bath and nearly kill you."

Mary laughed. "I don't think so."

"Think harder."

She looked down at the card and sighed. "Thank you for the offer." Then she bobbed, smiled a regretful goodbye and left him.

"Wednesday! Remember?" he called after her.

He was engaging but was he mad? Go alone to the studio of a stranger? Never.

Even so, Mary was flattered. For the rest of the evening she thought of them all and what they'd said and how they'd looked at her as she dutifully handed coats to their happy, champagne-filled owners. They had been drunk, of course, Rupert Thornton and William Hunt. Drunk and extravagantly admiring. Mr Felix Dawson had seemed more sober but he'd turned out to be the maddest of them all.

꧁ ꧂

Mary turned the stiff visiting card over in her fingers in the carriage home. Through the window a low moon was playing hide-and-seek behind chimney pots and treetops. The moonlight gave each tree and building a special silvery sheen. It reminded her of the delicacy with which Millais had painted every blade of grass and wild flower on the riverbank around Ophelia, and the equal care with which he'd painted Lizzie Siddal.

What must it be like to be looked at and captured in such a way? Mary imagined the Italian girl who sat for Titian's *Venus*, posing in only a half-draped velvet robe. And in her dream she saw a pair of dark eyes staring into hers. The eyes came closer, closer...

"Hey! Get up, girl! Hurry yourself."

She woke up with a start. They were back in Pimlico already and the disgruntled coachman was addressing her from the carriage door. She had no idea how long she'd been asleep, head resting against the window frame. Slipping out of her seat and avoiding his eye as she stepped down, she felt almost as guilty as if her dream had really been happening.

Chapter Eight

By the next morning, the whole night seemed like a dream to Mary. One look at Annie and she knew she could never share it. It was bad enough when she wore a well-made dress. What would happen if she let slip that gentlemen had been singing her praises in front of a famous painting?

That didn't mean the evening wasn't discussed in the steamy kitchen. It was, in great detail. Despite her distaste for the coach builder, Annie was eager to know all the intricacies of the house that she so disapproved of and Cook always loved to hear any detail about rich people's lives. When Mary happened to be passing they pressed her for news of the fashions, the décor, the flowers. They simply assumed she had spent the evening in the hallway, taking coats, and she did nothing to suggest otherwise.

She hid Felix Dawson's card at the bottom of her trunk but got it out occasionally, when there was little chance of Annie intruding on her, to run her fingers along its edges and convince herself the night had been real.

Rupert Thornton smiled at her in a cheerful, complicit way when he next came to call on the professor. Mary flushed and bobbed and tried to keep a straight face. It only made his smile broader. She didn't know whether to be cross with Rupert for almost getting her into trouble or grateful to him for showing her the painting.

Over the following days she often thought of *Ophelia*, and the painters she had met or heard talk about. She wanted to learn more about William Hunt and Millais, or any of their circle. They seemed so different from everything she knew. They broke the rules of dress and decorum, and some of them at least consorted with servant girls. Now that she knew the names to listen for, she discovered to her delight that they were often the topic of conversation around the table in St George's Square, especially when Rupert was among the dinner guests.

They were quite famous, it seemed, and called themselves the Pre-Raphaelite Brotherhood. They were ex-students from a place called the Royal Academy and, as well as Hunt and Millais, they included another artist called Dante Gabriel Rossetti. *This Rossetti must be the 'Gabriel' they kept talking of,* Mary thought to herself. According to Rupert, they rejected anything classical or conventional in art, as taught since the days of Raphael and Michelangelo. Mary didn't know about those artists. She wondered if the Brotherhood liked Titian, as she did, but as she only saw Rupert in the company of her master and mistress, she couldn't ask.

"They've quite simply saved painting, in my opinion," Rupert observed one evening at dinner, when Eliza's brother and his wife were visiting. "They paint nature, and truth, and history, and love. They remind us of the greatest stories."

The professor strongly disagreed. "Mawkish tales, badly told. They're all syrup and romance. I'll have none of it. Give me a decent landscape, not some fairy dell dotted with flowers. And those women! The things they get up to that no decent lady would contemplate. It's shocking, I tell you. Scandalous."

Sometimes, after discussing the Pre-Raphaelites, he was driven to draining his claret glass in vexation and calling for another. Mary grew accustomed to having the decanter ready to pour him a fresh glass. Rupert respected his teacher in most things, but not in this.

"There's more life in their paintings than anything since the great masters. More colour, more intensity. And what's wrong with romance, eh, Prof? What do you have against it?"

"Nothing, per se," the professor admitted. "But look at them! Marrying each other's wives. Carrying on with chorus girls. Carousing in insalubrious bars…"

"Not in front of the servants, dearest," Eliza murmured with a mild glance to her husband and a nod towards Mary, who carefully studied the patterned rug at her feet.

"And yet everyone wants to meet them," Eliza's brother said. "Prince Albert himself defended their art, did you hear it? He said it cost them 'the highest effort of mind and feeling'. The great Windus himself has several fine pieces, I'm told."

Yes, I've seen them, Mary thought. Luckily she managed to stop the words before they reached her lips. She glanced up to find Rupert watching her, his eyes dancing merrily. Despite herself, she couldn't help returning a fleeting smile.

"Indeed he does," Rupert agreed. "He has the finest collection in London. Although I hope to rival him one day. I already have some rather fine drawings and a painting or two."

"Do you really?" Eliza asked, leaning forwards fascinated. "I've always wanted to collect art. Haven't I, Philip?"

The professor gave an embarrassed cough. "Yes, you have, my dear."

"I have a very good eye, I'm told. If you need any help, Rupert, you have only to ask me, you know."

"You're very kind, Mrs Aitken," he said. But Mary saw his hidden horror at being advised in any matter of taste by his hostess – the mistress of a dozen china shepherdesses and not one decent painting. This evening her dress was a pattern of black and blue diamonds so brash it risked giving her guests a headache. When Rupert caught Mary's eye again, she had to bite her lip to keep her face straight. Eliza, too, looked up and saw her. Mary feigned an itch to her nose. Even so, the mistress frowned. *She is right to be irritated*, Mary thought. *What an ungrateful servant I am! And Rupert Thornton brings out the worst in me.*

Two weeks went by and a cold and foggy spring gave way to the first warm hint of summer. Mary noticed the change as she kneeled on the black-and-white tiles outside the front door, polishing the knocker to a shine.

Back in Westbrook you always knew what part of the season it was – almost to the day. Fields needed to be furrowed; crops needed to be sewn and tended and harvested; pigs were fattened and slaughtered; baby lambs were born and grew into sturdy sheep. Here in London there were only the trees and market gardens to give any hint of the cycle of nature. Without hedgerows, thick with birds and burrowing animals and wild flowers and lambs in the fields, what would summer mean? The air would still be thick with coal dust, and the streets still busy with the same tradesmen and workers, doing jobs that never changed. There would be no May festival – no maypole to dance round. For a few days, Mary longed for Kent. She carried on with the drudgery of her daily tasks in the tall white house, grateful only that not so many fires needed to be laid.

And yet, London had its own magic to perform.

She noticed it two Sundays after the first summer breeze. And she noticed it *inside* St Gabriel's church not out. That day it was as if the pews themselves were blossoming. Suddenly all the ladies were wearing new fashions. Vivid hues had given way to pale pastels. Heavy capes had become fine wool shawls. Silk bonnets were replaced with wide-brimmed straw hats. Even the gentlemen's waistcoats were nattier shades of bright spring colours.

How do they know? Mary wondered. How could they tell? Was there some sort of secret London telegraph? In Westbrook you wore years'-old work clothes for the fields and farms and only adjusted your layers according to the weather. London was a fashion parade of new-season designs. In church Mary's eye gleefully took in the sloping shoulders, the trend for pintucks, the particular shades of palest green and yellow that looked so outstanding on some lucky young ladies and did no favours to their friends. If she'd had a chance to work at a shop like Mr Foster's here, what fun she might have had, recommending colours and designs. Or, even better, sewing them herself. She couldn't concentrate on the service at all. Afterwards, she marvelled to Harriet that everyone looked so smart and gay.

"Don't they indeed?" Harriet agreed. "Mrs Harrington spent two days last week finalizing her new wardrobe. Isn't her dress the nicest in the garden?"

Harriet was always so loyal to her mistress. Mary followed her gaze to where Mrs Harrington was talking with her son Edmond. The sunlight from behind cast a gold halo round them both. Tall, fair and smiling, they reminded her of angels again. Although Mrs Harrington looked bell-like, too, in an enormous lemon-yellow crinoline that could have hidden a small village under its capacious hoops.

As always, Mrs Harrington looked better than Mrs Aitken, whose skirt was not quite as broad and whose crimson silk was not one of the new season's colours. Not for the first time, Mrs Aitken was out of sorts on the way home, complaining about the 'show' of some of the 'flashier' families.

"I do wonder that Jane Hillier thought that leghorn hat appropriate for church. How was anyone supposed to see around it? If Lydia Elson's skirts had been any wider, her family could not have fitted into the pew.

She wouldn't give me the name of her seamstress, you know, Philip. Said she was too busy to take on new commissions. We all know she just wants to keep the woman to herself. So rude. I would quite exclude her from the invitation list if I could."

Mary suppressed a groan. The 'invitation list' was to a supper party to celebrate Philip's fortieth birthday. Cook was preparing a feast to feed twenty. The house had to be cleaned, tidied and re-cleaned from top to bottom. Eliza spent her time worrying about everything from the style of her new evening gown to the quality of the roast beef to the shape of the champagne coupes.

In a bid to get everything ready, Mary and Annie were going to bed an hour later than usual and rising half an hour earlier. Tempers were frayed and even Cook, who was normally placid and happy, shouted at Annie on a regular basis. Annie's furies with Mary took place almost hourly.

❧⁓❧

Mary was counting down the days: six until the party itself and seven until next Sunday – her second day off since she'd arrived in London. She was going to spend the afternoon with Harriet, exploring London, and the rest of the time catching up on sleep. Meanwhile, keen to avoid the fractious, unhappy household, Mary had volunteered for all errands that would take her away from it.

"You can get the flowers the day before," Annie had told her, with a grim smile.

"With pleasure."

"It won't be. You've to walk to Covent Garden, which is a good hour away."

"What time?"

"Six in the morning, to get the best blooms. So leave the house at five. And the grates must be done before you go."

"Yes, Annie." Mary sighed.

"You'll need several baskets. The mistress wants enough flowers to make an arbour. It's easy to get robbed at that time in the morning – there's all sorts about. So look after your pocket book and keep it safe. And when you get back, I'll have a list of jobs for you as long as your arm, so mind you come home sharpish. I'll know if you've been lingering."

That morning Mary woke up with the three o'clock bell from St Gabriel's church and couldn't get back to sleep again. She rose early, dressed quietly and did her chores by candlelight. They were easier now she was used to them – and had the muscles to do them properly – but what made them easier still today was to know that soon she would be outside, doing something else entirely.

The walk Annie had explained to her, through the dark streets from Pimlico to Covent Garden, was cold, but not so frightening. The beggars on street corners were still asleep. A few drunken youths caroused in the road but it was easy to avoid them. Carters drove by with loads of coal and beer, creating a steady rumble along the cobbles. Mary's route took her past a slumbering Buckingham Palace and through a misty St James's Park, on to the great open space of Trafalgar Square, where the hero Nelson surveyed the city from the top of his column, surrounded by wisps of fog.

Mary fell in love with London in the early morning. She had always enjoyed walking and her shawl kept out the chill. The city spread around her like a magic carpet of discoveries. She pitied Annie, still fast asleep, wilfully missing it all.

Covent Garden itself was another world – a hive of activity, full of noise and bustle just as busy as if it was the middle of the day. Carts rolled in from every street, full of fresh flowers, fruit and vegetables. They were offloaded by colourful costermongers with a series of shouts and arguments. Mary marvelled at the pointed yellow boots and silk neckerchiefs of the men, the gaudy shawls and bright feathers of the women. Here they had a fashion all of their own and were proud of it.

Horses snorted into the cold morning air, which was alive with the smell of animals and dung, pollen and herbs, coffee and stale beer on the breath of the workers. Every now and then the carters would stop to catcall or whistle as an extravagantly dressed woman passed by, with a wasp-tight waist and painted face, sometimes on the arm of a drunken-looking gentleman. Not only fruit and vegetables were sold here, Mary reflected, with a sudden jolt of understanding. She found herself just standing and staring for minutes on end, watching it all as if it were a play. Only the sound of an Irish accent at a nearby stall jolted her into activity, reminding her of Annie and what would happen if she didn't get home soon.

Finding the right flowers took a bit of time. "Pink," Eliza had instructed. "And blue. Lots of roses. And orange, to match my dress." Mary knew better than to point out that pink, blue and orange might look disastrous together, more like a vicious argument than a harmonious arrangement. Instead she focused on choosing the finest examples of each and bartering the stallholders down to a decent price. She was one of the first customers that day, so she had the best choice, and the flowers were dew-fresh and magnificent. The array of colours seeped into her brain and she closed her eyes to imprint the picture there, and the rich pure scent of them, too. Annie had said to rush but she couldn't. She'd have stayed there all day if she could.

Eventually her baskets were full, her pocket book was almost empty and the market was so busy she worried about her carefully chosen blooms getting crushed in the thickening crowd. It was definitely time to go home. The baskets were too heavy for Mary to walk. Not wanting to risk them on an omnibus and without the money for a cab, she called among the carters to try and hitch a lift in the direction of Pimlico. But all, it seemed, were heading the opposite way.

Starting to panic, Mary ran from one cart to the next. She thought she heard her name and turned round, but it was impossible. Who would she know here? She turned back to the row of carters, begging now for anyone who was heading west to take her. Finally one agreed to let her ride with him as far as Westminster. She was just stepping up when she heard the shout again.

"Mary!"

The carter stared over her shoulder. "Looks like you're wanted, dearie."

She turned round. There, running towards her as if his life depended on it, was a young gentleman. At first she noticed the rich, dark curls under his hat, then the kingfisher blue of his waistcoat. Then, as he drew closer, she recognized the sharp-boned face of the young artist from the Windus house.

"You never came!" he shouted.

"I beg your pardon?"

"Mary. Mary, isn't it? I gave you my card. You let me down."

Beside her, the carter turned surly. "Look – if you're going to have an argument with your gentleman friend, you can do it on your own time. I've a job to do."

"But—"

"Down you get, dearie. Hop it."

He started throwing down her baskets any old how. Mary had to jump to the ground to save their precious contents, before the carter cracked his whip and took off down the street.

The gentleman stooped to help her pick up a basket and she turned on him furiously.

"Go away! See what you've done?"

"No," he said, frowning.

"That was my ride home. Now I'll be late."

"It doesn't matter," he said, taking her arm. He was smiling now. "You're here. I've found you. It must be destiny, don't you think?"

"N-no," Mary answered. She was still angry. But she couldn't help softening at the way his dark eyes crinkled with surprise and pleasure at seeing her.

"I waited for you all day that Wednesday. You said you'd come."

"I said I wouldn't!"

"You said 'thank you'. That means yes, surely? Midday gave way to dusk. Still no sign of you. I begged Rupert Thornton for your address but the dastardly fool wouldn't give it. He said he didn't trust me. The dolt! I want you for art, not nefarious purposes."

"Oh!"

Mary's throat went dry at the mention of 'nefarious purposes'. She looked away. He placed a gentle finger on her chin and turned her head to look at him again.

"It's destiny," he repeated softly. "You have the most fascinating face. Your eyes are outrageously green. Your lips a series of tantalising curves. Your neck is endless. Your hair is the colour of sunrise and fate keeps throwing us together. Sit for me, Mary." His voice was low now, pleading. "I promise I'll look after you. Let me paint you."

Mary almost crumbled. She thought of Titian's *Venus* and Lizzie Siddal. *Hair the colour of sunrise.* "I wish I could," she mumbled. "But I can't. I'm late already. If I don't get home soon—"

"Not today. I'm busy anyway – sleeping off last night, that is. We got a little sidetracked at the club. That was quite a dinner. How about tomorrow?"

"Oh no! My mistress has a party."

"The next day."

There was a pause.

"It's my day off," Mary admitted. Her first in a month. *Was* it fate that she should be free so soon?

"Well, that's settled. I'll see you at two on Sunday. Make it three – I'm usually up by then. You can spare me two hours, surely? You still have my card?"

Mary nodded. She remembered every line: 'Felix Dawson, Artist, 24 Walton Street'. It was wrapped in ribbon at the bottom of her trunk.

"But I'm supposed to be seeing my cousin," she said, still a little scared by his excitement.

His lips formed into a perfect, sculpted smile. "Who would you rather see? Your cousin, whom I wager you see every week, or the best young painter in London?"

"And the most modest!" she scoffed.

"Great art isn't about modesty. It's about talent."

"And who says you have talent?"

His smile faded slightly. "A few people. No one important yet. What I need is the right muse."

"Can't you have Lizzie?"

He laughed. "No, I can't! And you're much, much

more interesting than Lizzie Siddal."

"I'll think about it."

"While you're thinking, here's the money for a cab home. I'm sorry I've kept you so long." He pressed a shilling into her hand. Mary stared down at it. "Oh, and I pay for modelling sessions, too. The going rate. You'll earn it, I promise. It's harder than it looks."

Before she could decide how to react, a smart brougham drew up, drawn by two matched black Friesians in shining harness. A round red face poked out of the window, topped by an immaculate silk top hat.

"Felix! Do hurry up! You've been talking to that girl for hours. I need my bed!"

"Roly, this is Mary. The one I was telling you about."

"With the eyes and the hair?"

"She has more than those, Roly, you chump."

"And you're a wastrel. Tell the lovely creature you'll see her tomorrow and let's go home."

Felix turned to Mary. "Not tomorrow – Sunday. At three. Promise me this time. I'll make you the talk of London."

"Is that a good thing?" she laughed, remembering the conversation around the Aitkens' dinner table.

"It is if you're with me."

Mary hesitated for a moment. "I promise." She rushed the words, before she could change her mind.

With a grin, he stepped into the brougham. Mary gathered up her baskets and quickly found an empty hackney carriage to take her home. She sat with his shilling in her hand, surrounded by the scent of roses, watching London pass by at a trot.

The flowers lay massed at her feet, a carpet of colour. She picked out a single, fat burnt-orange rosebud and held it. Today it was tightly furled but tomorrow, in the warmth of the parlour, she knew it would bloom into a perfect shape. For a few days, it would be a miracle of nature – then she would be asked to throw it out, with the others, on a heap at the bottom of the garden where its fresh beauty would be quite forgotten. Was she to live her life like this: vibrant, unknown, shut up in a wedding-cake prison, worn down by dirty laundry and unpolished floors? That didn't feel like her. It didn't feel *right*.

Fascinating … tantalizing … more interesting than Lizzie Siddal…

What Felix Dawson wanted seemed impossible …

but was it? Why shouldn't she use her free time to do as she wanted? Why should she be governed by the petty cares of the likes of the professor and Mrs Aitken, when it was the passionate lives of the Pre-Raphaelites that excited her? Why not step outside her normal life for a few hours, and become immortalized?

Mr Dawson's talent as an artist would have to be prodigious to match his flattery and promises. Mary smiled to herself and tucked the rosebud into her bodice. Maids could have secrets: Annie O'Bryan had taught her that. There was only one way to find out if this young man was as good as he said he was.

Chapter Nine

Sunday came. Mary had sent word to Harriet that she was otherwise engaged. She heard the bells in a distant church strike three as she knocked at the door of a pale blue Chelsea villa in Walton Street.

She still blushed at the idea of spending two hours alone with a man she barely knew, but how was she to be painted, if not like this?

A young maid came to the door and bobbed a curtsey.

"Are you here for Mr Dawson, miss? He said a young lady would be calling."

Mary looked at her, surprised. *Young lady?* She saw the maid cast a longing eye at the peacock sateen of her skirt – carefully washed and mended since the day she arrived in London – and raise her glance still further to Mary's face and radiant hair, worn loose under her bonnet and brushed today until it shone. The girl gazed at her as if she was some exotic creature.

"Um, yes," Mary said, straightening her shoulders. "Can you tell him Miss Adams is here?"

Before the maid could answer, there was a clattering of feet down the stairs and along the hall. "Mary! Mary! You came!"

Felix had spoiled her dignified entrance, but he looked so delighted to see her that she forgave him. The maid bobbed politely as Mary stepped inside. Felix looked dishevelled from whatever he had been working on, with paint splatters on his shirtsleeves and a palette knife still in his hand.

"I rent on the top floor," he explained. "Where the light is. North-facing. Perfect for painting. They're the best rooms in London – wait till you see them." He led the way. After three flights of stairs, he stopped at the open door to a separate apartment. "Here we are."

The flush in his cheeks brought out the dark Byronic beauty of his face. Mary marvelled again at how a man should choose to be a painter when he was so obviously born to be painted himself. Today he wore a soft white linen shirt with a scarlet neckerchief. Nothing about his appearance was careless but everything was carefree.

He was like no man she'd ever met in Westbrook.

Two hours. Alone. Mary suppressed a shiver.

"What do you think?"

"I … um…" She licked her lips. Then she realized he was indicating the room. She looked around carefully and ended up laughing.

His face fell. "What's so funny?"

"It's just…"

After the neat grandeur of the villa from the outside, Mary had not expected this. Her eyes darted from the tin bath in one corner, piled high with unwashed dishes, to the Chinese screen draped with drying underclothes. On a mezzanine floor above the bathtub, she could just make out an unmade camp bed surrounded by empty wine bottles and piles of open books. There were no curtains, no comfortable chairs, just canvases and paints and brushes everywhere.

Felix stared at her. "Well?"

"You must admit, it's very messy for somewhere so bare."

"Messy? Bare?" Felix gestured around the room. "Well, I suppose it lacks a certain feminine je ne sais quoi. But I despise tidiness – it's the work of the devil.

And furniture. Why spend money on furniture when I can spend it on paint?"

Mary stopped laughing. Why should she care about furniture and dirty dishes? Hadn't she wanted to be liberated from petty cares and normal lives?

"It will do very well," she said resolutely.

At that moment the grey clouds parted and a shaft of sunlight fell through the vast, high window that dominated the room. It lit up a trestle table piled chaotically with pots and paints. She noticed that among the brushes and paint-stained rags were little glass jam pots filled with lilacs and palest pink chrysanthemums. A grass-green bowl held three bright lemons and some exotic fruits she didn't recognize. Everywhere colours fought and danced. Just looking at them all, she felt her heart beat faster. Something inside her began to unfurl, ready to take flight.

The next thing she knew, Felix's hands were in her hair. She felt them sweep it aside to expose the nape of her neck to the air.

"Ah!" It came out as a gasp. No man had ever held her hair like this before – not since the boys used to pull it in the schoolyard, in the days when she wore it plaited with daisies and they called it the colour of rust.

He sensed her hesitation. "I-I have … ideas," he murmured, "for how I want to style it. When I draw you."

Mary stood stock still while he lifted the heavy locks and played with them, feeling her chest rise and fall with each breath, not wanting or daring to move or speak. Then, as he let the tresses fall back loose around her shoulders, his fingers strayed to her collarbone, just above the neckline of her bodice, and rested there. The warmth of his skin and the shock of his touch sent tremors through her.

Mary jolted away, startled at his boldness and the fire of her response. "I… I can do it myself. It's easier that way." It took a moment for her voice to become steady. The skin still burned where he had touched it. And not in an unpleasant way. But the only thing she had was her reputation and it was more precious to her than gold. She was here so Felix could paint her – nothing more.

"I … yes…" He coughed. "Of course. Let me get you a comb."

He rummaged around in various messy piles, and eventually found a tortoiseshell hair comb embellished with silver and seed pearls.

Mary admired it in surprise. "What does a young man need with such a pretty thing?" she asked, gently teasing, as she pulled her hair expertly into a coil at the nape of the neck and fixed it in place.

Felix instantly flushed and looked away. "Someone left it here," he said vaguely. "A sitter."

What sitter would forget her comb? Mary asked herself. But by now Felix was leading her towards a plain, large trunk positioned underneath the tall window and adjusting her posture until he was happy with the way the light fell on her face.

"Don't look at me," he said. "Look over there." He indicated the trestle table groaning under its chaotic mess of paints and jars of flowers. "And think about something you want but can't have."

She glanced up at his face, staring intently at her, and saw the exact look he was asking for in his own dark eyes. It was easy to summon up the emotion.

Felix worked in silence for a while, his eyes flicking back and forth between the paper and her face. He drew her with her hair caught up in the comb and then asked her to take it down again, fanning it out around her. As time passed, Mary's thoughts couldn't help but wander. They turned to the trestle table and the riot of colours there. Felix must be very successful, she decided, for someone so young. After all, even though he lived like a pig in a farmyard, he could afford this studio on an elegant square and expensively engraved wine glasses, like the one that held a single, perfect peony. He must have sold a lot of paintings. Who else, she wondered, had sat for him and taken that comb from her hair?

Eventually Felix interrupted her reverie by stretching his arms to the ceiling. "Lord, my arm aches. That's enough for today. You must ache, too."

Mary rolled her shoulders. Felix was right: she ached all over but she hadn't noticed until now. She had been too busy drinking in the details of the studio.

"You have a remarkable stillness," he said. "It makes you easy to draw. But your eyes – they're always dancing. It'll take me a month to capture them. Even so…" He looked at the sheet of paper in front of him with more than a hint of satisfaction.

"May I see?" Mary asked, getting up and walking over to the easel.

"Only if you promise to be kind. I still haven't quite caught the jawline the way I—"

"Oh!"

The creamy paper was covered in sinuous pencil lines, thick with shading, and out of it all grew … a girl. No – not just a girl. A princess or a queen, or a sensuous goddess with a noble nose, sculpted lips and a swirling cloud of hair that threatened to spill off the page and into the room.

The likeness was startling, but Mary had never seen herself like this. She was magnificent, compelling. Like Lizzie Siddal, yes, but so much more. Was Felix Dawson better, she wondered, than Millais and Rossetti? Was that possible?

"It hardly does you justice," Felix said. "Next time, I must capture you in paint."

She eased her shoulders and stretched out her back.

"Next time, I must bring a cushion,"

"Next time, I'll put stars in your hair." Careful not to touch her skin this time, he traced the edge of his fingers along the outline of her glowing mane, caught in a thin shaft of light. "I see you as Guinevere. Or possibly Astraea."

The sun was low in the sky. The afternoon was nearly over. "I must go," she said, not wanting to.

"When will you come back?"

"My next free afternoon is the third Sunday in June," she explained, retrieving her shawl and bonnet from the back of a chair.

"That's impossible! I can't wait four weeks for you!"

"You'll have to. I'm new to my job. I can't ask for special favours."

"Then I'll ask for you."

"No!" Mary spun round to glare at him.

"Why not?"

Men were so stupid sometimes. Apart from the fact that the professor disapproved so heartily of Felix's friends, no respectable servant would ever be allowed to sit for a man like him, alone, for a drawing such as he had done of her. Artists' models were thought of as 'no better than they should be'. Everyone would assume the worst, especially with money involved. "Because Mrs Aitken must never know about me and you. Do you think she'd keep me on if she knew I was doing this?"

"Why wouldn't she?"

Mary sighed. "I'm already taking a big risk coming here today."

Felix's face clouded for a moment, then lit up with

sunny confidence. "Trust me. When it comes to my art, I know what I must have. And I will have it."

She hardly dared meet his eyes. What 'must he have'? Did he just mean her likeness? Or was he thinking about those 'nefarious purposes'? Mary thought about them and knew she was wicked for doing so. She tried to push the very idea from her mind and got ready to leave. As she wrapped her shawl round her shoulders, he took the peony from its glass and presented it to her, like a token.

"Think of me," he said.

How could she forget?

As she left the house, she realized he hadn't paid her. She was about to turn back, but heard the clock strike six – not five, as she had supposed. *Three* hours had somehow passed, not two. She would have to rush if she was to get back before dinner. As she ran through the busy, dirty streets of Chelsea to Pimlico, her mind was full of questions about how to see him again, and the lies she must tell Cook and Annie about how she had spent the afternoon.

Chapter Ten

The peony seemed to light up the attic, resting in an old bottle of smelling salts that Mary had rescued from the collection for the rag and bone man. She sat it on the washstand so that it would catch the few rays of sun that filtered through the chimney smoke. It was quite as beautiful to her as all the flowers Eliza Aitken had arranged for the birthday party.

Annie was instantly suspicious of it.

"Where d'you get that from? Your fancy man?"

"Oh yes, I've been in London ten minutes and I have a fancy man," Mary said scornfully, tossing her head and willing her neck not to give her away by flushing. They faced each other across the floorboards, still tired and fractious from the week of extra work.

"So what happened? Did you steal it?"

"I found it."

"Found it where? In the street?"

"Yes," Mary said brazenly. "It fell from a grand straw hat." She held her gaze steady, imagining the hat that might have lost such a bloom: wide and shallow, held in place on pretty blond curls by a wide satin ribbon. She could picture it exactly – the bloom falling and herself innocently retrieving it.

I am not a thief, but I'm a good liar, she decided as Annie nodded uncertainly and dropped the subject. Even so, the sensible side of her wanted to hide the flower or get rid of it, to stop Annie from wondering about her. But she couldn't bring herself to do it. That, and his card, were all she had of Felix, and they mattered to her too much.

He had the drawing of course, and she pictured him obsessively, wondering how often he looked at it and what he thought. Would he call for her again in a month? Would he feel guilty about not paying her? Had he felt the same jolt of dangerous pleasure as her when his fingertips brushed her neck? She felt sure he had, but then, there might be other girls … other women… He was young and beautiful, full of life and bursting with talent. He could have any girl he wanted.

And what did *she* want?

Another picture? Another heady afternoon in his colour-soaked studio? Or would just the brush of his fingertips be enough?

She wasn't sure. But when the peony died a few days later, she certainly never missed a flower so much.

✦

The day after she had sacrificed her flower to the compost heap, she was in the scullery, scrubbing a salmon, when Annie came helter-skeltering down the stairs.

"Saints in heaven! You must see this, Mrs Green! The carriage outside! Go and look a minute!"

She ran back the way she had come. Cook hurriedly brushed the flour from her dress and walked up some of the concrete steps outside, clutching her skirts and puffing until she could get a good look at the street above. Mary followed, unable to contain her curiosity.

There, standing to attention and taking up half the road space, were four gleaming black horses, their harnesses jangling as they tossed their heads and flicked their glossy tails. They were hitched to the smartest carriage Mary had ever seen. It was a boat-shaped landau with its roof up: not large, but polished to an impeccable shine. Even the windows shone like crystal. To Mary's astonishment, Eliza Aitken was standing in the street, on tiptoe, talking to somebody inside. She never came outdoors to greet guests – that was Annie's job. She was so engrossed in her conversation that she didn't seem to notice half the street was watching.

Annie appeared and Mrs Aitken spoke to her for a moment, then turned back to the carriage. Mary wondered who on earth could be inside. She could just make out a gold and yellow crest on the nearest door. Might it even … her imagination ran away with her yet again … be royalty?

"Ow!"

She felt a sudden, sharp jab at the back of her ribcage. Whipping round, she saw Annie standing right behind her, ready to poke her again. She'd been so engrossed in watching the carriage, she hadn't heard the girl return.

"I was in the kitchen, calling," Annie said crossly. "Why are you out here?"

"Looking," Mary said.

"Well, you shouldn't be. You're wanted. By the mistress."

"Who? I…? *Me?*"

Mary didn't move. She was confused. How could she be wanted when the mistress was busy talking to the Queen or whoever was in the landau?

"You. And get a hurry-on. They're waiting."

"What for?"

In answer Annie simply grabbed her hand and pulled her, dragging her past Cook and up the concrete steps.

Wiping her free hand, still wet and raw from the fish, Mary followed in absolute puzzlement.

"Ah, at last," Eliza said, turning to see the girls approaching.

"I'm sorry. I couldn't find her," Annie explained, adding darkly, "She wasn't at her duties."

"Never mind," Eliza said. "She's here now. This is Mary, Lady Emmeline."

She reached out a hand and pushed Mary down by the shoulder to ensure she curtseyed as deeply as possible to the people inside. Mary looked down to make sure she didn't fall over. When she looked up again, she was staring into the bright, periwinkle blue eyes of a golden-haired girl who did not seem much older than herself. For a brief second, she thought she saw a glimmer of laughter in the girl's expression, but she quickly became distant and perfectly composed.

"Good afternoon, Mary," she said, nodding graciously.

"Lady Emmeline," Mary acknowledged, bowing her head.

"Ooh, no!" the girl laughed.

"That is my great-niece, Kitty Ballard. *I* am Lady Emmeline," said a strange voice, coming from the shadows of the carriage. Mary peered in its direction.

A head turned to her under one of the most enormous coal scuttle bonnets Mary had ever seen. It had a brim a foot long, shading the face from view. All Mary could make out were some tight grey curls peeping out underneath and thick lips that seemed surprisingly rouged. The body from the neck down was hidden under a high-collared cape in a purple tartan. Not royalty, but certainly intriguing.

"Lady Emmeline DuLac is a person of noble heritage and a distinguished philanthropist," Mrs Aitken said to Mary, in her grandest voice. "Do you know what that is?" Mary shook her head. "She gives extremely generous sums to the charities I serve. We are honoured by her visit."

"Not at all," the great lady said in a wavering voice. "It is you who do *me* the honour."

Mary waited, still wondering why she was there. Mrs Aitken usually tried to keep her well hidden from guests, unless she was serving at table. The mistress read the look on Mary's face and seemed uncomfortable.

"Lady Emmeline has a special request for us. She has asked to see you specifically. It seems… It seems that you might make yourself useful." She frowned as she spoke, as if not sure about what she was saying.

The niece, who had been silent until now, spoke up.

"My poor aunt is terribly unwell. We're lucky she was able to come out today at all, aren't we, Aunt Emmeline? She needs someone to sit with her and read to her, and take her mind off the worst of the pain. I come when I can, but…"

"You have your life, dear Kitty," the old lady warbled from beside her. "I can't impose."

"And her own servants are getting old. One is French. One is deaf. She needs someone young. My brother saw you at the Windus ball last month and said what a helpful girl you were."

Mary stared. Was this true? Who even was this brother? The niece smiled with angelic sincerity. Back in the shadows, the old lady fanned herself. "Pretty, *pretty* thing," Mary thought she heard her say, like a parrot.

Eliza Aitken beamed. "May I just say that we, as a family, would of course be delighted to do whatever small thing we can to assist."

"You're so terribly kind. My aunt would pay her for her time, of course."

"Oh no! I insist on it. Nothing at all. We are glad to be of service, aren't we, Mary?"

"Um, yes, ma'am," Mary said, biting her lip. *How easy it is for you, who have so much, to offer my services for nothing,* she thought. The money would have been very useful. But rich ladies like to show their charitable nature to even richer ones.

"You can read, can't you, Mary?" Eliza asked, as an afterthought.

"Yes, ma'am."

"Excellent. Just send for her whenever you need her, Lady Emmeline."

"Oh, call me Emmeline," the bird-like voice replied. "We are friends now."

Eliza beamed so broadly the look quite transformed her face. Mary bobbed to the carriage. She thought she saw one more glint in the pretty niece's eye as it moved off smartly, but dismissed it as a trick of the light.

***

Back in the kitchen, opinion that evening was divided.

Annie, who tended to think the worst of everything, was certain there was something wrong with Lady Emmeline.

"That voice! Did you hear it? It gave me the shivers."

"What shivers?" Cook scoffed.

"There was something not right about her. I know these things."

Mary tended to agree but Mrs Green, who was an expert on London society, took a different view.

"You know nothing, Annie O'Bryan. Lady Emmeline DuLac is famous for her respectability. Two of her brothers are bishops. Her father was a baronet. She gives more money to the church than you've had hot dinners. And I know how many you've had, my Annie, because I've cooked half of them myself, right here in this kitchen."

"I've heard her reputation," Annie acknowledged reluctantly, "but there was something weird about her, I'm telling you."

"Oh, you and your strange ideas," Cook said dismissively. "You're just jealous. Help her load the tray, Mary. And try not to spill as much water as yesterday. I'm telling you, Annie – this is young Mary's chance."

"She'll ruin it," Annie muttered. "She'll say the wrong thing or break something. Of all the people to call for!" She swept upstairs carrying a freshly laundered tablecloth.

Mary finished loading a wide wooden tray with glasses, napkins and cutlery for the evening meal and followed Annie upstairs. The bizarre creature in the carriage had scared her a little, it was true. But then, the great-niece had been charm itself. Either way, she would be out of this house for a while, and that could only be a good thing.

She tried to imagine Lady Emmeline's house. Would it be as grand as the Windus place? As usual, her daydreaming led to dropping a handful of forks and scratching the polish on the dining table before Annie could lay out the cloth. Annie chided her furiously and even walloped Mary on the arm with a spoon.

Down in the scullery, rubbing her shoulder to take the sting out, Mary couldn't help feeling she didn't belong here. She wasn't made for service and service wasn't made for her. If God had meant her to be a drudge all her life, surely He would have made her good at it? Her dreams turned to Felix's studio and the drawing he had done of her. The girl in that sketch would never be hit by a servant or sent to a mad old lady's house to read to her. It seemed forever until she could be that girl again.

Chapter Eleven

The first call from Lady Emmeline was delivered by messenger two days later. On lavender-scented notepaper, with the DuLac family crest embossed in gold, a hastily handwritten note begged Mary to come and read that evening, saying a servant would be dispatched to fetch her at eight o'clock that evening.

"You are excused serving at dinner," Mrs Aitken said, holding the note up to the light to admire the crest. "Annie can do your chores this evening and you can work hard tomorrow to make up for it."

"Yes, ma'am."

"You must wash most thoroughly and wear your best clothes. Put your hair up in a cap properly for once. Borrow one of Annie's. Get her to do it – it will be a disaster if you try. Call Lady Emmeline 'my lady' and don't speak until spoken to. Don't sit down until she asks you. Oh, what is she thinking of, choosing a country girl?"

When the time came, Mary scrubbed her skin under the freezing tap in the scullery and put on her sateen dress. Annie took great pleasure in viciously twisting up her hair to ensure as much of it was covered by her cap as possible. Downstairs the tradesmen's bell rang with an off-key clatter as the clock in the hall struck eight. Clutching her shawl tight round her shoulders, Mary followed the waiting coachman up the tradesmen's steps, her heart beating wildly.

She glanced along the street. The only carriage she could see was surely too large to be sent for a single servant girl? It was an elegant Clarence with yellow panels marked with a family crest, drawn by two matching bays in perfectly polished tack. Mary was amazed when the coachman opened the door for her to climb inside.

To her astonishment, three people were already sitting there. One of them leaned forwards so her face was caught in the light. It was Lady Emmeline's great-niece, who smiled at her encouragingly. She was dressed for the evening in jade green satin, trimmed with matching bows. Mary curtseyed deeply from the pavement. The girl patted the seat beside her.

"It's good to see you, Mary. I'm Kitty, remember? Don't be frightened! Come, sit next to me."

Speechless, Mary complied. She was aware of the silhouettes of two gentlemen in evening dress sitting opposite. Had Rupert Thornton arranged this, the same way he had fixed for her to visit the Windus place? She half expected to see his face smiling at her from the opposite seat. And who could the other man be?

But Rupert wasn't there. When she looked at the face under the silk top hat, Mary gasped out loud. Felix Dawson, as beautiful as ever, grinned back at her. He looked extremely pleased with himself. The man next to him, fat and round-faced, was, if anything, even more smug. He laughed aloud as Mary settled herself down.

"I don't believe it! We did it! Felix, you owe me half a guinea. I'm a genius!" He leaned forwards and tapped the panel behind Mary and Kitty with the silver tip of his cane. "Drive on, William."

The carriage moved off smartly down the street. Mary was too confused to say a word. Was she being kidnapped by these glamorous young people? If so, she didn't mind. It felt wonderful.

"You see?" Felix said happily. "I told you I'd find a way to see you again soon. And here we are. And you're wearing your peacock blue again. It's lovely, but we really must get you some new clothes, mustn't we, Kitty?"

"Yes, we must." The pretty girl beside Mary looked even lovelier than before. Her hair, caught up in a crown of flowers and lace, shone like spun gold. A delicate necklace of seed pearls and peridots sparkled on her collarbone. Her family must be infinitely grander than the Aitkens and yet here she was, sitting next to a servant girl. "I can't think of anything more delightful."

"However," Felix went on, "you will do perfectly for Cremorne Gardens, as soon as we relieve you of that truly ghastly cap. Kitty, will you do the honours?"

Kitty leaned forwards and unpinned Annie's cap with delicate fingers, making a better job of it than Rupert had. As her hair tumbled round her shoulders, Mary began to find her voice.

"Cremorne Gardens? Aren't we going to Lady Emmeline DuLac's house?"

"Goodness me, no," the round-faced man laughed. "That way disaster lies."

"But isn't she expecting me?"

"I hope not," Felix said. "I don't believe she's ever heard of you. Has she, Roly?"

"Not to my knowledge," his friend replied. "I don't see how she could have. She never goes out."

"But…" Mary's eyes darted from one to the other, then pleadingly to Kitty. "She asked for me… You were there."

"I was indeed," Kitty said, with the same gleeful glint in her blue eyes that Mary had noticed before. "But my great-aunt was not. As Roly says, she never leaves the house. She's a martyr to a thousand ailments. I don't know how she survives."

"So who…?"

"Who do you think?" Felix asked. They were all grinning so hard: so pleased with themselves, so delighted with her confusion. Mary realized they had pulled off a trick of some sort and her mind raced to catch up.

Someone else had pretended to be Lady Emmeline in the carriage. If the old lady never left the house,

Mrs Aitken might have no idea in the slightest what she looked like. If Kitty really was her great-niece, that would probably act as proof enough. It could have been anyone under that enormous bonnet.

"Was it someone I've met?"

"Yes…" Felix acknowledged. "Though now I think you were so understandably captivated by me that you don't remember." He laughed as the friend beside him dug him in the ribs.

The round face turned to hers. She suddenly noticed the familiar, fat lips, and imagined them thick with rouge. "You're the man I saw with Felix in Covent Garden. Oh…" Mary grinned. "You looked very fetching in your wig, I must say."

"Ah! She's got it! Clever girl!" He reached out for her hand and kissed it. "Roly Ballard. Pleased to meet you properly at last. A most excellent wig, that. Belongs to a friend of mine in Chancery. He used it for a terrible legal case last week. And my cape – what did you think?"

"I thought it very … large."

"It covered a multitude of sins. Eh, Felix? Ha ha!"

"And purple."

"Oh yes, isn't it? I had it made especially for some

theatricals last year. I was even more fetching then than I was in Pimlico. But what a triumph, Felix! I spoke to that wretched Aitken woman for a good ten minutes and she'd swear I'm a lady. Lent me her maid without so much as a murmur. And now you may do with her as you please."

There was a brief silence, broken by his laugh. Not everyone was as unshockable as Roly Ballard. *Nefarious purposes* echoed through Mary's head.

Then Kitty took her hand and said, "Ignore my brother. He's far too full of himself in general and he'll be insufferable tonight. I did all the work. He couldn't have done anything without my help and face creams. I only did it for Felix, because he wanted to see you again so badly. *He*'s a gentleman."

Felix turned to Mary. "Not wanted to see you – needed to. I can't possibly wait another month or whatever insufferable time you told me. Rupert Thornton gave us the idea with his Windus scheme. Even he has the odd sensible thought occasionally."

"Do you know him?"

"Oh yes – everyone knows Rupert, don't they, Roly?"

His friend nodded dismissively. Felix turned back

to Mary. "This way, a note from 'Lady Emmeline' will arrive every time I need you. Or when there are adventures to be had. You seem like someone who's made for adventures."

The look he gave her was so intense that Mary felt her temperature rise. His eyes had an effect on her that she'd never experienced before. *Made for adventures*. That felt so much more real to her, and true, than 'made for laying tables', or 'made for cleaning grates'. To be here, now, with the balmy summer air rushing by them and the carriage full of Roly and Kitty's laughter – *this* was living. Mary was soon laughing alongside them. The impossible had just happened and they made it seem easy. Her heart sang, the way it had in Felix's studio.

<figure>❦ ❦</figure>

Cremorne Gardens was only a short carriage ride along the riverbank from Pimlico. It was a pleasure park, full of music, lights and dancing. As Roly cheerfully bought tickets for them all, families were leaving with sleepy children in their arms and more young people were arriving, ready to enjoy the night.

The next few hours passed in a blur. One minute they

were watching a theatre performance outdoors. Pierrots and harlequins leaped about in front of waterfalls and mountain peaks, in a lively, noisy show that nobody seemed to understand. Then a bell rang and the crowd rushed to see a man on a small platform, hitting blocks of wood with hammers.

"I think he's supposed to be a musician," Kitty giggled, but it was like no music they had ever heard, and soon they wandered off to drink foul-tasting fizzy punch and get hopelessly lost in a maze.

Mary wondered that the punch didn't make her tipsy, as Roly guided them ever onwards, leading the way down leafy paths between tall trees, pointing out the boat lights on the river beside them, and finding the best vantage point to watch the evening's fireworks. She had never imagined that such a place could exist or that so many people could have the leisure to enjoy it. They weren't all fine gentlemen and ladies like Roly and his sister, in silks, top hats and buttonholes, but shop girls in their smart clothes and jaunty hats, and tradesmen in their working tweeds. Anyone could have a good time in London, it seemed – if they had the money to pay for it.

The fireworks started perfectly on cue and lit up the velvet evening sky with bursts of gold and silver, to the sound of orchestral music and *oohs* and *aahs* from the crowd. They culminated in a thrilling battle between two ships made of fizzing light, firing rockets at each other in a dazzling recreation of Nelson's victory at Trafalgar. The crowd bellowed their approval now, but Mary hardly heard them. She was *in* the battle, in a golden ship, raining down cannonfire on the perfidious French, watching the explosions burst into life not far above her head. Her face was bathed in their light.

Only when the last rocket had fizzed and died did she notice that Felix was watching her, not the sky. She assumed that he would say something but he didn't. He seemed as awestruck by her as she had been by the display.

Being watched by Felix was different from being noticed by any other man. Sometimes such attention made her uncomfortable, like when Rupert stared at her at dinner, but when Felix watched her she felt like a work of art. There was reverence in his gaze, as well as desire. She felt herself glow.

"Come, come!" Roly instructed, taking his friend roughly by the arm and pulling him on. "Enough admiring the scenery. I hear the band playing."

Kitty took Mary's arm as if they were old friends and they walked companionably together. Mary had so many questions to ask the other girl but she hardly dared talk to her.

Kitty sensed her hesitation. "You must think I'm a dreadful reprobate, running around with my brother like this."

"Oh no," Mary said. "I love it."

"The fact is, I suppose in a year or two I'll be married, and have babies and a house of my own and… I do love adventures, don't you?"

"Yes. Like nothing else."

"You never know what you're going to find. Especially with Roly. He's a terrible flirt and a liar. He has the worst reputation in London and yet somehow he manages to persuade our parents that we live the most impeccably decorous lives." She laughed. "He assured my mother we were going to dinner with several of his married friends. I'm quite well-behaved really but I love to imagine…" She stopped on the path and turned to Mary with a wistful look in her eye. "Look at you, in that lovely dress, with your hair loose and no need of a chaperone. I could picture you and Felix having a thousand escapades."

Mary was flattered and embarrassed, and certain that Kitty's envy was misplaced. "Look at *you*! In the latest fashions with those jewels and the prettiest face. I don't think I *can* imagine how perfect that must be."

"It's not perfect at all. It's very dull. But thank you for saying I'm pretty. Roly assures me on an hourly basis that I'm a hideous crone."

At this, Mary could only laugh.

Soon they arrived at a bright red-and-green Chinese pagoda, surrounded by tables where groups and couples sat to eat and drink. A large platform nearby was full of people dancing. It took Mary's breath away – lit as it was by hundreds of gas-fired bulbs, which made the night sky glow almost as bright as day. Hundreds of couples were whirling around to the music from the band. Roly bought them all more punch, then took his sister's hand and led her to join the dancing couples. Mary cringed as he promptly crushed Kitty's skirts and stood on her toes, while she somehow remained a picture of elegance and refinement, moving as if on wheels.

As Mary took another sip of punch and watched,

a hand touched her elbow. The music was irresistible and before she knew it she was dancing, too, with Felix expertly guiding her while somehow never taking his eyes from hers.

This is heaven, she thought. *I must have gone to Lady Emmeline's after all and been horribly murdered, because I'm in paradise.*

She felt fuzzy but happy, following Felix's lead, feeling the steady pressure of his hand on her waist, sensing the crowd beyond them as a dizzy blur. Her long hair swirled around her shoulders and down her back. The handsomest man in the Gardens was her partner. When she closed her eyes she saw fireworks.

"Are you glad we abducted you?" Felix asked, leaning in so she could feel his warm breath on her cheek.

"I…"

She wanted to tell him how very, very glad she was. But she was interrupted.

"Felix Dawson, by my soul! I thought it was you. Introduce me to your charming partner. My, what a beauty!"

They had been stopped in their tracks by a wide, drunk-looking, grey-haired gentlemen in perfect but dishevelled evening dress. He grinned at Felix and leered at Mary, before giving her what he clearly thought was a subtle wink. She felt faintly disgusted. She had the sense that at any moment he would lean in and kiss her, and stood as far back as she could.

A flash of panic crossed Felix's eyes. "This is … ah … Guinevere Arthur. An actress from Italy. Gwinny, this is Sir John Kilkenny."

"Gwinny, eh? Give me your hand." Reluctantly Mary held her hand out and the old man pressed his wet lips to her fingers. "Charmed, fair lady." Mary bobbed a small curtsey, not sure what to do, not wanting to speak. "Foreign, eh? If you ever want a guide about town, I'm sure I can find you a chaperone."

"She's busy. Very busy," Felix said hastily. "Good to see you, Sir John."

"Call me Johnny, old man. An artist like you. Future star of the firmament. A pleasure to meet you, Gwinny, my dear."

With a final leer he ambled off, and Mary and Felix both breathed sighs of relief. They caught each other's eye and their faces collapsed into laughter. Soon they were laughing so hard they had to sit down.

"Guinevere?" Mary said, when she could breathe enough to speak. "*Gwinny?*"

"I'm sorry, I panicked. It's the first name I thought of. Sir John's a terrible old soak. An art critic, with a fine knowledge of Arthurian legend. He likes the classics, too, so I imagine he's an acquaintance of Philip Aitken." Felix looked sheepish. "We should have thought of that."

Mary gasped. "What if they find out? They'll throw me out in a heartbeat!"

"As you quite rightly pointed out last time. So they mustn't find out. When you're with us, you can't be Mary Adams. We'll have to think of something better."

"Not *Gwinny*." Mary flashed her eyes teasingly at him and he blushed.

"What's this? Who's Gwinny?"

Roly and Kitty had finished their dance and come to join them at the table. Felix quickly explained the brief encounter with Sir John and Roly mocked him roundly, too.

"Girls from Italy are not called Guinevere, you nincompoop. And actresses are women of doubtful reputation. Mary, as we know, is a paragon. Why, she reads to old ladies out of the goodness of her heart."

"You think of something, then."

Roly considered the problem.

"Aurora. After the dawn. Aurora Begorra, from Ireland."

"Ghastly," Felix pronounced.

"Tiziana Magnifica, from Rome."

"Hideous."

"Ariadne Lavelle," Kitty offered.

"Oh, I like Lavelle," Felix acknowledged.

"Thank you. Lavelle's syrup is very soothing for the throat."

"But Ariadne's all wrong. It makes me think of spiders. Besides, she was abandoned on Naxos. I have no intention of abandoning Mary."

Mary felt her temperature rise again. "Who was Ariadne?" she asked. "Why was she abandoned?"

But conversation was temporarily suspended. Roly looked around, then at his sister, and announced it was time to go home. As they made their way out of the Gardens, Mary felt her head start to swim. Even so, she noticed that many of the ladies were not society girls, like Kitty, any more, or shop girls. An increasing number wore very low-cut dresses and bright powder on their faces. Several of them were cuddled up to gentlemen as they walked. Kitty pretended not to notice them but Mary watched openly and marvelled that such bright, indecent creatures were allowed to mingle so openly with the crowds.

I am a little bit drunk, Mary thought. *And Cremorne Gardens is a little bit disreputable.*

She was grateful as Felix took her arm to steady her and they searched for their carriage among the waiting queue of vehicles in the street. Once they'd found it and settled themselves inside, Roly said to her, "You asked me something. I forget what. Something important."

"She asked about Ariadne," Felix said.

Mary fought through the fog of the punch in her brain and remembered. "That's right. The abandoned girl."

"Not just a girl," Roly corrected her, searching in the pockets of his coat and pulling out a cigar. "A princess. A Greek one."

He paused to get his cigar to light and ignored Kitty as she coughed and tried to wave the smoke away. Mary didn't mind the smell or the smoke. She was happy to be riding in a large, comfortable carriage while an eerie mist settled over the River Thames beside them.

"So. Ariadne," Roly said, when the cigar was lit to his satisfaction. "The daughter of the legendary King Minos of Crete. Her father was a cruel and powerful ruler. Other kings had to bow to him, including the king of Athens. What was his name, Felix?"

"Aegeus."

"Indeed – Aegeus. Every year, like the others, King Aegeus was required to send seven young men and seven young women to Crete, just to show King Minos he was the boss. Each year, he set them loose in a labyrinth built by King Minos. Now, in the centre of that labyrinth lived a terrifying monster. It was the hideous offspring of the king's wife and his favourite bull, and was called the Minotaur."

Mary gasped. How could men even imagine such a thing? She was horrified yet gripped by the story.

"Yes?" she whispered.

"The Minatour killed his young tributes in bloody and horrible ways. Theseus was furious that his city should have to provide this sacrifice."

"Who was Theseus?"

"Aegeus's son. Our hero. Keep up, girl." Mary nodded

meekly. "He demanded to go with the next set of tributes so he could put an end to the monster. Well, as soon as he arrived in Crete and stated his intention, he had a bit of luck. The daughter of King Minos, Ariadne, fell in love with him. Before he went into the labyrinth she secretly gave him a ball of thread, explaining that he would need it to find his way out again. So in he went. And soon he found the Minotaur, or rather, it found him."

Roly paused again. It was clear he had a taste for amateur dramatics. He waited while Mary held her breath and grinned at the effect he was having.

"But Theseus was the son of a king. He defeated the monster with brute strength and courage. The problem now, though, was how to get away. In the fight, he'd dropped the end of Ariadne's thread. He was doomed to be lost there forever, until at last he found it again."

"And escaped?"

"Indeed. Ariadne was waiting for him at the entrance. 'My father will never forgive me for helping you,' she said."

"In a quavery voice like that?" Felix joked.

"I do an excellent female impression, as I have just proved, so shut your tatur-trap, Mr Dawson. Where was I? Oh yes. 'Take me with you,' she purred, in sultry, feminine tones. So Theseus took her on his ship, ever the gentleman. But he wasn't as smitten as she was. On the way back to Athens he got his crew to stop at an island called Naxos and he left her there, the blackguard. She was rescued in the end, mind you," Roly added. "By Dionysus, the god of wine. Always my favourite god, good old Dionysus."

"I could be Ariadne," Mary said softly. To rescue a hero from a maze? To flee from an angry father and end up with a god? Right now, Mary felt she could do that. She wanted to.

"No, no," Felix argued. "Not Ariadne. We need something else. Something without bulls and wine, Roly."

"Oh, I don't know. Wine seems very appropriate." Roly's face was redder than usual from all the punch he had been drinking. "We're dragging her into the Underworld. We might as well admit it."

Felix thought for a moment. "Ah! Roly! You have it!"

"Have what?" Roly asked, frowning.

"Mary's new name. I'd been thinking of an English tale, but Greek will do. She can be Persephone. It's perfect."

"Per-*sef*-oh-nee," Mary repeated, sounding out the name to herself. *Persephone Lavelle.* She liked it. It was beautiful and mysterious. And very, very different from the ordinary name Pa had given her. "Yes. I'll be Persephone. What's her story?"

But as Felix and Roly vied with each other to tell it, the carriage came to a smart stop with a whinnying of horses.

"We're here," Kitty sighed, looking up at the gas-lit stucco of St George's Square. Her disappointment spoke for all of them and they sat for a moment in silence.

Mary rose unsteadily to go. Felix leaned forwards and caught her fingers in his gloved hand.

"The next note from Lady Emmeline will come soon, I promise."

"I am at her service, sir."

"Goodbye, dear friend," Kitty said sweetly, pulling her in for a quick embrace.

"Don't do anything I wouldn't do," said Roly. Which didn't prohibit much, Mary thought. She left the carriage laughing.

It took several loud knocks to wake Mrs Green, who was snoring in the rocking chair, waiting to let Mary in. But by the time she reached the tradesman's door and unlocked it, she was bristling with curiosity.

"How was it, Mary? Magnificent?"

"It was … unexpected," Mary said mysteriously. "I'll tell you all about it in the morning." Of course, she would do nothing of the sort. But she would have fun imagining what Lady Emmeline *might* be like.

Ten minutes later she was asleep in her narrow bed, dreaming of labyrinths and fireworks, without even the energy to undo her stays.

Chapter Twelve

"Excuse me, sir."

A few days had passed since the illicit trip to Cremorne Gardens. Her headache was gone – though she vowed never to drink punch like that again. She had lied vaguely and effectively about her night with 'Lady Emmeline', then Annie had told her off a thousand times for dreaming. She had waited for the chance to find the professor alone and not too busy. It had taken until now. Mary stood nervously at the door of his study. Professor Aitken looked up from his papers, surprised.

"Yes?"

"Excuse me for asking, but I…" Mary coughed, willing the words to come.

The professor's grey-flecked brows drew together. "Continue, Mary."

"I… Please, can you tell me…? Who is Persephone?"

The brows knitted themselves still tighter.

"I don't understand your meaning. Does my wife have a friend by that name?"

"No. I thought she might be Greek."

She had been thinking about the name ever since Felix first mentioned it. Her secret life required a new identity: *Persephone Lavelle.* Could Persephone's story be as good as Ariadne's? If she was going to be this girl, she wanted to know.

"Oh!" Philip Aitken paused for a moment, startled. "Do you mean the goddess?"

That made sense. Mary nodded.

He smiled a rare smile. "Come in, Mary. Don't be afraid. The Greek goddesses are something of a passion of mine. Persephone, or Proserpine as the Romans called her, was one of the the daughters of Zeus, chief of the gods. How do you know about her?"

Mary had prepared for this. "On my day off, sir. I went to the Royal Academy to see some pictures. I heard men talk of her there."

"Did you now? How very educational. Well done. Let me see … which version to tell? Ah yes… Persephone's mother was Demeter, goddess of the harvest. Persephone wanted to devote herself entirely to nature – she was not interested in gods or men. Demeter was fiercely protective of her beautiful daughter. She tried to hide her away to keep her safe, but nevertheless, the god Apollo fell in love with Persephone. So did Hades, lord of the Underworld. Persephone was gathering flowers one day when Hades suddenly appeared from below and dragged her down to be with him. One minute she was there, the next…" The professor curled his fist in the air. "Gone."

He stopped. Mary realized he was looking at her, to check she was still listening. She had been silent for a long time, but not because she was distracted – quite the opposite. So *this* was his subject at university? She had always assumed what men studied there was dry and dull. But a girl kidnapped by the lord of the Underworld? Like Ariadne's story, this was anything but.

"Please … go on."

He smiled. "Now, Demeter had no idea what had happened. Her daughter had disappeared and nobody could tell her where to look. Zeus could have told her, of course. He was the girl's father, after all, but I'm afraid Zeus is very often neglectful in these stories. The gods behave quite irresponsibly much of the time. Where was I? Ah, yes. Demeter searched high and low, asking everyone she met. But Persephone was nowhere to be found. Wild with grief, Demeter abandoned her harvest duties. Fields produced no crops. Trees were bare. The land became barren. The people had nothing to eat and eventually Apollo, hearing their cries of anguish, told Demeter where her daughter was.

"She rushed to the Underworld straightaway to plead for Persephone's return. But Hades was very much in love with the girl. He refused to relinquish her. God and goddess prepared to fight, until Zeus intervened. This time, he took pity on Demeter. He decreed that Persephone could go home with her mother on one condition: she must take nothing from the Underworld."

He paused again. Mary sensed hope, but also tragedy. "Yes?"

"Well, Demeter joyfully agreed and Persephone prepared to go home. It seemed so close, so bright… But the gods play games. While in the Underworld Persephone had taken a single bite from a pomegranate. She had eaten six seeds and Hades argued that this meant she must stay with him. Mother and daughter's anguish increased. Zeus ruled, in the end, that for each pomegranate seed she had eaten, Persephone must spend a month of the year beneath the earth with her new husband. These months became winter, when grieving Demeter misses her daughter. The other months, when Persephone can return to the land of the living, are our spring and summer." The professor leaned forwards, his chin resting on his steepled fingertips. "It's a charming story. The details vary according to sources. Ovid tells it somewhat differently but I believe I have captured the basics."

Suddenly Mary, who had been lost in the Underworld, reaching for her golden, light-bathed mother, was back in the study, dutifully bobbing a 'thank you' curtsey to the master. He seemed very pleased.

"Did you like it, Mary?"

"Oh yes, sir!"

"Well, I am glad you appreciate the Greeks. Not everyone does. Sometimes I struggle to get such rapt attention from my students." He looked at her wistfully. "Now, off you go. I'm sure you have duties to attend to. Fires and whatnot. Don't let me keep you from the important things."

But nothing could be more important, Mary thought, than stories like these. They filled her head as she scrubbed muddy vegetables for supper and scraped the rough scales off slippery fish. They made the endless journeys up and down stairs more bearable, because she could imagine she was Demeter searching for her daughter, or Persephone rising each springtime to see her mother again.

Felix was right: Persephone's story was better than Ariadne's, because instead of being abandoned by a man, she had gods fighting over her. And she was the more tragic because she didn't want them to. *Did Persephone like Hades?* she reflected. *Did she come to love him?* He was her husband after all, but the story didn't seem to linger on her feelings in the matter.

 ⚜

The following evening after supper she was called back to the study. The master was alone tonight. Rupert had dined with him earlier and then gone on to a ball somewhere. Annic gave Mary a quick, almost sympathetic glance. But when the professor greeted her, the face behind the beard was smiling. She bobbed.

"You asked for me, sir?"

"I did indeed, Mary. I wanted to give you this. You can read, I take it?"

"I know my letters, sir."

"Good. This is a book I got for Alice some little time ago but she has shown no interest in it. You may borrow it until she does. It is written for children, so I believe even servants might understand it. It contains some of the more interesting legends – appropriately adapted for simpler minds. It's nicely illustrated, too. Step forwards, don't be frightened. Here you are."

He held out a large, thin volume, bound in pale linen stamped with gold. It said *Greek Legends for Boys and Girls* on the cover, above a gold line drawing of a man in what looked like boots and a short skirt fighting a monster with the head of a bull. *Theseus!* Mary thought to herself. And the Minotaur. How vivid the stories became when you knew them.

"Thank you, sir," she said, curtseying deeply.

The professor looked quite moved. "You are most welcome, my dear. It is indeed a joy to share these tales with someone who appreciates them. I can certainly find others when you're ready."

As she took the book from his hands, she felt a bond between them. She sensed that she alone in this household saw his true love of his subject and the excited boyishness behind his grim façade. His children and Annie were too frightened of him to notice, and his wife was not interested in gods and goddesses when she had dinners and friends and household expenses to worry about.

Was it an unseemly bond? Mary tried to decide, as she ran up the servants' stairs to her room, to hide the book under her pillow. Not unseemly, perhaps: the professor was interested in training her mind, not admiring her face. But even so, it felt like something she mustn't talk about or even think about too deeply. She felt instinctively that no one in the household would approve if they found out.

❦

That night the book, like the paintings, became a key to the magic world. Hunched up in bed with a candle, Mary read about goddesses who could summon storms and kill sailors who displeased them; heroes who would travel the world for ten years, battling gods and monsters to return to the woman they loved; mortals who married gods; humans transformed into a tree, a stag, a spider.

For thousands of years, it seemed, humans had been transformed. You didn't have to end where you started. Mary thought of Lizzie Siddal and the girl in Felix's drawing, and wondered who she could become.

Chapter Thirteen

Felix called for her four days later. Four nervous, excited days. Eliza Aitken tutted solicitously as she read over the message.

"Lady Emmeline has a chill. She would like you to read to her this afternoon. Take a bottle of lavender water from my store and say I find it soothing on the pillow. I have asked Cook to bake her some *petits gateaux au chocolat*. Take them with you in a basket and assure her of my sympathy for her condition."

Up in his studio, Felix put the lavender water on his handkerchief and pronounced it 'very soothing'. The look he gave Mary as he breathed in the scent made her feel the opposite of soothed. They ate the chocolate cakes with beer, then he drew her as the goddess Astarte with stars in her hair, as he'd promised. But he wasn't happy with his work that day and crumpled it into an angry ball – though Mary had thought it beautiful.

"The light's wrong. My touch is off. Sometimes it happens. Nothing to be done. Let's hire a cab and go somewhere."

He told the coachman to take them to Highgate Cemetery. Mary knew about his Pre-Raphaelite set and the scandalous things they got up to, and wondered if she should be shocked. She was certainly surprised. Of all places in London, it was the last one she would have chosen.

What she wasn't ready for at all was the utter wonderment she felt as soon as they walked through the huge, wrought-iron gates.

"Why, it's beautiful!"

"Of course it is. I worship only beauty. Come, walk with me."

The cemetery was built on a hill overlooking the north side of London. It was quite new – unlike the crumbling, ancient graves outside St Michael's church in Westbrook – but already moss and lichen were starting to invade the stones and turn them green. What stones they were! Not simple tombs and gravestones, but veritable palaces for the dead, with Egyptian pillars down one pathway and Gothic archways down another. Stone angels stood guard or lay sleeping on the burial place. All around, creeping woodland provided gentle shade. Squirrels watched them pass before scampering into high branches. Birds sang. Mary shivered at the loveliness of the setting.

They walked along in silence between the vaults and tombstones for a while. Felix didn't take her arm but she felt his presence and his deep appreciation for the atmosphere, like hers. She sensed their hearts beating in time.

Eventually, after stopping to look up at one of the mossy angels, its feathered wings caught in a shaft of sunlight, he turned to her.

"Not many girls I know would be so content to come here."

"It reminds me of *Ophelia*."

He nodded. "Millais? Yes, nature in all her glory. Death, of course. That frightens some people."

Mary nodded back. "It frightens me but it happens. To know that it can be so peaceful once it's done..." She looked around, soaking up the dappled light, the birdsong, the stillness beneath the stones.

Felix stopped and leaned against a moss green pillar, one leg bent, his foot resting on the stone behind him. His voice was low.

"Clearly the blue river chimes in its flowing
Under my eye
Warmly and broadly the south winds are blowing
Over the sky."

Mary smiled. The words took her back to Westbrook.

"One after another the white clouds are fleeting;
Every heart this May morning in joyance is beating
Full merrily
Yet all things must die."

She gasped at the last line. She was also confused. He'd said 'This May morning', but it was June already. It took her a moment to realize he was quoting poetry. Beautiful, beautiful, sad lines. She shivered again.

"Did you write those words?"

He grinned. "Ha! Me? Thank you, but no. That was Tennyson."

"Oh. You'll have to teach it to me."

"With pleasure."

Mary nodded to herself, thinking. "Tenny-stone…"

"Tennyson," he corrected.

"Tenny*son*, I mean. Yes, of course. I've often heard Rupert speak of him."

Felix's eyes narrowed. "Rupert Thornton? Often? When?"

Was that a hint of jealousy? Mary smiled, but pretended not to notice. "Oh, at dinner. He's a regular at our table."

"I wonder why," Felix muttered sarcastically.

Mary played the innocent. "He's a very good student. Devoted to his professor."

Felix laughed without humour. "And to his professor's maid, no doubt. Well, I pity you."

"Oh? Why?"

"Having to listen to him pontificate. He often hangs around Gabriel and Millais but he has no idea about life or art, you know. He likes to think he does. But if he came to this place, his first thought would be to find an excellent, tasteful spot for his own mausoleum and a good sculptor to decorate it."

Mary giggled. This was quite possibly true. Was this dislike the reason Felix hadn't come over to introduce himself that first night? Whatever the case, the very thought of Rupert seemed to prompt him to head down the nearest pathway at marching pace. She struggled to keep up with him. He walked with an athletic stride, not at all like the frail gait Mary had imagined an artist might have. But then, she had seen him drawing. Art was a physical activity, much more so than she'd realized. He had powerful shoulders, too... She found herself thinking about the body under his white linen shirt and was so distracted that she only realized how fast they were going when she ran out of breath and had to rest on a nearby empty plinth, begging him to wait for her.

He turned back, alarmed, and ran to kneel at her feet.

"I'm sorry! I didn't mean... Are you all right?"

"Yes. Just a little dizzy."

"I wasn't thinking. Not true. I was thinking too much."

So was I, Mary agreed silently.

"We should probably head home. 'Lady Emmeline' will be needing her nap shortly, I dare say."

"Yes, we should."

They stayed where they were, though: Mary seated and Felix kneeling beside her. His face was in shadow but she could still make out where stray curls that touched his cheek were slightly damp with exertion.

A part of her wanted to brush them, gently, from his face and rest her fingers there.

"You have no idea how magnificent you are," he said in a low voice. "In this light, with eyes like malachites and your hair glowing against the trees. You really are a goddess, Mary."

She gave him a little smile. "Persephone. It suits this place. Taken by Hades and living with the dead."

"My Lord! You know the story? We never got to tell it to you."

"I asked the professor about it."

"Did you, by god? And you love Tennyson and talk of Titian… Are you sure you're a country girl?"

"Absolutely! With a farmyard for a garden."

He took her hands and stood up, pulling her with him. "How can you be so perfect? Girls who look like you are silly and vapid, and that's all right, because we draw them and make them wonderful, but you…" He stared deep into her malachite eyes. "You … really are wonderful." A hand strayed to her hair and stroked it. "Persephone. Goddess of nature…"

He trailed off and turned away. He had stared into Mary's soul, it felt like, for five long seconds. She had counted them in her head without breathing, sure he was going to kiss her. But instead, he had stepped back and walked off into the shadows.

Had she done something wrong? She was sure she hadn't. Did she *want* him to kiss her? Her lips tingled at the thought of it. She stood on the spot, in the dappled light, breathing fast and shallow.

When he turned back, it was as if he had completed a puzzle. His eyes were bright. He spoke fast and clear, gesticulating as he talked.

"You're Persephone Lavelle, a mysterious young lady whose parents are dead, brought up in Italy. That explains why nobody has met you. It also explains your feeling for poetry and art."

"Wait!" Mary laughed, holding up a hand. "I can't speak Italian. I don't know a word. I don't even know what it sounds like!"

"Hmm." He acknowledged the problem.

"How about this?" Mary suggested. "I am Persephone Lavelle, my mother died when I was young, brought up in Kent by my beloved father." She liked the idea of a beloved father. She was sure she could imagine one if she tried. "I grew up in a small village. *That* explains why no one's met me."

Felix laughed. "Touché. Lies close to the truth are the best. But your father was French, which explains your lovely surname."

"Yes, but he didn't speak it to me," Mary said firmly. "He had a lot of money but lost it." She was warming to her task... "Now I'm dependent on the kindness of distant relatives."

Felix laughed again. "Yes, yes, yes! Now it's my turn. We met ... at a party... Why not? It's true. But the most important thing is, I know how I shall paint you. I've seen it as if it's already done. You're the goddess Persephone herself – a girl caught between life on earth and the Underworld. You think you're about to rejoin your mother but, tragically, you've already sealed your fate. A half-eaten pomegranate lies on the ground and Hades waits in the background, ready to claim you. Come on! I need to get home so I can block it out."

He took her hand and swept her back down the paths towards the entrance. His mind was already in his studio, she could tell.

"I need to get back to Pimlico!" she warned him.

"Yes, yes. I don't need you today. I can do some of

the preliminary work from memory. But I will do soon. Explain to your mistress that Lady Emmeline has taken a turn for the worse and will be calling on your services more frequently in the days ahead. Can you do that?"

"Of course."

They reached the cemetery gates. It was late in the afternoon and the only passers-by were an ancient gardener raking the gravel and a young ragamuffin eating an apple off the tree. Felix put his arm round her, talking happily about his new ideas. The gardener and the boy surveyed them as they passed.

At the gates, Felix stopped and turned to her, and she saw the look of intent in his eyes. This time he wasn't going to be distracted by thoughts of painting or anything else. He drew closer and she felt the warmth of his breath. This time Mary was prepared. Before his lips could reach hers, she turned away.

Sitting for him was dangerous enough. Anything more was begging for disaster – she had to be careful. As a gentleman, he seemed to understand.

"I'm sorry," he mumbled. He made do with running his fingers through her hair. She shuddered with the pleasure of it.

"I am, too."

He pulled back. "I think you'd kiss the way you look," he murmured.

"Tired?" Mary teased him.

He shook his head. "On fire."

PART II

THE WHITE DRESS

Chapter Fourteen

Despite the warmer weather, poor Lady Emmeline was very sick throughout the month of June. It caused Annie no end of problems and even Cook had to be drafted in sometimes to help with some of Mary's lighter duties, she was called away so often.

"I don't have to go if I'm needed here," Mary told Eliza Aitken, feeling guilty when a messenger came for the third day in a row, though she was desperate to see Felix. She saw Kitty and Roly sometimes, too, but it was Felix she really wanted.

"No, no! We'll manage without you. Lady Emmeline's need is greater than mine. Be sure to tell her how much we pray for her swift recovery. If she would ever like us to visit her, too, to lighten her darkness. The children, perhaps…"

"I'll tell her, ma'am, certainly."

"And books… Can we give her any new ones? Philip has so many. What are you reading at the moment?"

"Tennyson, ma'am."

"Oh? What?"

"'The Lady of Shallot'."

Felix had given her an anthology of poetry after her third sitting. She had been reading the poems every night ever since. Tennyson was there and Shakespeare. A poet called Donne, who talked of suns and fleas – Mary couldn't understand a word – and another called Marvell, whose words were just as difficult. 'The Lady of Shalott' was thrilling and romantic. It was about a lady forced to weave all day, in an enchanted tower in Camelot. She was courted by Sir Lancelot and struck down by a curse for leaving her loom to look at him through the window. Mary had read it four times already and knew much of it by heart.

"You're reading Tennyson to Lady Emmeline?"

Mary panicked. She had momentarily forgotten the context of the question. "Yes, ma'am. She's very fond of it."

"How extraordinary. I'm sure my husband has other things that are more appropriate. Some interesting tracts from St Gabriel's, perhaps?"

"I'll ask her, ma'am."

"And Mary – please don't keep her up too late. It can't be good for her health. Annie tells me you read to her till past two this morning."

Felix had taken her to a party at one of Roly's clubs to celebrate great progress on his drawings for the new painting. There had been dancing and champagne… Roly had drunk so much he had to be carried to his carriage.

"She finds it hard to sleep, ma'am. But I'll see if I can calm her."

"I'm sure you will. You're a good girl, Mary. It's very noble, what you're doing for us all."

"Thank you, ma'am," Mary said, curtseying, as her neck turned the ruby red of the Turkish rug.

And yet, the strange thing was, when she was with Felix in the studio, what they were doing together did indeed feel noble. There was little drinking, except a sip of beer or wine, and no dancing. Their excitement rested in his talent with a pencil and brush, and her use of her body to sit still, to hold a pose and catch the light. It was demanding; it was exciting; it was work; it was art.

He hadn't tried to kiss her since the visit to Highgate Cemetery. Felix didn't talk about that moment but she sensed he thought of it as often as she did. She still wanted to but, if they let it happen, one kiss would surely lead to another and who knew where it would end? Mary knew she wasn't ready to become his mistress. She might gain him but she would lose everything.

Meanwhile he contented himself with painting her.

He had completed the preliminary sketches and prepared a canvas for the painting that was taller than himself and four feet wide. The sketches, which were scattered around the room, featured Persephone life-size, her lips stained with pomegranate juice as she stared up towards the distant light of freedom. In one of them, Felix had indicated armies of dark green trees behind her, with the shadowy figure of Hades himself half-hidden in the background, watching. Standing out against the shades, he said that Persephone would shine like a beacon. Her skin would glow in flesh tones, but apart from her face and tumbling russet hair, the picture's light and focus would come from a white dress with flowing panels and billowing sleeves, encapsulating the young goddess's ancient purity.

Felix was excited about the dress. He had designed it in his head that moment in the graveyard and since then a local seamstress had brought it to life, using ten yards of white silk damask, woven with a design of ivy leaves. Mary, who was used to Philip Aitken saying 'very nice, dear,' to his wife's latest excesses, had never thought a man could be so interested in a woman's clothing. But Felix was fascinated, and sure of his ideas.

The dress arrived just as he was ready to start work on the canvas itself. At first, struggling into the white silk behind the screen in the studio, Mary was convinced he had no sense at all of women's fashion. The dress had no corset and came all in one piece, unlike the usual bodice and skirt that she was used to. The only way to do it up was to ask for Felix's help with a row of buttons at the back. Truly he was dragging her to the Underworld! They didn't speak while his delicate fingers worked on each one and she wished the birdsong outside would drown out the sound of her rapid breathing.

"There," he said when he was finished. "Turn round and let me see."

Mary took a moment before turning. When she did so, he was standing too close. Her mouth went dry. They stared and laughed and both stepped back, so he could judge the effect of his creation.

He looked at her for a long time.

"Yes," he said, nodding slowly. "Yes."

That was all.

He led her out into the studio, where she glanced into a full-length mirror leant precariously against the wall.

Yes, she thought. *Yes.*

Felix may have no sense of fashion but he had every sense in the world of what suited her. The new dress showed off her neck and shoulders. It formed the perfect foil for her hair. Looking down, she admired the way the simple panels flowed, gathering in volume from her waist until they fanned around her feet.

Up until now she had admired gowns for their complexity. Her favourites had been those, like Kitty's, with the narrowest waists and widest hoops, the cleverest tucks and gathers, the most sophisticated dyes. Yet the white dress's very simplicity was what made it exceptional. It was comfortable too, without the boning and underskirts of normal clothes. She felt almost naked moving around in it, and blushed as she walked. For all sorts of reasons, she was reluctant when the time came for Felix to help her unbutton it at the end of the session.

"I'm not sure about the neckline," he said, reaching for a glass of wine to wet his dry lips as she disappeared behind the screen again. "It keeps pulling."

This was true. The seamstress, though quick, had not been very accurate with the yolk.

"I'll fix it," Mary offered. "It won't be hard."

"You sew, too?"

"Exquisitely. It's what I do best."

"I doubt that very much, Mary Adams."

"Persephone Lavelle," she reminded him, letting the dress fall to the floor.

"Very well, *Persephone*. But still, I wager five guineas there are many things you do better than sewing."

"I don't have five guineas and neither do you, but you're wrong. I've been sewing since before I could read… And before I looked like this, since I know what you're thinking."

He laughed. "You're right about that. But wrong about the five guineas. I can certainly afford it – with a little help. And if you can fix the dress, then you've earned it."

"*Five guineas?*" She popped her head round the screen. "Don't be ridiculous. That's ten times what I earn in a year."

He looked back at her from over his wine glass. "I admire your mathematics. But Roly lost more than that last month at the races. And won it back at cards."

"Ah, but we're not Roly," Mary pointed out, back behind her screen, lacing herself safely into her bodice.

"I will be one day," Felix said wistfully. "Through my paintings. Not as red-faced and insufferable, obviously. But as rich. And in the meantime … there are ways."

"What *are* those ways?" Mary asked, hooking on her skirt. She'd wanted to know ever since her first visit here. Felix hadn't sold a big painting yet, so how was this studio paid for? Who funded the wine, the paints, the fruit and flowers, the fine clothes and carriage rides with flame-haired models, the silk damask dresses?

"There are … ways," he repeated evasively. Mary stepped out from behind the screen to see if she could stare him into submission but he wasn't looking in her direction. Instead he was gazing at a canvas half-hidden behind a chair piled with dirty clothes. All she could make out were the sandy paws of a dainty dog, set against the thick folds of long black skirts.

When he sensed her looking at him, he spun round, shook off his thoughts, whatever they were, and smiled. "Talking of guineas, I owe you your wages. Here."

He took a silver coin from a pile carelessly tossed on the trestle table and crossed over to press it into her hand. She opened her fingers to look at it: a crown. Five shillings. It was what she earned in a week as a maid and twice what he'd paid before.

"Are you sure?"

"Money's good," he said. "And going to get better. You need – *Persephone* needs – more clothes. And you worked hard today. I told you you would. Most girls sigh and fidget. You never do. You're totally still, unless I need you to move. I only struggle to capture those eyes. Those malachite eyes…"

He looked into them again. His own were brown, fringed with long lashes. Under the right one, a pattern of three small moles ran along the top of his left cheek. Without thinking, she lifted a finger to stroke them. She felt his breath quicken and her heart beating rapidly.

It took a great effort from both of them to pull away.

"Thank you for the money." Her mind was suddenly a mess. She was about to leave when she remembered the white dress. He put it into an untidy package for her and she waited while he tied the string, watching his hands and aching for them to touch her.

"Here." He handed her the parcel.

In her confusion, she left her bonnet and shawl behind.

Chapter Fifteen

She didn't sleep that night, or much the night after. She longed to talk to someone about the roiling feelings inside her, and the look of Felix as he watched her, and the magical way the painting was taking shape. But who could she tell? Annie was as cold and hard as always. Cook, she was certain, would love nothing more than to know the gossip from an artist's studio and would repeat it to half of London before the day was out, which would be the death of everything.

So when Sunday came and she finally saw the warm, cheerful figure of her cousin coming towards her in the churchyard, arms open for an embrace, Mary struggled to stop the words from tumbling out.

"My, you look bright-eyed!" Harriet said, marvelling at her. "The summer weather has given you a glow."

"Thank you," Mary said guiltily.

"You must tell me all about what you've been up to in London."

"I wish I could…"

"Well, today we have all the time. You know the Harringtons are taking lunch with the Aitkens?"

"Yes. Cook's been attempting to prepare lobster in their honour. It wasn't as simple as she hoped."

Harriet grinned. "Did she tell you that Mrs Harrington suggested I should come along to help out? She thought we'd like the opportunity to see each other."

"Really?" The elegant, fashionable lady in the churchyard gained in perfection in Mary's eyes. "My! Isn't she kind?"

"Oh, the whole family are. All except Joe." Harriet tucked her arm into Mary's. "Always in trouble and always in debt, but the rest of them are darlings. I only wish you could be as lucky as me."

"Don't worry about me. I'm glad for you, Hattie, really."

Mary marvelled once again at the change in her cousin since coming to London. They walked home in cheerful procession behind their mistresses and set to work in the Aitkens' busy kitchen.

With Harriet there, everything was different this morning. Cook was glad of the older girl's deft and ready help. Even Annie was in a good mood as tasks were done well and on time, without her asking. Mary realized how truly hopeless she was at carrying out her duties. She almost felt sorry for Annie, who so often had to clean up after her.

The room was steamy with the smell of roast beef and boiled ham. A whole salmon – Mrs Green's *pièce de résistance* – lay set in aspic on a silver platter, along with the experimental lobster mousse, made in moulds shaped like cockle shells. While she worked on the three-tier fruit jelly for dessert, Cook chatted happily to her new audience.

"Of course this must all seem very plain to you, Mary. Oh, the things you must see at Lady Emmeline's table! Tell your cousin all about them."

Mary flushed salmon-pink. "Lady Emmeline eats very well, of course. She's partial to pigeon and ice cream. But I generally only see her bedchamber. She likes me to read to her there."

"Lady who?" Harriet interrupted.

"Lady Emmeline DuLac!" Cook shook her head in

surprise. "Didn't you tell her, Mary? You shouldn't hide your light under a bushel. Mary's practically been mixing with royalty." She sighed at Harriet in mock despair. "She is very subtle, your young cousin. Most discreet. She hardly tells us a thing. Yet she spends more time with the great lady than she does in this house."

"*Do* you?" Harriet asked sharply.

"Yes, I do. But she swears me to secrecy," Mary gabbled. "There isn't much to report."

Harriet's face took on the same sceptical expression that Annie so often wore. What young girl would visit the house of one of London's great dames and not want to recount every detail? Cook might be convinced that Mary was naturally 'subtle and discreet', but her cousin knew better. As soon as they were alone in the scullery, she closed the door and pulled Mary to her.

"So?" she asked in a hoarse whisper. "What's happening? Tell me the truth."

Mary chewed her lip. "I can't. I'd love to but I can't."

"There is no 'Lady Emmeline', is there?"

"Oh, there is, but I haven't met her. Promise not to tell a soul!"

"So... Where do you go? What do you do? Is *that* why

I never see you on your days off?"

"There is … someone." Mary hung her head. She would rather examine the hem of Harriet's dress than look her in the eye.

Harriet squeaked. "Mary! You're not running off to meet up with some stable boy?"

"No! No!"

"Nothing good will come of it! I promised your ma—"

"He's not like that, I swear. He's a gentleman. He only wants to paint me." Mary skated over the trips to Cremorne Gardens and the cemetery, and the clubs and cafés, and the hackney carriages.

"*Paint* you?"

"Yes. Like Lizzie Siddal."

"Who?"

"She's a famous artists' model. They hung her picture in the Royal Academy."

"And you? Are they going to hang your picture in the Royal Academy?"

Mary chewed her lip some more. "They might. I don't know. But it's very good, I know that. He's the most wonderful artist, Hattie. Promise you'll keep my secret. Swear."

She waited anxiously. The words had come out in a tumble but she was terrified of her cousin's answer. Harriet would never stand for the slightest misbehaviour when they were little. How would she cope with this?

And yet Harriet's face did not become a thundercloud. There was kindness in her eyes. And something else, too. Mary couldn't place it.

"Yes, I'll keep your secret," Harriet said with a grin. "But mind you don't forget your place. You're a maid, not a model like this Lizzie-Whoever-She-Is. It's all you've got and you're lucky to have it, painting or no painting."

"I know," Mary agreed.

Harriet reached out her hand and tucked a stray coil of hair back into Mary's cap. "I hope he's good to you."

"He is!"

This kindness, this recognition, was not what she'd expected at all. And then she saw it. The bright glow around Harriet that she'd noticed the first day she arrived in London. Finally she knew what it meant.

"*You* have someone! A sweetheart! I should have known it."

"Don't be ridiculous!" Harriet went the colour of

beetroot juice and hid her face against the mangle.

"You do!" Mary persisted. "Of course you do. I hope he's good to you, too."

They heard footsteps in the corridor outside. Annie was approaching, calling out their names.

"He is," Harriet whispered quickly, glancing at the scullery door. Mary had never seen her so happy.

"London's been good to us both," she grinned.

In later days, Mary often thought back to that moment, before Annie burst in on them. The look of pure joy on Harriet's face seemed set to last forever.

It was the last time she saw it.

Chapter Sixteen

The sharp, bright blue of June skies gave way to hotter weather in July. Complaining of the uncommon heat, Mrs Aitken took the children to visit her mother by the sea in Norfolk, which made Annie and Mary's lives in London much easier.

The next time Lady Emmeline called, the carriage took Mary not to the studio, but to an address in Mayfair, in the fashionable heart of London. Standing beside a tall Georgian townhouse in dark-painted brick, with dozens of white-framed windows, she marvelled at its grandeur. It even had a turning circle for carriages. The coachman indicated a side door where a maid was waiting. She led Mary inside and up the servants' stairs to an airy floor of family bedrooms.

"Where am I?" Mary asked.

"Didn't the coachman tell you? This is Balfour House,

the Ballards' 'ome. Miss Catherine's been looking forward to your visit. I'm Winnie, by the way. She's told me aw' about you."

"Oh? What did she say?" Mary asked.

"What good times you 'ad at the Gardens and how you're a model for one of Master Roly's young friends. Oh, and 'ow she wants to disguise you as a lady." Winnie turned to Mary with a look of resignation. "She asked me to try it meself once and I told her in no uncertain terms. But Miss Catherine does love her japes. 'Ow she's going to behave when she's married, I don't know. It won't be long now, if her mother has anything to do with it. 'Ere she is."

Winnie led Mary into a large, silk-lined room with an antique four-poster hung with gathered muslin. Light poured in through three tall, narrow windows and bounced off several mirrors. Skirts, petticoats, bodices and shoes were scattered around the floor, the bed and various chairs. Kitty looked up from the middle of it all, dressed only in her stays and underskirts, and beamed at Mary.

"You're here! I haven't seen you for an age! Felix is so selfish. But he has lent you to me for the afternoon.

Do help us, Winnie. Now the fun can begin."

With Winnie's evident disapproval, the fun did indeed begin. The first task was to choose an appropriate outfit for Persephone Lavelle to go shopping with her new friend. Persephone, Kitty decided, would wear duck-egg blue taffeta and a wide straw hat to shade her face from the sun. Stepping into Kitty's spare hoops, Mary felt herself suddenly taking up four times more space than she was used to. She kept on accidentally bumping into things. The taffeta that went over the petticoats was so light and crisp it seemed liable to take off or tear at any moment. Kitty told Mary not to worry: such things could always be replaced.

She herself wore a lilac gingham dress, fresh from Paris, which used more fabric in its pleated skirts than Mary had worn in a lifetime. They made up their faces with touches of cream and grease, selected parasols from Kitty's vast collection to match their outfits, and finished off with matching summery shawls, gloves and hats.

Mary hardly recognized herself in Kitty's long mirror. She was a real lady and a fine one. With her raw fingers sheathed in gloves and her freckles hidden by powder, you would never guess she was a country girl who had spent the morning swabbing the kitchen floor. She twirled round and Kitty clapped delightedly.

"I knew it would be perfect. All we need to do is gather up Aunt Violet and we can be on our way."

"Aunt Violet?"

"My chaperone. Mama insists. She's my great-aunt, really." Kitty thought for a moment. "Like Lady Emmeline, I suppose, but Aunt Violet is very different from the real Aunt Emmeline. She's seventy-three and deaf as a post. How she's supposed to defend my honour when Roly's not around I don't know, but I'm not allowed to order the carriage without her. It's most trying. But she's a darling and does what she's told. She won't get in our way."

Aunt Violet was duly rounded up from wherever she had been napping in the vast house, and appeared looking sleepy but amenable in the hall. Kitty introduced 'Persephone' and Aunt Violet nodded and smiled. She was small and plump, dressed in complicated black silk ruffles with a white lace collar, somewhat in the style of Queen Victoria. She didn't faint with shock at the sight of Mary in her borrowed dress and accessories, which Mary took as a good sign. Her own heart was pounding: *impostor impostor*. But nobody turned a hair as she followed her friend and their chaperone outside.

Kitty called for one of the manservants to accompany them and carry their purchases.

"Now, where shall we begin?" she asked as they joined Aunt Violet in the open landau, which Mary realized was the one used for 'Lady Emmeline', but this time with its roof down so they could take the afternoon air. "The Duke of Northumberland lives round the corner. We might bump into him on a sunny day like this."

"No – please!" Mary begged. She was still learning to walk and sit in her tighter stays, and trying to remember not to rub at her powdered nose. The last thing she needed was to bump into a duke.

"But I want the world to meet Persephone." Kitty pouted. "You look so lovely. Not lovelier than at the Gardens, I admit – you were just as beautiful then. But more presentable. I want to present you!"

"I wish you wouldn't," Mary pleaded. "Not yet. Can't we practise first? Is there somewhere else we can go? Somewhere without dukes?"

"Hmm," Kitty pondered. "I know! Let's cross the river. There are some surprisingly good fabric shops in

Southwark. I know them because Roly has arty friends down there." She raised her voice. "Take us to Borough High Street, William."

The coachman nodded and tapped the horses with his crop. Kitty sat back, satisfied. Looking down, Mary marvelled at her own blue skirts, filling the carriage like pools of sky, and the lace-gloved hand adjusting the ivory handle of her parasol to shade her from the beating sun. It was the hand of Persephone Lavelle: hers and yet not quite hers. It occurred to her briefly that while she had never felt right as Mary-the-drudge, she felt equally out of place as Persephone-the-society-girl. Perhaps it was just a matter of getting used to it.

But soon she stopped thinking about herself. In the open carriage, she was easily distracted by the view. London was as busy as ever – an endless building site it seemed. The Thames flowed relentlessly dark and grey beneath them as they crossed it on a wide stone bridge. Looking east, towards the sea, steamers and barges steadily plied their trade. West were the Houses of Parliament, a nest of stone and scaffolding, nearly finished after the fire. London was all about changing and making things. Mary found it as compelling as she had the first day she arrived.

Once they reached Southwark, the clamour of the tenements spoke of a very different London from the West End. Here, there were ragged children begging on every street and washing hung out to dry between high windows in crumbling buildings. Omnibus drivers fought for road space with carts freshly loaded with goods from the docks. The stink of the river hung rank in the air, mixed with the foul smell of tanneries and drying leather, intensified by the summer heat. Several workmen, caked in brick dust, turned to stare at the ladies in their smart, open carriage. Mary shivered with self-consciousness but Kitty ignored them with ladylike composure.

Soon they turned off the main street to a side road near the river, where Kitty took her to a large draper's shop. Its stock wasn't as fine as Mr Foster's – he had the best eye for silk and wool in Kent, people said – but there was much more of it and it was still a paradise to Mary. With Aunt Violet looking on benignly, she and Kitty spent an hour choosing a fabric for Persephone's first evening dress.

After much deliberation, they went for an ivory silk moire, which took most of Mary's money. Mary had never worn anything like it but Kitty pronounced it perfect for a new society girl of mysterious origins. She also said she could get her seamstress to make it to Mary's measurements. Though Mary could have sewn it herself, she was grateful for Kitty's offer. It would be hard to explain to Annie what she was doing. It had been tricky enough explaining the white dress she'd brought home to mend. She'd told Annie it was 'for a friend of my cousin who's getting married' and didn't like the piercing look Annie had given her.

In the carriage on the way back, surrounded by parcels, Mary began to feel more at home in her hoops and gloves. As the journey took them along the wide thoroughfare of Piccadilly, she built up the courage to practise being Persephone.

"How about if I speak like this?" She lowered her voice and gave it a mysterious lilting tone, along with a more cultured accent – she hoped – which she based on Kitty's own.

Kitty clapped her hands and laughed with delight.

"I love it when you talk that way! It goes with your eyes and your queenly look…"

"I look queenly?"

"Of course you do! Poor Felix is quite enchanted. Oh look, Roly's friend Samuel is nodding to us. There – across the street. His father's the finest surgeon in London and he's wooing my friend Maria. Wave to him!" Mary wished Kitty didn't get so easily distracted. Nevertheless she waved and the elegant young gentleman tipped his silver-topped cane to her in acknowledgement.

"And that place behind him," Kitty continued, "is the Royal Academy." She pointed to the grandest building on the street: a huge stone affair with several balconies either side of a great archway, leading to a courtyard beyond.

"Oh, I see!"

"I must take you soon. Piccadilly is very good for shopping, too. It's where I…" Kitty broke off. "Boots!"

She shouted this last, surprising word. Even Aunt Violet heard her and stared in confusion.

"What do you mean?" Mary asked.

"Stop the carriage, William! We're getting out."

The coachman obeyed. Surprised and confused, Mary followed her friend out of the landau and waited while the manservant helped the aged Aunt Violet descend. When they were all on the street, Kitty threaded her way across the wide expanse of Piccadilly, through the busy traffic.

"Boots!" she repeated to Mary above the sound of the wheels and horses. "You need them. Yours are half worn through. The best cordwainer in London is right here. Last week I saw the loveliest style in ivory kid, with a heel and satin laces. And you really need slippers, too, for dancing."

"I don't dance," Mary shouted back. At least, not enough to need special shoes for it.

"Persephone does." They waited while poor Aunt Violet and the manservant took their chances between a cart and a large red omnibus. "And gloves, of course. Your own parasol. An evening shawl – but you can borrow one of mine. We've hardly started!"

Mary laughed. "I have three shillings, Kitty, not a thousand pounds."

Kitty frowned. "We'll do it slowly. I'll buy you presents and you'll earn lots more from Felix, won't you? I wish

Papa were more generous with my allowance. Come and look at the styles, anyway."

They spent an enjoyable ten minutes in the cordwainer's shop and five more in the glover's next door. Mary didn't spend any money but she imagined for a while what it must be like to be Kitty, with a hundred pretty new things to admire every day and only the worry of which to choose.

As they were leaving the glover's, two grand ladies in great tiers of ruffled skirts stood aside to let them pass. Kitty gave a little gasp and curtseyed deeply.

"Mrs Prinsep. Lady Wentworth."

Mary curtseyed, too. This was it. Oh, goodness. She was being Persephone in daylight! She wanted to giggle and run but instead she curtseyed with all the grace she could muster. The taller woman, whose grey hair was piled high under her extravagant hat, smiled back at them both.

"Kitty Ballard, isn't it?" she said. "How you've grown! Please give my regards to your mother."

"I will. May I present Persephone Lavelle? She has recently arrived from Kent. Persephone, this is Mrs Sara Prinsep."

"Good afternoon," Mary said in her new Persephone voice. She had never spoken in this way to a lady before. Her heart fluttered like a trapped butterfly and she hardly dared to look up for fear of trembling. Mrs Prinsep's eyes rested on her.

"She is quite the *vogue*," the tall lady announced eventually. "I assume your brother collected her. Does Gabriel know her?"

"Mr Rossetti? No, not yet," Kitty said, tacitly admitting that Roly had indeed 'collected' Persephone. "But Felix Dawson is painting her."

"Aah." The word was long and drawn out, like a sigh. "That is something I'd like to see." At last, she turned back to Kitty. "It was good to see you, my dear. That colour suits you."

"Thank you," said Kitty, eyes sparkling with pleasure as the older ladies took their leave.

"How was that?" she asked, as soon as they were out of earshot.

"Terrifying."

"But you did it."

"Yes." Mary felt the warm glow of pride at having passed the test.

"And to the best hostess in London."

"Lady Wentworth?"

"No. Mrs Prinsep. She's one of the Pattle sisters. They're known as Beauty, Dash and Talent."

"And she's Beauty?"

"No, Dash. You should see her sister Virginia! And she liked you, I could tell."

Mary glowed with pride.

Kitty checked her pocket watch. "Come, let's find William and go home. Wait! What's happened to Aunt Violet?"

They looked around. But there was no sign of the plump old lady or the manservant. She'd left the shop ahead of them and should be standing right there. Mary scanned the street several times in a panic. Kitty bit her lip in frustration. Officially Aunt Violet was responsible for her young niece but in reality it was the reverse. They had been talking less than five minutes – where could she possibly be?

"I'll go this way," Mary suggested, pointing north. "You go that."

Kitty nodded.

Mary ran up the street, as fast as her skirts and

decorum would let her. Eventually, turning round, she saw Kitty at the corner of Piccadilly, waving her parasol. Mary ran back, fanning her flushed cheeks.

"You found her?"

Kitty indicated a quite unflustered Aunt Violet, who was standing a few feet away. She was taking leave of a pale, straight-backed woman, who was also dressed in black. The other woman was bending down towards Aunt Violet's face, mouthing a fond 'goodbye'. Her face fell in shocked surprise when she saw Kitty waiting nearby, however, and Mary a few steps beyond her.

"This, um … is … Persephone Lavelle," Kitty said, stepping forwards. This time, unlike before, she was a picture of awkwardness. "Mary, this is Mrs Lisle." Mary curtseyed and the other woman dipped her head.

"Persephone," she said thoughtfully, as if it were hello and goodbye, and a thousand other things besides. She nodded again and moved away in the direction of the Royal Academy. Only then did Mary notice the little black dog with tan paws and nose, trotting obediently at her side.

At that moment, William drew alongside them with the landau, having somehow turned it round and crossed the street. As they climbed back inside, Mary found herself scanning the pavement for another glimpse of the lady in black. Why had Kitty behaved so strangely? The skirts reminded her of something. And the little dog…

And then she remembered.

Mixed with Kitty's sudden awkwardness, it all made sense. Those were the black skirts and the dog from the portrait in Felix's studio. She could now put them together with a woman with dark blue eyes and straight black hair, elegantly styled and lightly streaked with white. Was she the owner of the tortoiseshell comb? She must have been a beauty in her youth.

"Tell me about her," she said to Kitty in a low voice. Though there was little chance of Aunt Violet hearing her, servants listen, too, as Mary knew only too well.

Kitty flushed. "Do you really want to know?"

"Please, tell me."

Kitty's anxiousness made Mary pause for thought. If Kitty wanted to spare her the story, it couldn't be good. But yes, she wanted to know.

"Well, then," Kitty said, also speaking low and glancing nervously up at the coachman behind her.

"Her name is Mrs Lisle. She's a rich widow and has been these past ten years. Not rich like Sara Prinsep but quite rich like Mama. She's known for her love of art. She also supports ... artists. According to my brother. An artist."

"She's the one who pays for Felix's studio?"

Kitty nodded and looked down. Mary's thoughts raced. "*There are ways.*" This was the person responsible for the endless paints and canvases, the coloured wine glasses, even the scattered coins on the trestle table. Mary's hand went to her heart.

Kitty looked at her kindly and said nothing. She knew what Mary must be thinking.

"I had assumed it was a man."

"Anyone would."

"Is she...? Does she...?" Mary's thoughts were a jumble. "What else do you know about her?"

"She lives in a grand house in Chelsea, on the King's Road," Kitty said. "Mama took me once. You would never believe it to look at her but she has a stuffed tiger in her drawing room and chandeliers as big as a man, made of red Venetian glass in the ballroom. She lives alone apart from her servants and her daughter. Actually, the girl is her sister's child, I think."

Kitty stopped but Mary wanted more. "You said she was a widow?"

Kitty frowned. "I think she grew up in Scotland. She married the local laird, very young. One day he was shooting on one of his grouse moors and a guest somehow accidentally killed him. She buried him on the family estate, packed up the house and came to London, and never went back again."

"Why did she come to London?"

Kitty thought hard, mentally rifling through her index of society gossip. "I seem to remember Mama saying that he used to bring her here for the Season but he locked her in the house every night and left her. Even so, she must have fallen in love with it here. They say he was not kind," Kitty went on, "if you know what I mean."

Mary nodded to herself and said distantly, "I know exactly what you mean."

"They said she wasn't sorry when he died. People do say the most terrible things at parties. The most terrible, *fascinating* things. She could have married again, I'm sure, but still she wears black, ten years on. She's mistress of her own fate. I admire her for that. She's an expert on modern art, she's even friends with the Prince Consort. She goes about town without a man at her side or a care in the world. Mama doesn't approve, of course."

Mary grinned. "My mother wouldn't, either. She would be horrified."

"I must admit, I like her," Kitty said, looking almost apologetic about it, knowing how Mary felt about Felix.

"Then I shall like her, too," Mary said.

Why shouldn't she? She admired everything about the woman that Kitty described, from her love of art to her unusual independence. Having met her briefly, she even admired her gracious bearing, her rich but subtle shawl and gown, her taste in dogs. She had no need to be jealous: she knew how obsessed Felix was with painting her and how close they felt whenever they were together. It was only the thought of the tortoiseshell comb, casually abandoned in the studio, that made her pause.

Chapter Seventeen

The perfectly adjusted Persephone dress lay folded in Mary's basket, where Annie paused each night to look at it.

"When did you say your cousin's friend was getting married?"

"I'm not sure."

"You'd think a girl would need her wedding dress."

"You would," Mary agreed, avoiding Annie's eye. "I'm sure she'll ask for it soon." At least she had a vague excuse for this lie. Harriet had not been at church on Sunday. There was no news of her, but Mary assumed she'd been unwell. In a way, she was glad not to have seen her cousin recently. Harriet was bound to ask her questions that she didn't feel like answering.

To Cook and Annie's great relief – and Mary's disappointment – Lady Emmeline hadn't called for her the day after her trip with Kitty. Nor did she send a message in the week that followed. Now each day dragged slowly, a pale imitation of the day before.

Rupert Thornton called round several times to see the professor, often dining with him alone. Without Mrs Aitken or other ladies present, they didn't need two servants to wait on them, so Mary hardly saw Rupert unless the they needed port in the study. Then he was reduced to his usual silent stare of longing. She tried to avoid his eye. It wasn't Rupert she wanted to be stared at by.

Why did Felix not want to see her? What had happened? She had no way of finding out and there were ten long days until her next day off, when she could run to Walton Street and find out for herself. The wondering was torture. He had seemed so tender the last time they were together. Had she spoiled it by not kissing him that last time in the studio? Or by wanting to? Had she misunderstood?

Mary took refuge in the book of poems he had given her. Though 'refuge' was perhaps the wrong word. It intensified her feelings, which made them harder to bear. She read the anthology every night, tucked inside her bible so Annie wouldn't see it. She had moved on from Tennyson to Byron.

She walks in beauty, like the night
Of cloudless climes and starry skies;

The words transported Mary to the dark walk in the cemetery.

"What are you reading?" Annie asked, from across the attic room.

"The Book of Job."

And all that's best of dark and bright
Meet in her aspect and her eyes.

"I never saw the Book of Job make a girl look that way."

"Then you don't know your bible."

She read the lines over and over, learning them by heart. It was impossible not to picture Felix watching her as he drew her. She tried to hide her tears and when that failed, she told Annie she was homesick.

"Ah, the Book of Job does that to a girl," Annie commented sarcastically.

For once Mary wished she could just talk to her. She was lonelier than she'd ever been, now that Lady Emmeline was well.

It was almost a relief when Eliza got home with the children after two weeks away and the busy house left Mary little time to speculate. And yet, with ironic timing, not two days later, the messenger was back again.

"She needs you this afternoon," Eliza Aitken said with a cluck and a sigh. "Which is most unfortunate. Why could she not have wanted you when I could spare you? I was counting on your help to mend my undersleeves. Annie tells me you sew better than she expected. But so be it. Give Lady Emmeline our warmest wishes. Come home as soon as you can."

With the white dress safely folded in her basket, Mary prayed the carriage would take her to the studio and not Mayfair. Fond though she was of Kitty, it was Felix she needed to see. The questions that had plagued her every night still echoed in her head. *Why did you drop me? What did I do?* She feared the answer but had to know. She sank into the cushions with relief when the coachman turned the corner at the pottery, heading for Walton Street.

The villa was its usual cheerful self – pale blue and tranquil, under a summer sky. Felix met her in the hallway as if nothing had happened. She wanted to melt into his arms, but in front of the maid she merely curtsied. By the time they'd reached the top of the stairs, she'd mastered her emotions.

He, however, was in the best of moods. He turned to her at the door and grinned, flashing his teeth.

"You're back! At last we can carry on!"

I never wanted to be away, Mary thought, but said nothing. She noticed that his teeth seemed whiter because his skin was darker. Two stout new walking sticks leaned against the wall, one taller, one shorter. *He's been out in the sun. Not alone.*

"You look as beautiful as ever," he added. "More so. Paler."

"I've been working," she said, still trying to understand his absence and to manage her melancholy. She would not give him the advantage of letting him know how much she'd missed him. If he could be indifferent to their attachment, then so could she.

"You brought the dress?"

She held out her basket. "Here it is."

"Let me see. I've been dreaming about you in it."

Felix moved around the studio, arranging the plinth where she would sit, and the chair. Meanwhile she carefully put on the white dress behind the screen, doing up as many of the buttons as she could.

"You've been busy?" she asked, with studied lightness.

"Oh … you know…" He sounded evasive. Guilty, too. Or was she imagining that? "A friend suggested a holiday. I couldn't say no. Beautiful weather up by the lakes. I painted for hours."

Ah! It all made sense. Mary looked at the walking sticks again and noticed that the shorter one was made of elegant ebony. He talked on and she tried to stop jealous thoughts from racing through her head. She *took him there. With her black skirts and her little dog. It must have been soon after I met her. She spirited him away and he couldn't disobey her. He's as much at her beck and call as I am at his.*

"And did your friend paint, too?" she said. She didn't care, but a 'he' or a 'she' in his answer could put her thoughts to rest – or drive them on.

"A little," he said. "Not well." He laughed but Mary noticed he'd nimbly avoided giving anything away.

She couldn't think of a way of asking again.

"I'm ready."

She stepped from behind the screen. He was standing by the trestle table, waiting, but didn't smile when he saw her. Instead his face was a mask of concentration. His eyes traced every part of her, from the top of her head to her hair, cheeks and eyes, to her shoulders and upper chest, her neat bosom, and down past her flowing skirts to the tips of the ivy green slippers he had found for her. *Whose?*

When he met her eyes again, he let out a long sigh.

"Perfect. You are, in every way imaginable, ideal."

She didn't answer. She liked to be looked at by him but she didn't want to be ideal. She wanted more.

He moved forwards and she remembered the buttons, turning her back to him and sweeping her curtain of hair aside. His fingers brushed the fine hairs on the back of her neck. She shivered as before, involuntarily. Her mind had not forgiven him yet, but her body had. She held her breath for every button, while her blood turned to molten gold.

At the end, his fingers rested on her skin far longer than they needed to. "Ideal..." he murmured. "Even if you didn't quote Tennyson and sew like a wonder."

She turned round to face him, hiding her feelings with a teasing smile. "So you admit that I do? Then you owe me five guineas."

He grinned. "Absolutely. But you were quite right: I haven't got it."

"Oh?"

He took her hand and guided her to the chair. "Money's tight. I must be careful."

"Did you spend it on your walking holiday?"

"Something like that." There was an awkwardness in his voice and he wouldn't meet her eye.

She has reined him in, Mary thought. *He has done something wrong and she's punishing him.*

As she sat down, another thought occurred to her. *Could it be me?*

His long absence, the lack of funds – all this had happened since Kitty had introduced her to Mrs Lisle on Piccadilly. Could *she* be the source of his punishment? But they had only met for the briefest of moments and Mrs Lisle couldn't possibly know about her feelings for Felix. He wasn't even there. She dismissed it as a coincidence.

"I brought you a present," he said, going off into a corner and returning with an ancient hatbox.

"Oh?" Mary said.

"Well, it's for Persephone really. For the painting. I made it from things I found while walking. Here."

He lifted something out. At first it looked like a bundle of dried leaves. But as it reached the light she gasped with pleasure: it was a crown, made of twigs, leaves and ivy, held together with wire and painted silver, gold and copper.

"The goddess's headpiece. Will it fit you?"

"I think so."

He watched anxiously as she put it on her head and leaned over to adjust it on her hair. Then he relaxed and grinned with satisfaction.

"Will it do?" she asked.

"You look magnificent."

He brought her a hand-held mirror so she could admire the effect. The gold and silver glittered against her hair. The crown gave her a stately air, like a May queen, or a goddess of the seasons. "It's beautiful," she said. "Thank you."

She noticed, as she handed the mirror to him, that its

elaborate silver back was engraved with the letters 'JDL'. Mrs Lisle left her looking glass here, too… Yet Mary couldn't stay jealous for long. Felix had foraged a crown for her, even while he was supposed to be 'walking'. If there was some kind of competition, surely she had won?

Felix's energy was infectious as he flitted round the studio, adjusting the canvas, setting up his palette, putting Mary into position and fortifying himself with cold coffee. There was no mistaking the light in his eye as he focused on her, getting back into the rhythm of his painting. He had been nothing but joyful since he'd seen her again.

As usual, once he got to work, she felt her muscles relax. She was at peace here, surrounded by his canvases and tubes of paint, his brushes and rags: a little squalor and a riot of colour. She loved the smell of coffee and linseed oil and turpentine. She loved to watch the sweep of his arm, the cut of his collar, the drape of his jacket. Today it was sand-coloured linen, made bold by a silk scarf at his neck of cornflower blue, which matched the cheerful country flowers nodding in a jar on the trestle table behind him. She was as at home in this studio as she had ever been in a field in Kent.

As always, the time flew by. Two and a half hours later she climbed down from the plinth, stiff in every joint and sinew, and surprised that she should be so. Felix's face and hands were streaked with paint. He looked exhausted.

"Are you hungry?" he asked. "I have cake. It's quite old, but I think we can still eat it."

"Can I see the painting first?"

His face clouded. "I wish you wouldn't."

"No – please. Let me."

Eventually he relented. "Look but don't judge. I still have so much to do on the face. It's getting there, but the balance is wrong…"

They stood side by side. For a long time, she stared at it silently.

"Mary?"

The girl on the canvas already glowed with life. He must have worked on it since her last sitting, despite not seeing her. The darker background was still only sketched in, but the portrait of her face and neck was well advanced, despite what Felix said. The skin and hair shone with a dozen different shades of red, pink and gold. The uplifted eyes shone like jewels. The dress, which he had started, shimmered with light.

"Mary?"

She shook her head. This took his talent with the first drawing to a new level. In oil, life-size, she looked like Titian's *Venus*, yet herself, and new. He was making her mythical.

"Mary!" He didn't understand. He spoke to her gently, through her hair. "It will be good, I promise. Trust me."

"I know," she whispered.

He turned to her and took her head in his hands, searching to reassure her. At his touch, the room seemed to tilt and shift. She stopped thinking about the painting and thought only of the moles on his cheek and the warmth of him, and how much she had missed him and how unbearable it had been.

He sensed the change in her immediately. This time, as he bent his head, no muscle in her body resisted. His lips were soft on hers at first and feather-light. His hands caught in her hair. She lost count of the kisses but soon they became deeper, harder. She didn't know whose need was greater: hers or his.

When finally the last kiss ended, her lips were bruised. She couldn't speak. He stared at her for a moment, with the back of his hand to his mouth. She could tell he was willing himself to be honourable. She willed it, too, because she didn't know how much strength she had. Just enough to turn round, it seemed, and sweep her hair aside.

He didn't move for a while. Then he seemed to come to himself.

"Oh, yes," he babbled as he undid her buttons, fingers shaking, taking even longer than before. "It will be good… The face, I mean … on the painting. I haven't mastered the shadows yet and I've overworked the lips, but I can rescue it. We made a big advance today…" He groaned as he realized his double meaning and Mary smiled to herself. Her blood still felt like molten metal. "I'll need you again…" His breath was hot on her neck. Eventually the final button was undone and she took refuge, disappearing behind the screen.

When she was ready at last, they managed to say goodbye without touching. The air seemed to crackle with the strain of it. What they had started could not end well. And yet she could only feel joy. His feelings were as strong as hers, she knew it now. If she suffered, he was suffering, too. She finished the session in the same good humour as Felix's when it had started and as she decided to walk home under the hot summer sun, she felt as if she was floating on a cloud of happiness.

Which meant she wasn't prepared at all when a dark figure stepped out of the shadows two streets from home and a menacing voice rasped out:

"Mary Adams? I want a word with you."

Chapter Eighteen

Time slowed to a trickle as Mary glanced around her. There were people in the street but they were already averting their eyes and hurrying on. The man sounded dangerous. Though her instinct was to freeze in fear, she summoned up every scrap of courage she had and burst into a run. Her basket was light and there wasn't far to go to reach the safety of St George's Square. But though she was fast, she was hobbled by her skirts and he was faster. He caught up with her in three strides and pinned her arms to her sides from behind. She struggled but he held her fast.

"A word, I said."

"Let me go!"

"Don't be a fool." His fingers pressed into the flesh above her elbows.

"What do you want?" she asked, still struggling.

"Calm down and I'll tell you."

The more she struggled, the tighter his grip. She reduced her fight to a tremble.

"That's better," he said. He turned her round to face him and she recognized the silhouette of his cap, and the extravagant collar of his thin tweed coat.

"You're Annie's fancy man!"

"Ha!" He threw his head back. "Not fancy man. I'm her brother. Eddie O'Bryan, at your service."

He gave her a mock bow. Mary recognized the same lilting Irish accent as Annie's and the same freckled nose – though his had been broken more than once and a bruised eye suggested he'd been in a fight.

"What d'you want with me?"

He smiled. "Well, now. There's a question. It's not me, Mary, so much as my sister. She's been wondering about you for a little while. You and your grand old lady, who seems to need you whenever there's a job to be done at home. Who makes your eyes shine, Annie says, like a girl at prayer. What kind of old lady does that, I wonder?"

"Lady Emmeline DuLac," Mary spat defiantly. "Let go of me!"

"I would but you'd run. You see, the thing is, Mary…
I've been standing outside Lady Emmeline DuLac's
house this very afternoon. Mighty grand it is, too.
I went there as soon as Annie told me about the message.
Stayed there to wait for your arrival. And you never
came."

"I did!"

"You did not. It sets a man to wondering. Where do
you go now? So I asked some questions. I know people
all around this city. People who know things. They
know, for example, about a red-haired girl who goes
dancing in the Gardens with a certain artist and his
friends. So I ask some more questions. And they tell me
about another red-haired girl — or is it the same one,
I wonder? — who goes to the artist's house and stays
there for hours. All alone." He looked at her and tutted.
"Naughty Mary. What would your mistress say, now?"

"That wasn't me!"

"Would you like to go and prove it? Shall we ask the
old lady?"

Mary tensed. She was trapped and not just by his
strong hands. "What do you plan to do?" she asked
reluctantly.

"My duty as a brother is to tell my beloved sister everything," Eddie said. "It's only right."

"And yet...?" Mary asked. He didn't sound very dutiful. It gave her a shred of hope.

"And yet ... I like you, Mary. You're just a girl, having a good time, earning some money perhaps?"

Mary struggled again. "You want me to pay you? I won't!"

"Just a shilling or two."

"Never!" If it was money he wanted, he was out of luck. She could not pay and would not. It would never stop.

He cocked his head and his smile became speculative. "Then how about you pay me in some other way?"

At this Mary struggled harder. "No! I wouldn't touch you!"

"Just a kiss, Mary!"

"Get *away* from me!"

He let her go. "Only joking," he said, looking hurt. "You're not my type anyway. But if you won't pay me, I'll have to tell Annie what I know."

"Then tell her. See if I care."

He shrugged. "If you say so. Off you go now."

He gave her an ungallant mock-bow as she picked up her fallen basket. She walked away with her head held high and her body still shaking from the shock.

She cared very much what he said but what else could she do? Annie could destroy her. She would have to face up to her somehow. But right now she was too confused by Felix's kiss and this confrontation to think of anything except getting home.

⁂

Annie disappeared halfway through serving dinner. Mary, guessing that Eddie had called downstairs, carried on with shaking hands and spilled the master's claret. When Annie finally reappeared, carrying the blancmange for pudding, she had the look of a contented cat. Mary knocked the water jug off the side table and broke it. The mistress sent her out in a fury.

As she trailed into the kitchen, Cook took one look at her and sighed. "You've been a mess since you got home this afternoon. Go upstairs and read your bible. You're no good to me tonight."

"But I—"

"You'll only break something else. Go on now."

Mary crept upstairs to the little attic room. A flat, grey evening light cast chimney shadows on the wall. She got Little Miss Mouse out from the trunk under her bed and sat her on the blanket, staring vacantly into the familiar dark glass eyes that stared blankly back at her. Her mind still couldn't process what had happened in the last few hours. Missing Felix; the impossible, wonderful kiss; her body on fire; the way he wanted her; the absolute lack of shame she felt wanting him. And then the shock of Eddie O'Bryan's ambush. It could have been much worse but it was bad enough.

If her brain was confused, her body was worse. She had run and fought and felt every emotion from elation to terror, and now she was simply exhausted. She wanted to sleep but she couldn't. She needed a plan to deal with Annie.

She was still sitting on her bed, fully dressed, with Little Miss Mouse beside her, when Annie joined her after the family had gone to bed. It was dark by now and Annie lit the candle. It made her face glow like a jack-o'-lantern and new shadows danced on the wall.

"His name is Felix Dawson," Annie said calmly. "An artist."

"Yes."

"Is he painting you?"

"Yes."

"Is *that* what you call it?"

At this Mary, who had felt purely exhausted, sat up with fire in her eyes.

"Yes, I do, Annie. Because that's all I do. I sit and he paints me."

She didn't mention the kiss, of course, but why should she? It had only just happened. And it could have been so much more but it wasn't. She was trying to be good but a girl like Annie would never understand.

"If that's what you say," Annie sneered, unbelieving. "When I think of all the times I've scrubbed and cleaned for you and done your dirty work when you weren't here. I always knew there was something. You could hide it from them but not from me. With yer books and yer flowers and yer fancy dress…"

Mary gasped. Annie was right. Sharing a room with a girl with a sharp and suspicious mind, how had she thought she could ever get away with it?

"You owe me something," Annie said, picking up the candle and coming closer. "That picture – it'll be worth a pretty penny, when it's done?"

"I don't know." Mary hadn't really thought about the money. But she remembered Felix saying that painting would make him as rich as Roly one day. Collectors like Mr Windus had a lot of money to spend. "Perhaps," she granted. "Why?"

"I want ten pounds when it's sold."

"What?"

"You can ask your Felix for money then. You can find a reason. I've a need of it for my brother. Eddie owes someone from a boxing match – someone you don't want to owe money to. But if he knows it's coming he'll wait."

She was entirely calm, as if asking a scullery maid for ten pounds happened every day of the week.

"I can't possibly get it!"

"You can. You're a clever girl, Mary. Sly. You've got a brain on you – and a face. I've watched you all these weeks. Men do things for you. You're not like the rest of us."

She stared at Mary through the glimmering candlelight. It flickered on her pointed chin, her sallow complexion, the mouse-brown hair that fell in thin, limp strands. Mary realized guiltily that she had always felt a little superior to raggedy Annie. She felt ashamed.

"I-I'd help you if I could. I have some money…"

Annie shook her head. "It won't be enough. Ten pounds or I'll tell the mistress. I could tell her tomorrow if I wanted to."

Ten pounds was a fortune! Felix would never give it. She couldn't ask.

"Annie, please! Have pity!"

"Why should I?" Annie put the candle down and steadily began to unlace her stays. "At least you can stop pretending in front of me. You can read those fancy books he gives you to your heart's content. And stop hiding those bright new shillings and sixpences where you think I won't find them."

Mary picked up Little Miss Mouse and held her. Annie really missed nothing. She felt her whole life stripped bare. Then she remembered that there was one weapon in her armoury. She didn't want to use it – but she had to, in self-defence.

"If you say anything, I'll tell her about the food you steal for your brother. I know it was him I saw you with. See what she thinks of *that*."

Annie frowned. She seemed rattled for a moment, but took a breath and calmed herself. "So. Who d'you think they'd believe – you or me?"

Mary sank back. Annie could prove her suspicions by calling in Lady Emmeline. Mary had no proof at all.

When Annie blew out the candle she got hot wax on her fingers and cried out in pain. *Serves her right*, Mary thought, getting up to undress in the dark, before lying back down with Little Miss Mouse held tightly to her cheek.

Chapter Nineteen

The secret of Persephone Lavelle had changed its nature. It was no longer a golden glow inside, but a dark thundercloud overhead. Every look Annie gave reminded Mary that she could give it away whenever it suited her.

However there was one advantage to the new situation and Annie herself had pointed it out: Mary no longer needed to lie to her. When Cook asked for details of Lady Emmeline, Annie threw her a subtle glance and Mary felt a strange complicity. Upstairs in the attic room, she attended openly to her hair and didn't need to find an excuse for her new dress when it arrived from Kitty's seamstress.

As Persephone, Mary recklessly devoted herself to enjoying her transformation while it lasted. July flew by in a flurry of outings. She drank wine and went to the theatre, where young men queued to give her compliments. She wore fine gloves and flowers in her hair. Felix liked to take her out. In the studio, it was hard for them both to be alone together without wasting the day in kissing, though Felix was keen to finish the painting, so they tried.

In the end, to force himself to concentrate, he asked Roly and Kitty to come to the studio, so they could unknowingly act as chaperones. Mary sat under the tall, north-facing window while Felix arranged the handmade crown of leaves in her hair. She was pleased to see her friends but would have been more pleased to be alone with Felix. There were places on her arms and neck that longed to be caressed but today he was focused on the painting. She saw the steely look in his eye of an artist at work. It was going well and he wanted to get on with it.

"I must say, you've almost caught her likeness," Roly said, pouring himself a glass from the bottle of champagne he'd brought. "Just a few more touches around the eyes perhaps ... some healthy pink blobs on the skin..."

"Shut up, Roly, you know nothing," Felix said

smoothly. "Thank God you've never touched a paintbrush."

"I have!" Roly protested. "I painted a whole boat up at Oxford. Two delightful shades of red and green. It even floated. Jolliest thing on the river."

"Well done."

"We should go there soon. Your friend Gabriel's doing some mural thing at the Union with Morris. We should stop in on them."

"We must," Felix agreed vaguely, adding red and brown to yellow on his palette to achieve the shade of gold he wanted for her crown.

"But of course we'll see them before that," Roly went on. "I've heard Gabriel's invited to the Prinseps'. Are you going? *Tout le beau monde* will be there."

Felix nodded without looking up. "I have my costume all ready." He indicated a chair in the corner, where a rich, embroidered Ottoman coat was laid out alongside the usual pile of dirty laundry.

"A costume party?" Kitty asked, eyes wide. She had been wandering around the studio, picking up trinkets. Now she was all attention.

"Mmmm," Roly said. "Tomorrow. Val Prinsep's back

from Turkey and the Holy Land. He's been on quite the tour. Helped discover some old relics in Halicarnassus."

"Oh, yes!" Mary said, breaking her pose, unable to contain herself. She had been very good so far, staring steadily at the Chinese screen.

Felix harrumphed in exasperation. "Hopeless! Why can't you sit still?"

"I'm sorry. But Halicarnassus… They've found a whole lost city."

She remembered standing in the shadows at dinner in St George's Square when Rupert and the professor had discussed the discovery. According to Professor Aitken, it contained one of the Seven Wonders of the World. She had tried to hide her fascination but the professor himself had caught the brightness in her face. She longed to talk to him about it more but, of course, she couldn't.

"Well, Val's back in all his glory," Roly went on, "and his mother is celebrating in style. Oh Lord, and I nearly forgot – I saw her the other night and she asked me if I knew Persephone Lavelle. I said of course I did – one of m'best friends, no less – and she said good, she thought so, and would I please tell the young lady, as she didn't have her address for correspondence, that Sara Prinsep would be delighted if she could attend her little *soirée*. By which of course she meant what promises to be one of the most jolly and extravagant parties of the season. And that her sister would like to take your photograph. So there we have it."

He smiled absently and took a long drink of champagne.

Mary's eyes, through this speech, had grown rounder and wider. But her growing bubble of delight was popped by a sound from nearby.

"Oooooooooh!"

It was not a happy noise. Kitty was pursing her lips and narrowing her eyes. Her crinoline moved with the sway of a young woman stamping her foot.

"Is there a problem?" Roly asked.

"Of course there is! My disreputable brother may do as he likes but, because Mama is incredibly dull and refuses to enjoy herself at parties, I'm not taken anywhere good. *You* may go, Mary, because you're new and exotic. I may not." There was definitely the sound of a stamped foot this time. "And don't smile at me, all of you. I'm allowed to be furious."

"I'm so sorry," Mary said.

"Well, you should be."

"Should I stay at home?"

"Of course not! You must go! You'll have to tell me all about it. Roly's hopeless. He can remember every wine, while I drink cordial, but not what people wore or any of the gossip. And Sara Prinsep knows everyone. It will be *divine*."

This sounded even more impressive than the Windus ball. Though Mary felt very sorry for poor Kitty, she couldn't help grinning at the thought of mixing with the finest in society, at the personal invitation of the hostess, in her new silk gown. Felix quite gave up on the painting and threw his brush aside.

"I can't do it. All your fault, Roly. You're never to watch us again."

Roly, quite unrepentant, handed Mary a glass of champagne.

"Thank God that's done. Now, back to the party. The theme is 'Exotic Araby'. It wouldn't be the same without Persephone. You must come as a Nubian maid. It's all the rage. They'll love you."

Chapter Twenty

What on earth, Mary wondered, was a Nubian maid? Was it an exotic kind of housemaid?

It took fifteen minutes of searching in the professor's study to find a learned tome on Egypt, whose colour plate illustrations showed dark-skinned young women in loose clothing and veils, walking barefoot but adorned with great hoops of gold jewellery. 'Nubian' seemed to refer to the desert land they came from. 'Maid' simply meant girl. Mary chided herself: she should have known that from her poetry books.

While Eliza was out and Cook and Annie were busy, she raided the house for clothes. She felt reckless at the thought of seeing Felix again and in such glamorous circumstances. On an upstairs landing, Eliza kept a trunk of shawls she rarely wore. One of these, in blue shot-silk with a gold edging, would make an ideal veil.

A linen tablecloth over her chemise would do for the dress itself. For the jewellery, she borrowed a spare watch chain from the professor's desk to put around her neck.

Roly, in his excitement, forgot to send a message from Lady Emmeline, but it didn't matter. Eliza and Philip Aitken were going out for the night anyway. They were attending a small dinner party with friends. Eliza had heard about the evening at the Prinseps' and longed to go to that instead. "After all, you're an expert on ancient history," she complained to her husband. But they did not know Sara Prinsep. Mary smiled to think what Eliza would say if she knew that her scullery maid had received a formal introduction on Piccadilly. Meanwhile, for the Aitkens, beef Wellington and trifle at the house of a mere lawyer who lived in Islington would have to do.

Mary paid no attention as Eliza called Annie every five minutes to help with her appearance that evening. She was busy enough with her own. She had fashioned a charcoal pencil from coals in the kitchen fire and used it to outline her eyes. A curtain rope did as a belt for the tablecloth dress, which she held in place with a few hidden stitches. The veil Mary artfully arranged in various styles, admiring its effect in the hand mirror she had bought with one of her shillings.

When Annie finally came up and saw it all, she took a step back in shock, before recovering her composure.

"Off to your fancy man again?"

Mary nodded. She had given up trying to explain who Felix really was to her.

"Fancy dress, too?" Annie peered at the tablecloth. "Are you an angel or a Roman?"

"A Nubian maid," Mary explained.

"What's one of those when she's at home?"

"A girl from the Arabian desert, collecting water."

"Well, mind you look after those borrowed things. And where are your boots?"

"I'm going barefoot."

"Surely not? Like a beggar? You'll catch your death."

"It's summer. And desert girls don't wear boots."

Annie shook her head and laughed.

Mary was astonished that she didn't have more to say. As she watched Mary fix the veil at its most becoming angle, Mary began to suspect that Annie was starting to enjoy her adventures vicariously.

The Aitkens' hired carriage set off at eight o'clock. Twenty minutes later, a small brougham arrived for Persephone. Roly had at least remembered to send a carriage. It wasn't the usual one she rode in, though, and she realized he probably needed that for himself. The ride took her past neat, terraced rows of little cottages and large, ugly brickworks, whose fires never seemed to go out, down Chelsea lanes bordered by hawthorn bushes and apple trees and on towards the new palace-sized mansions being built by Mr Ballard and his friends in Kensington.

To her delight, as the carriage drew close she discovered her destination was larger still than any of these, with acres of garden surrounded by a brick wall. A plaque beside the gates said 'Little Holland House', but there was nothing small about it. Carriages queued to enter under an avenue of lime trees. Mary could just make out hundreds of coloured paper lanterns strung between smaller trees in the distance. She felt as if she was about to enter another time, another world.

The liveried footman who took her shawl marvelled

for a moment at its rough, shabby fabric, but was too well trained to stare for long. Another man in livery asked for her name, ready to check it against the handwritten list he held.

"Persephone Lavelle," she said in a throaty, lilting voice.

He looked at the kohl-rimmed eyes under her shot-silk veil.

"Welcome to Little Holland House, Ma'amselle Lavelle."

"*Merci.*" It was one of the only two words of French she knew. Felix had taught it to her. The other was *baiser.* A kiss. It didn't seem quite so bad to talk about kissing, if you did it in French.

A moment later, she was caught up in the crowd. The rooms were already full of people talking and laughing. All around her, guests wore elaborate coats and tunics. Men jangled with sabres sheathed in jewelled scabbards dangling from their belts. Women wore gold headdresses of vaguely Oriental design, decorated with feather plumes, and cascades of pearls and diamonds over their high-fashion ballgowns. Mary at once felt shy and underdressed, in her simple tunic and veil.

She regretted going barefoot. *Why* had Roly mentioned Nubian desert girls? To hide herself, she quickly drew her veil over her face.

At first she badly missed the company of Kitty and wondered if it had been a mistake to come. However, as she wandered from room to room, it was impossible not to admire the bright colours and secret corners of the Prinseps' house. The rooms were painted vivid shades of red and blue, and were full of treasures. Tables shaped like elephants; statues of many-limbed gods; vast, multicoloured lanterns made of glass; a stuffed peacock so lifelike Mary thought it may be about to sqwawk… She was busy admiring its iridescent feathers when a booming voice rang out: "Persephone Lavelle! My dear! It's you!" She looked up to find Roly bearing down on her.

"You look glorious," he said, kissing her fingers. "That blue scarf thing is a work of genius. Let me look after you."

He led her into yet another room full of people. In Roly's company it was impossible to be shy for long. He introduced her to many moustachioed, sabre-wearing friends as, 'Persephone – the latest stunner to hit London.'

They jostled for her attention and shone like beacons whenever she deigned to talk to them.

Roly had not been so stupid after all to suggest her costume. It was a positive advantage, she soon discovered, to be dressed as a desert girl, not a fashionable lady. Her bare feet and 'brave' outfit heightened Persephone's mystery – men almost queued up to admire her. The hostess herself, in the make-up and gold headdress of Cleopatra, graciously smiled when Roly introduced her, and pronounced her: 'Quite ridiculously lovely. Take her from my sight, Roly. She makes me green with envy'.

"She doesn't mean it," he assured Mary with a laugh as they continued their passage around the entertaining rooms. "That's her highest form of compliment."

Mary believed him. She was tipsy on champagne and in love with Sara Prinsep's universe. Every two minutes, Roly pointed out an artist or poet or politician. He even claimed to have seen Tennyson himself in another room. And around the famous people were lively acolytes, dripping with jewels, talking about art and poetry and affairs of state. Eliza Aitken would die with pleasure to be standing here.

But Mary couldn't completely enjoy herself. She had

assumed that Roly was taking her to Felix but they had toured the whole ground floor of the house twice now and he was nowhere to be seen.

"Has he arrived yet?" she asked, having scanned the room they were in for the seventh time.

She forgot to say who she meant but she didn't need to. Roly, who had been Dionysus himself in his jollity up to now, stopped sharply. For a moment he looked almost serious.

"Um…"

It was enough. Mary's heart contracted and she grabbed Roly's hand. Something was wrong.

"Tell me."

"Well, here's the thing. He *is* here. But he's rather busy…" Roly cut himself off, lapsing into an embarrassed silence. Mary felt her good mood evaporate. The taste of champagne turned sour in her mouth.

"He's with her, isn't he?"

Roly looked at her sympathetically. "He'd rather not be. But duty calls, you know."

She nodded and fought back stinging tears. She hadn't thought about Mrs Lisle since the studio. Now the memory made her bitter. First the walking trip to

the lakes and now this. Could she not leave Felix alone?
But … did he want her to?

Mrs Lisle had impressed with the elegance of her dress
on Piccadilly. She was not bad looking, even though
she was twenty years older than Mary, at least. Perhaps,
on nights like this, she made herself irresistible to him.
Roly seemed not to think so … or was he just being
kind?

"Can I see them? Please?"

"What?" Roly looked horrified.

"I promise I won't cause a scene."

"You mustn't," he said in a low voice. "He needs her."

"I know. I'll just look. From a distance. *Please*, Roly."

He sighed and slumped his shoulders. "As London
knows, I cannot deny a beautiful woman anything."

⁓

In a glazed orangery at the side of the house, a string
quartet played lively tunes. Beyond them, under the
lamplit trees, people walked and talked and laughed
in twos and threes. The air was warm and balmy.
Roly took Mary past a laurel hedge that led towards a
yew-lined alcove with a little fountain. A stone bench

had been carefully placed there to enable visitors to enjoy the sight and sound of the water.

Looking at it through the glistening spray, Mary made out two ladies sitting on the bench and a small group of men and women standing nearby, drinking champagne. Roly nudged her. She looked at the champagne drinkers and there he was, his long hair curling over the collar of the Ottoman coat.

From the shadow of the laurel hedge, Mary watched. Felix and another man were talking to a woman a few years older than herself, dressed in an outfit made of fringed silk shawls. Light from a nearby lantern lit her narrow nose and neatly styled dark red hair. The conversation seemed friendly, nothing more.

"That's Effie Gray," Roly whispered. "Another stunner. Effie Millais now, I should say. Effie Ruskin, as was…"

"Oh?"

"Ah, yes," Roly grinned. "The muse of a thousand husbands. Well, two. Mr Ruskin didn't appreciate his prize. He left her far too long in the company of the charming Millais. That other man's George Watts, who lives here with the Prinseps. Another Pre-Raphaelite.

And … look! My goodness – that's Lizzie herself. Sitting down. I didn't know she was in London. Isn't she fine?"

Mary turned to the bench, where the woman on the left drew her attention with clouds of long copper hair and a pale, still face, lit up with green-gold eyes. So this was Lizzie Siddal. Mary was mesmerized.

The model had made no effort either to be fashionable or to dress in 'Exotic Araby'. Instead she wore a high-necked dress of amber velvet with no waist or corset, which hung on her as if she were a boy. Its simplicity reminded Mary a little of the Persephone dress but she had never thought to wear something so plain in society. However, looking at Lizzie Siddal, she saw how it made her stand out in the garden, almost as much as her loose hair and bright eyes. Mary promised herself not to be swayed by fashion again.

Lizzie was 'fine' indeed. Her skin had a delicate pink glow and her deep-set eyes seemed lit from within. She wasn't pretty, like some of the women here, all pin curls, jewels and smiles, but oh, how lovely! Once you saw her, it was hard to look away.

So, for a while, Mary didn't glance towards the other woman on the bench. However, when Lizzie leaned forwards to say something to her companion, she instantly recognized the oval face and smooth black hair of Mrs Lisle.

It stunned Mary that she should have been so close to Felix's patroness for so long and not even have noticed her. Alone, she was distinguished, but next to Lizzie she seemed quite ordinary. She, too, had avoided fancy dress. But her black ballgown, though stylish, looked conventional beside Lizzie's amber dress. Her jet necklaces, though tasteful, seemed excessive next to Lizzie's bare porcelain skin.

Felix, Mary noticed with relief, was still tête-à-tête with Effie Millais, seemingly indifferent to Mrs Lisle's presence. As Mary watched, the widow glanced up at him not once but twice. *She needs him more than he needs her*, Mary decided, allowing herself a little smile.

He did glance round in her direction, however, and peered through the fountain for a moment. Mary longed to join him but Roly reached out and touched her arm. She realized how intently she was staring, and how dangerous it was. Reluctantly she let him pull her away.

"I thought he seemed … quite happy," she said as they

wandered back into the house.

Roly laughed. "You mean he didn't seem interested in the widow. I told you so. She's far outshone by Lizzie and to be quite plain about the matter, Lizzie will soon be outshone by you, my dear. Her bloom is fading; yours has barely begun. Good Lord – speak of the devil! Her great admirer. Gabriel! Over here, man!"

Roly raised a hand in salute and a bearded man with short, receding chestnut curls waved in return, turning towards them. He was dressed in long, elaborate robes, under which Lizzie sensed a body heading for stoutness.

"Roly Ballard!" he called out. "The most dangerous man in London! Has Lizzie changed her dress? My God!" He took a step back as Mary pulled down her veil. "Not Lizzie at all! My, my, my... How extraordinary."

"This, Gabriel, is Persephone Lavelle," Roly said. "Persephone, may I introduce Dante Gabriel Rossetti?"

"Ah," the artist murmured as Mary curtseyed. "So this is the much-renowned Persephone."

Mary flushed with embarrassment and delight that the great Pre-Raphaelite should have heard of her. At the same time, she hid her surprise that this stoutish man with receding hair should be the scandal-maker that everyone talked about.

"Enchanted," he said, staring at her in the way Felix did. "Quite enchanted."

It didn't have quite the same effect as when Felix watched her, but still, she shivered.

"Hands off her!" Roly laughed. "Felix has plans for Persephone."

"I'm sure he does. I'm curious to see them." The eyes glinted wickedly then glanced up, distracted by something in the room behind her. "Ah! Hi! Rupert! Come and join us."

At first Mary was simply annoyed that her big moment with the great man should be so soon interrupted, but then she saw the horrified look on Roly's face and her heart skipped a beat. *Please, not…*

But it was. She turned round to find a pair of familiar bushy eyebrows two feet away.

"Rupert Thornton, may I present Persephone Lavelle?" Rossetti said.

Rupert viewed her in great confusion. She stared back, just as nervous. He could ruin everything, but it was too late to hide.

"Isn't she a stunner?"

Rupert coughed and nodded. "I must admit, I'm stunned."

His eyes searched hers and they were clouded with hurt. He lapsed back into silence. Soon it grew embarrassing.

Rossetti laughed. "I sense you know each other already. Well, I'll leave you to it. Come, Roly – tell me what you've been up to lately. Is it true you lost ten guineas on a race between raindrops?"

He took Roly off, and Mary and Rupert were left alone. Rupert coughed again. It was a nervous tic that irritated Mary. It made him seem like an awkward schoolboy and contrasted with his appearance, which she admitted was magnificent. He had come as some kind of sultan, Mary thought, in a fat turquoise turban a foot tall and glowing silks of red and gold that hung to his rich leather boots. For the first time, she was truly struck by his wealth. He wore it lightly at the Aitkens' house but here she began to realize that he was rather grand. As always, he looked at her as if no one else in the room existed. As usual, it made her uncomfortable.

"I'd heard talk of Persephone for a while," he said at last. "But I didn't know..."

"You weren't supposed to know."

He looked wounded. "You could have told me."

"How?" she asked, defending herself. "You're my master's friend."

"You could have trusted me. I'd do anything for you, Mary."

"Persephone," she corrected him snappishly.

"Persephone. Remember that first party? It was me who found you, Mary. Persephone, I mean."

Mary sighed. "I suppose you did."

"And now Rossetti himself is recommending you to me!" He laughed. "And you're posing for Felix Dawson! My – it's you! They say his *Persephone*'s a wonder."

"Already?" Mary asked. "Who says so?"

"All his friends. Everyone. I want to buy it, when it's finished."

"Oh! Please – don't!" She was appalled.

Now he looked offended. "Goodness me – why?"

She fought to find the right words. *Because I don't want you to own me*, she thought. Out loud, she faltered, "Because it would be strange for it to belong to…"

He bent his head towards her. "A friend?" His hint of a smile was hopeful.

An idiot, she thought. *A rich one, who eyes me like a prize possession.* But she needed him to like her and not give the game away. "Y-yes. A friend. Exactly."

He bowed. She wasn't sure what he thought but the wounded look remained.

"Your wish is my command."

He seemed rather stiff. Moments later, he moved on. Mary chided herself for not being kinder and more flattering. But it was too late to change it now.

⋇ ⋇

With no one else to talk to, and afraid of bumping into another of her master's students in the brightly lit house, she found herself in the garden again, heading towards the fountain. But the little group was gone.

It was time to leave. Felix was not here and the party had lost its fairy dust. She went to collect her shawl.

In the carriage, her thoughts flitted between Lizzie and Mrs Lisle on the bench, Felix and Effie Millais, Sara Prinsep and the great Rossetti. For Persephone Lavelle, the evening had been a great success. But as Mary Adams, she couldn't delight in it as much as she wanted to. Why hadn't Felix warned her that Mrs Lisle would be there? At least she would have been prepared. And then there was Rupert. He was so attached, so pleased with himself for discovering her, and she had let him down. Would he be able to keep quiet about that? Would he want to?

First Annie and now Rupert. Her secret was unravelling, like Ariadne's thread.

Chapter Twenty-one

Eliza Aitken was quite put out. All her friends were talking about the Prinseps' party and she had not even been invited.

"Jane Hillier says the rooms at Little Holland House are bright and gay, and full of trinkets from India. Why don't we have anything from India? Anyone would think, from our house, that the British had never been there."

"Henry Prinsep is a director of the East India Company," her husband placidly reminded her over luncheon. "He lived there for years. I have often suggested that we should put out some of my treasures from Italy and Greece..."

"Oh, Greece!" she said peevishly. "Nobody cares about Greece."

"The whole party, I gather, was held to celebrate discoveries from Halicarnassus, a mere boat-ride from Kos."

"Don't bother me with *geography*. Annie, my shawl. I feel quite cold in this dark, damp room."

The professor ignored her, smiling wistfully. "I admit, I long to talk to young Val Prinsep. Halicarnassus was home to the tomb of King Mausolus, you know." His wife was busy cutting chicken away from a bone and didn't answer. "Quite spectacular. He had it built for himself and his wife Artemesia. Who was also his sister."

"Oh, *please*, Philip!" Eliza snapped, looking up from her plate at last. "We have no need to hear that kind of thing in this house. Really!"

"It was over two thousand years ago!" he protested. "And quite normal for those Persian—"

"That reminds me," Eliza interrupted. "A little scandal from somewhere much closer to home." She was smiling, Mary noticed, showing small, sharp teeth. "I heard it last night at dinner. Caroline Harrington wasn't there – did you notice?" She dropped her voice. "One of the servants. That household seems so right and proper but under the surface..." She nodded significantly. "Ah, thank you, Annie. You can leave the shawl next door. I feel much better now."

Mary marvelled that one of her friend's misfortunes

could actually warm Eliza Aitken like a fire. But her mistress had always been jealous of Mrs Harrington. Mary had seen it for herself in the churchyard, talking to Harriet.

Oh, Harriet!

One of the servants.

What 'little scandal' had hit the Harringtons' house? It couldn't be related to Harriet – it simply couldn't. She was the most sensible, loyal, hardworking girl. But even so, a nagging worry embedded itself in Mary's brain. She hadn't seen Harriet at church last week and it wasn't the first time she'd missed it. Why was that? Mary knew she wouldn't rest until she discovered the truth.

For the rest of the evening, every hour that passed felt to Mary like a week. The scandal was not referred to again by the family in her presence and she was exhausted by the pretence of not caring about it, while listening out for any word.

Cook, normally the first in line with any gossip, simply gave a little sniff when Annie asked her about the news, buzzing with her own curiosity. At least it meant Mary didn't have to ask.

"I'm not one to share the misfortunes of my neighbours," Cook told them with an arch look. "I like to keep my counsel."

"It's because she doesn't know anything," Annie muttered under her breath to Mary, who privately agreed. Mrs Green had never willingly kept her counsel before. Meanwhile, worrying and wondering made every job in the house more difficult.

That night Mary heard each passing hour chime. She felt trapped and useless. When a messenger arrived the next day with a note from Lady Emmeline, she nearly wept with gratitude. It was a chance at last to leave the house and find out what had happened for herself.

"She wants you this afternoon," Eliza Aitken said crisply. "Honestly, I'm almost glad. You've been even more reckless and thoughtless than usual this morning, Mary. I've never seen so many sooty fingerprints on the parlour hearth. I don't know what's got into you."

"Yes, ma'am. Sorry, ma'am," Mary said, bobbing.

"And Mary – do remind her about the children. She hasn't asked to meet them yet and I'm sure she'd find them charming."

"Certainly, ma'am," Mary said. She was so used to lying to her mistress now that she hardly noticed it.

When the carriage arrived, Mary spoke to the coachman quietly.

"Drop me at St Gabriel's. I'll walk from there."

"To Walton Street?" he asked, surprised. "You'll dirty your skirts, miss."

"No. I'm going somewhere else. Tell Mr Dawson … tell him I'm sorry, but there's something I have to do. I'll see him tomorrow, if he wants me."

She sensed the coachman's disapproval in the way he gee'd the horses after he'd let her down next to St Gabriel's. But she shrugged it off and ran as fast as she could to the Harringtons' house.

She hadn't been there before but she'd often heard Harriet describe it with smug satisfaction as 'the largest house on Queen Street, slightly wider than the rest, with a more ornate balustrade'. And there it was, with bay trees in stone planters either side of the front door and a freshly blacked railing running along the pavement.

Mary took the stairs down to the basement and rang at the tradesman's door. A young maid in a fresh white apron answered it.

"Yes? What d'you want?"

"Is Harriet here? Harriet Wilson?"

The maid's face clouded over. She pursed her lips and looked hostile. "Why d'you want to know?"

Mary's heart plummeted and yet still it seemed impossible. "I'm her cousin. I need to see her."

"Not here, you don't. Now get out, before I get someone to throw you out."

The girl made to close the door but Mary put her foot against it, to hold it back. "Please! What's happened? You must tell me!"

"I'll do no such thing. Go away!" She called behind her. "Jack, come here! Someone's causing trouble."

A large, jowly face above a muscled neck appeared in the gloom behind the girl. He moved the maid aside and bore down on Mary, pushing her roughly until she fell backwards to the ground.

"Get out of here, d'you hear? And don't come back!"

He slammed the door and Mary picked herself up, leaning for a moment against the basement wall to calm her trembling body and pounding heart. A thousand horrible images flashed in front of her: Harriet in jail... Harriet in a ditch... Harriet in a street gang's clutches...

What to do now? Where to go? She didn't know.

Shakily she climbed the steps back to the street and walked along the road, careless of which direction she was going in. Still in shock, she hardly noticed rapid footsteps crunching on the sand behind her. A hand grabbed her dress and held it. She gasped and nearly fell again.

"Hey! Stop there!" It was a young boy, not more than nine or ten. His face was grimy with what looked like boot polish and he wore a patched waistcoat and a tweed cap. He was out of breath from running after her.

"What is it?" Mary asked, cross and frightened, pulling her skirts from his hand.

"You the one 'oo was askin' about 'Attie?"

"Yes," she said cautiously. "Who are you?"

"That'd be tellin'."

Mary guessed he was the Harringtons' boot boy. "What do you want?"

"Well, I got information. It'll cost you." He tilted his head back and gave her a boyish 'hard man' look. Mary didn't have time for games. She dug in her pocket.

"Here. A penny. It's all I've got."

He rubbed it between his fingers, smelling it for good

measure, as if trying to judge whether it was real.

"Oh, come on," Mary snapped. "What's happened? Is she safe? Has she gone to the country?" She dropped her voice. "The peelers haven't got her, have they?"

He laughed. "She ain't in jail – but she's gone. Left yesterday. There was a right to-do. The missus cryin' and 'Attie cryin' and wotnot. The missus has been in her room all shut up ever since. 'Attie told me you'd come. Jus' before she went. Told me to tell you where to find her, if you was in time."

"How did you know it was me?" Mary asked.

"Oh, I know," the boy said, winking. "A girl like you…" The wink turned to a leer. On a ten-year-old, it looked ridiculous. Mary lost her temper.

"So, where do I go?" she snapped. "Where is she?"

"Covent Garden market. There's food there. People around. She said you'd know it."

"I do. How will I find her?"

He leered again. "Girl like you … girl like her. Shouldn't be difficult."

"Go home, nasty boy."

Despite his news, Mary regretted giving him her penny. She quickly turned her back on him and headed off on foot for Covent Garden – glad at least that she already knew the way.

❦

Mary hardly noticed the streets go by as she ran. Her mind was racing with speculation, but at least Harriet was safe. She was in London and not in jail: that was a start. By the time she reached Trafalgar Square – where a brewer's dray nearly ran her over in her distraction – Mary had decided it must be something to do with a theft. It was the only answer. Since coming to London, Mary had often heard stories of servants being dismissed for stealing from their masters – anything from snuff to the family silver. The one thing she was sure of was that Harriet was innocent. Maybe it was a simple mistake; perhaps one of the other servants was the real culprit. Mary felt sure that once the truth was known Hattie would be returned to the Harringtons. By the time she reached Long Acre and smelled the rotting cabbages that littered the roadside at this time of day, she felt almost cheerful with certainty that somehow, all would be well.

As long as she could find her.

Mary had forgotten just how busy and noisy the market was. Not quite so crowded now – it was the afternoon and most of the buying and selling was over – but still full of costermongers packing up their stalls and fine ladies and gentlemen strolling beside the buildings. She stood as close to the centre of the open space as she could and looked around desperately. How to spot one girl among all these people? Then she remembered what the boy had said and took off her bonnet. She fanned out her hair so that it fell to her waist, as wide and bright as possible. She scanned the scene for a glimpse of Harriet's neat black silhouette. Two minutes later, she heard a sharp cry behind her. As she spun round, Harriet launched herself into her arms.

Chapter Twenty-two

They held each other for a long time: two still black forms with matching copper hair in the middle of the bustle and colour of the market. Harriet clung to Mary as if for dear life.

"You came! You came!" she murmured.

"Of course I did. What's happened? What can I do?"

Harriet pulled away and shook her head. "Nothing." She seemed to sway.

Mary caught her, gripped by fresh concern. This was more than some mere misunderstanding. "Come with me." She led her to a low wall beside a packed-up stall littered with wilting lettuce leaves and squashed tomatoes. They sat on it side by side, uncomfortably. Looking at Harriet closely, Mary saw how pale and faint she looked. "Tell me everything," she said.

Harriet opened her mouth to answer but as she did so

her face seemed to crumble. Her body arched over in a vision of pain. Her lips opened wide but no sound came out. Mary felt her skin prickle. "What is it?"

But still Harriet couldn't talk. She stared up at Mary with dull, blank eyes. Mary leaned in and reached for her cousin's hands. "You must tell me!"

Harriet pulled her hands away and stared at the ground. She wrapped her arms around herself. Seeing her so cut off from human friendship, a slow-dawning fear crept up Mary's spine like a slithering snake, enveloping her in its coils.

"Has someone hurt you?" Harriet bit her lip. "A man?" She started to rock herself backwards and forwards. "Did he ... touch you?"

Harriet's head bowed. She nodded, but barely.

Mary's mind raced. Oh God. Oh Lord in heaven. An unmarried girl.

She took a deep breath. "One of the servants? Mr Harrington? Did he force—?"

"No! Not him!" Harriet's voice was suddenly passionate and loud. "Edmond! And he didn't force himself! I love him! He loves me!"

Harriet said the words as though they excused and

explained everything. But instead of relief, Mary felt the coils of horror squeeze tighter round her chest. She sat back.

"The master's son? He loves you?"

There was a sort of fierceness to Harriet now, though her lids brimmed with tears.

"He does! It was beautiful, Mary. I was his sun and moon and stars. Every night he came and—"

"*Every night*?" Mary whispered. Was her cousin mad? "For how long?"

"Since Candlemas. He came without fail and held me close. He was tender, Mary. True love like that … it's such a precious thing. No one said… I never knew…"

So *this* was where Harriet's happiness had come from. Mary made rapid calculations in her head. Candlemas was the beginning of February. That was seven months ago.

"Oh, cousin!"

Harriet was weeping openly now. The tears streamed down her cheeks and she made no move to wipe them away. They fell on the bodice of her plain black dress, where salt stains already showed. With her shawl hanging loose, Mary saw how the dress thickened at the waist, where every seam was straining. Her chest, too, Mary noticed now, had grown. She had a more womanly shape. Even her face was more rounded than before, though her eyes were sunken. Mary's hand reached unconsciously towards her cousin's stomach. Harriet looked down and shrank away.

"How long have you known?"

Harriet's eyes were panicked, like a horse about to bolt. "I *didn't* know." She dropped her voice to the merest mumble. "I thought it was happiness that made me fat. Everyone told me how London suited me. You did. I kept being sick but I assumed it was bad fish or a cold. Then Cook caught me in the scullery, throwing up on the dishes. She guessed straightaway what it was. She told me. I was so scared, Mary."

"Hattie, Hattie…" Mary murmured the words as she stroked her cousin's hair.

"They asked what I'd done. Who with… It was shameful. I denied everything to protect him, but two nights ago, the mistress came to me. She put her hand on my stomach and … it jumped."

"Jumped?"

"It kicked. That's what she said. I'd had the feelings

before. I thought they were indigestion. But she said she felt it kick her hand. She flew into such a fury."

Harriet recounted her story as if amazed by every step of it. Night after night that golden boy had come to her… *Didn't you think?* Mary wanted to ask. *Didn't you know this might happen?* Hariet was normally so sensible about everything. But it was clear that when it came to her lover she hadn't thought or hadn't understood. Had she not watched the animals at home, as Mary had? Did she not see what happened after?

"Did Edmond say nothing? Didn't he explain?"

Harriet's eyes, once so bright and trusting, slowly brought themselves up to meet Mary's again. "He said it was all right if we weren't married. He said you only got babies if you were man and wife. He said our love was a dream."

The pain in Mary's chest was now replaced by cold, hard anger.

"A dream? Oh, a dream – really? And now that he's been proved wrong? Now there *is* a baby?"

At the mention of the word, Harriet started to cry too hard to speak. While she wept, Mary's fury grew. Not at her cousin but at everyone else. Why did her mother not warn her of the possibility of such a tragedy? Could Edmond really be such a simpleton, or did his lust for his 'sun, moon and stars' come before any thoughts of common sense, any true care for her? And elegant Mrs Harrington – did she let her sons wander the house at night and her maids sleep alone?

"Soon everyone will know!" Harriet snorted through her tears. Her face was distorted with fear and misery. No artist ever painted this, Mary thought bitterly. This was not a girl serenely floating in a river, chanting songs, but one very much alive, made ugly with despair. With a baby, nobody would want Harriet. No one would employ her. How would she survive? Mary wanted to hit something, howl at something, break something.

Slowly Harriet brought her sobs under control. She was eager to speak in defence of her lover. "He-he … he's … so sorry. He never wanted this to happen. Yesterday he brought me a little posy of the prettiest flowers." Her eyes softened at the memory of it. "He'd marry me if he could. He's sworn he'll love me forever. But he'd be cut off without a penny. We'd have nowhere to live. He couldn't complete his studies. I can't ask that of him."

The thought of the flowers made Mary's blood boil

harder. He gave her a baby and then matched it with a *posy*?
"But Harriet, he's asking it of *you*. What will you do?"

Harriet's eyes were deep wells. The dim light was gone
again, at the thought of losing Edmond. "I … don't …
kno-ooow!"

The wail of despair seemed to echo for an age. Mary
knew exactly what would become of her – abandoned or
locked up, half-starved and worked to death. Meanwhile
Edmond would be sent away until the 'unpleasantness'
blew over. Then he would return to continue his gracious,
well-fed life. '*A little youthful indiscretion*.' A knowing
smile every now and then among the menfolk. The girl
would be dismissed as a worthless slut. The baby, when
it came, would die. Mary found herself weeping, too.
She clung to her cousin, her dearest friend, and felt her
heart breaking.

It was Harriet who recovered herself first. "I'm sorry.
I shouldn't have told you any of it. Please don't tell Ma.
I couldn't bear it."

Mary nodded. "Where will you go?"

"Edmond has given me a little money. Enough for a
room for a few nights…" She trailed off.

After that – where? No one in Westbrook would have

her. The whole family would be shamed. There was only the workhouse. Babies died there all the time. Or the streets of London…

Harriet sniffed and rose. "I must go. Edmond is leaving soon. He's meeting me to say goodbye."

"Leaving?" Mary asked sharply. "To go on holiday? Abroad?"

"Yes! To visit a relative in Rome to help with his studies. How did you know?"

"Oh, just a guess."

Harriet ignored Mary's sarcastic tone. "Think of me," she said. She straightened her dress, wiped her cheeks and held out her hands. "Pray for me."

"I will," Mary promised. And she would, every night, with all her heart, and her hands wrapped around her little bible. But she didn't expect God to answer. Not in any way she would understand, anyway. He never had before. Not through all Pa's furies and being sent to London or the deaths of all the little animals she'd loved as a child.

Harriet made to leave, her shoulders bowed as if the weight inside was too great to carry.

"Wait!" Mary called Harriet back with a shout.

The other girl turned her head slowly, as if moving through treacle. "I'll do more than pray. There's a way. We'll find a way. I'll come back in two days and find you, with the answer. Meet me here. Right here."

Harriet smiled at her sadly. Mary ran over and flung her arms round her cousin one last time.

"I'll help you. I have friends now. Trust me."

"I must go. Goodbye, dearest."

Mary watched in dumb misery as Harriet's cowed black frame was lost in the crowd.

PART III

THE UNRAVELLING

Mary must have slept that night but she heard the church bells strike three, four and five. She lay with her bible on her chest and felt the weight of it crushing her.

There were ways to get rid of a baby. Mary knew that they existed but not what they were. A teenage girl in the village had died when Mary and Harriet were small. The influenza, her family said, but there were whispers, rumours. A boy, a sin ... God's wrath ... a hot bath, gin... Mary didn't understand the details but Ma had taken the young cousins to Maisy Goodfellow's wake. The body was laid out on a table, dressed in her Sunday clothes, eyes closed, as if she were sleeping. She held flowers, too, like Ophelia in the painting. Wild poppies and forget-me-nots from the hedgerows. Her face was pale as a ghost and waxy as a doll. Mary had cried that day. "Just you remember," Ma had said in the lane afterwards. "Be a good girl or you'll end up like Maisy." Mary promised, even though she didn't know what exact kind of 'good' Ma meant at the time. She had understood since then.

But Harriet, apparently, had not. Perhaps she thought 'good' meant acting kindly, the way the rector talked about in Sunday school. Perhaps she thought it meant being in love. If no one had explained to her and her lover had lied to her, then how *was* she supposed to know?

⁊⁊⁊ ⁊⁊⁊

By luncheon no message had arrived for Mary. This worried her, since she had offered to meet Felix today instead of yesterday. She needed him. Needed his help and comfort. Why didn't he want to paint today?

Mrs Aiken pronounced herself relieved.

"Lady Emmeline has been ill-using us lately. I suppose, from her sickbed, she hasn't noticed. But though she's such a dear friend, I do wish she'd realize how much I depend on the servants. At least we have a full day's work from you for a change."

Downstairs, Cook hummed to herself as she clattered

about the kitchen with tins and trays. Mary willed herself not to panic. In two days, she'd said, she would go to Harriet with some kind of salvation. So far she had done nothing and one of those days was already half gone.

"Fetch me the sugar, Mary," Cook said cheerily.

Mary went to the larder, where the sugar jar sat almost empty on a shelf. A brown paper packet beside it, sealed with wax, was ready to refill it. She stood for a while, looking at the jar and the packet. A desperate plan had formed itself quickly in her head but she didn't know if she had the courage to go through with it.

"Come on, sluggard, what's keeping you?" Cook shouted.

Mary jolted herself out of her stupor. "I'm just looking for it," she said, reaching up and taking the packet. She hid it behind a stack of beer bottles on the floor, heart hammering, and reached up again for the almost-empty jar.

"Here it is," she said, going back into the warmth of the kitchen. "But I'm afraid there's not much left."

"There's a whole new packet."

"I couldn't see it."

"I bought it last week."

"I thought so, but it isn't there."

"Oh, come, girl, let me see!"

Cook bustled past her to the larder and stood in dumb confusion at the sight of the empty shelf.

"I could have sworn I bought one." She frowned.

"I'll go out and get some if you like," Mary offered.

"But it's Thursday. Half-closing day. The grocer's shut."

"I know of one," Mary offered. "A little further away, towards Chelsea. It won't take long."

Mrs Green sighed. She knew Mary was needed for all sorts of other tasks but once she had set her mind on making something – in this case, Italian biscuits for a trifle – she hated to be defeated. Mary knew this, and waited.

"All right then," Cook huffed at last. "Take some pennies from the jar. Promise you won't be long."

"I promise. I'll fly like the wind."

"And … thank you."

Mary blushed at this. Though she lied and cheated on an almost daily basis, it still felt odd to be thanked for doing so.

Upstairs in her room she grabbed a couple of shillings left over from her modelling work and used some of the money to pay for a hansom carriage as soon as she was out of sight of the house.

"Take me to Walton Street!" she instructed the coachman.

He rattled along at quite a pace, as if sensing her urgency. Halfway there, she heard and felt the loud patter of raindrops on the roof. She hadn't noticed the approaching thunderclouds outside but the air felt heavy with the promise of a summer storm. At the door to the pale blue villa, the maid let her in with a cocked head and eyebrows arched in surprise.

"Mr Dawson didn't say no one was coming."

"He must have forgotten," Mary said dismissively. "Don't worry, I know the way."

She rushed up without being asked and felt the maid's disapproving eyes following her as she went. At least the girl hadn't said he was out visiting. She knocked on the door at the top of the stairs but no one answered. Was the maid wrong? Had he slipped out without anyone noticing? Mary felt her panic rise again and knocked harder, shouting his name. "Felix! Felix!"

"I'm coming!" came an irritable reply.

Her knees almost gave way beneath her with relief. The door opened and there he was, in his shirtsleeves, pink-cheeked from sleep and his dark hair ruffled.

"Thank goodness!" she said, ready to run to him and hold him.

But his arms weren't outstretched to welcome her. He looked angry. She was confused. Was this to do with the party? Had he seen her watching him?

"You didn't come yesterday," he said coldly.

"Oh – I couldn't."

"I sent the carriage for you."

"I used it for something else. Felix—"

His eyes narrowed as he interrupted her. "You're not supposed to do that. The light was perfect yesterday. I had everything set up ready and so much I wanted to do. Look at it now." He flicked a glance behind him at the tall, north-facing window, which was thundercloud grey. "And I'm tired. I was out drowning my sorrows with Roly last night. You might as well go home."

"I can't!" Mary exclaimed. "Not yet. I didn't come

here to sit for you anyway."

"What?"

"I need your help. Listen."

She walked into the room uninvited. She felt cold in here for the first time, and it wasn't the thundercloud sky that was responsible. Felix closed the door behind her, folded his arms and glared. She still felt stung by his response, having been so sure he'd be as pleased to see her as she was to see him. It hadn't occurred to her that he would want to punish her for not coming yesterday. Truly, he was more dedicated to his work than she'd realized.

This made what she had to say more difficult but the sight of *Persephone and Hades* on its easel gave her courage. The painting was even more lovely than the last time she'd seen it. He'd captured her face perfectly and her copper waterfall of hair. The damask dress now glowed against the reds, pinks and golds with almost unearthly light. Could such a goddess ask a man a favour? *Yes*, Mary thought. If she was desperate.

Mary moved a pile of books off a rickety chair and sat down. Felix roved around at first but eventually pulled up an upturned beer crate and sat on that.

"Well. What is it?"

He was so close. She just wanted to reach out and touch him, and feel the warmth of him. She wanted him to shut out the world and make it better.

"I have a cousin…" she began.

This wasn't a Greek legend. Mary wasn't sure what words to use to tell Harriet's story but he was waiting and somehow words came. She found herself starting in Kent, running round the fields with her cousin, who saved her from endless trouble.

"Go on," he said, confused but softening.

She explained how Harriet had brought her to London and how she worked as a maid for the Harringtons.

"A good family. Joe's a friend of Roly's. I like him," he said, nodding. "He's a blackguard, though. Wait – he hasn't done anything bad, has he?"

"Not Joe…"

"Not Joe? It's always Joe."

"Not this time. Edmond…"

Felix frowned, then smiled. "The hard-working one? Surely not. He's the saint. The apple of his mother's eye, so Joe always complains."

Mary paused, searching for words again. Felix's

easy mood turned to mild curiosity, then doubt, then concern, as her silence explained what she couldn't say.

"Edmond ... and the maid? Your cousin?"

Mary nodded.

"Caught in the act?"

"Not quite. There's a child. There will be."

"Oh God. Is she certain?"

Mary hung her head.

He leaped up and the beer crate tumbled over. "The idiot! I'd have expected it of Joe, but hardly Edmond."

She looked up at him. "He told her that nothing could happen if they weren't married."

"And she believed him?"

"Yes."

"Then she's an idiot, too."

Mary rose to her feet, furious. "She trusted him."

He threw his hands up. "What a fool! You'd never do that."

Mary groaned. That was true. But it wasn't the point. "She has nothing. If we don't help, she'll die!"

"Don't be dramatic. Girls have babies all the time."

Despite herself, Mary felt overwhelmed by tears. She didn't want to cry in front of him but she was desperate and she'd been so certain of his help. Startled, he tried to comfort her, but she pushed him away.

"Mary!" he exclaimed. And then more softly, "What do you want me to do? Seriously – what do you think I can do?"

"You're rich. You're a gentleman. You can save her."

He looked at her with a sad, wry smile. "None of those things are true."

"Yes, they are."

He gestured at the studio. "Look around you. Look! Up there, down here, my paints and canvases, that table, this wine… None of this is mine. D'you understand? Until I sell paintings, I have nothing. I couldn't help her if I wanted to."

Mary reached out to him. "You're all I have. I need you."

"I'm just a poor artist. I couldn't save a drowning cat. I'm sorry."

She didn't know whether to cry or give in to the nausea that threatened to overwhelm her. Tears won but she refused to weep in front of him. Wiping her eyes with her sleeve, she ran blindly for the door.

"Don't take it like that!" he called out. "Look, stay.

Have some bread." She reached the door but he caught up with her and held it closed.

"I can't eat while my cousin is starving," she said in brittle, icy tones. She wanted to shame him but it didn't work. He simply stroked her face with his free hand.

"Don't punish yourself for what she's done."

"So you won't help me?"

"I can't."

He wouldn't even try. The full force of Mary's bitterness welled up inside her. "What is the point of you, then? You're just some widow's lapdog."

At this Felix's tender look vanished entirely. It was replaced by shock, then horror. Mary realized she had let slip for the first time that she knew who Mrs Lisle was. She thought he might hit her but instead he stood stiffly, with wounded self-control.

"I sacrifice everything for my art. Everything. My pride, my dignity, my security. You're right: there is no point to me, except my paintings. I can't help you. Though God knows I love you. You came to the wrong lapdog." He opened the door. "Goodbye."

Mary felt him disappearing from her, like a light vanishing into darkness. Too distressed to speak, she ran back down the stairs. She wept all the way home in another hansom carriage and through Cook's fury with her for not getting the sugar, which she had quite forgotten. In the larder, she curled into a little ball and cried herself out. By the time she 'found' the spare packet of sugar and produced it as a peace offering, it was too late for the trifle.

Cook and Annie took turns to scold her all evening but Mary hardly listened. Her heart was too full of impoverished artists and abandoned cousins and babies who died on cold street corners, and promises she couldn't keep.

Chapter Twenty-four

Mary thought that by bedtime she was all cried out, but as she climbed into her shift she remembered Felix's wounded look as she left him and it was hard to keep fresh sobs at bay. Red-eyed, she told Annie they were hiccups.

But Annie wasn't convinced. After an hour, she leaned up on her elbow and asked, "What is it? Come on, tell me. Has your fancy man thrown you over?"

Normally Mary would have maintained a dignified silence but tonight she was too exhausted and too sad.

"He might as well have," she admitted. "But it's worse."

"What's worse than that? Don't tell me – did someone squiggle on one of his precious paintings?"

At that, despite her grief, Mary found herself giggling. "No," she admitted.

"Come on, then – tell me."

So Mary did. Everything. She had kept too many secrets and couldn't hold them all in any longer. To her surprise, Annie listened without her usual carps and questions. She was so quiet that at one stage Mary thought she'd gone to sleep.

"Annie?"

"Still here," the Irish voice murmured. She sounded sad, too. Her reaction was so unexpected it made Mary's tears flow again.

"I thought … I thought…"

"Thought what? That I wouldn't care?"

"That you'd be the harshest of all," Mary admitted.

"Why now? Because I'm not your friend?"

"That. And because you're a Catholic."

"Ah, there now," Annie sighed. She got up and lit the candle, so they could see each other. "Let me tell you a little story about my family. My ma's devoted to the Church. Spends an hour every morning on her knees praying to the statue of Our Lady. She's eleven children and I'm number six, so by then she was busy. It was my eldest sister who looked after me when I was small. Another Mary, like you, but not with the hair – thank the Heavenly Father. Well, Mary met a boy and these things happen. She was with child. And Ma went to the priest to find out what to do."

"Yes?" Mary held her breath.

"Well, the priest condemned Mary as a sinner and told Ma to throw her out of the house. So Ma did, to please God. And they threw her out of the village, to please God better. And she starved for a while in a cow byre and eventually they found her in the river, stone cold and drowned, with the baby still inside her."

"Oh no!" Mary gasped aloud. She thought of the *Ophelia* picture but imagined a scene nothing like it. No delicate flowers floating. No fairy-tale dress. No hallucinating artistry.

"And Ma didn't even say a prayer for her," Annie went on in a low, flat voice. She didn't look at Mary, but at something in the darkness that only she could see.

"Why didn't she pray?" Mary asked.

"Because the priest said so."

"I thought you were supposed to pray?"

"Oh, he told Ma that Mary was beyond saving. She wasn't in purgatory – she'd gone straight to hell. A suicide, too, so they couldn't bury her in the churchyard. They put her in a field near the sea, with the cattle wandering over her. Ma wouldn't speak of it or even mention her name. Well, I couldn't stay at home then so I came to London, even though I was twelve and London seemed as far away as the moon to me then. But I knew what was right and what was wrong and the cows walking on my sister's grave…"

Annie's voice cracked at last. Mary moved across to sit on her bed and took her hand. "I'm so sorry."

"It wasn't right. It couldn't be. I never told Ma where I was going. She'd lost one daughter without caring – I thought she could lose two. Only … Eddie found me a few months ago. He's the next brother down from me. I'd sent a postcard once to a girl in the village and he saw it and traced me here. He's a clever lad, is Eddie. And he told me –" Annie squeezed Mary's hand – "he told me Ma was never the same after I went. Half her face stopped working overnight. She couldn't say her words straight. She walks with a stick now. So maybe she cared. But I'm not going back."

Mary held Annie to her for so long she lost track of time. She felt so fragile in Mary's arms, like a little bird.

Eventually Annie pulled away. "Now we have Harriet to think of," she said with a sniff. "I always liked her.

Hard-working girl – better than you!" She grinned and Mary smiled.

"It's true – I'm terrible. I'm sorry."

"It's not your fault. You were made to be enchanting to gentlemen, not to clean a grate."

"More than that, I hope," Mary said. Annie made it sound lovely: being 'enchanting to gentlemen', and at Little Holland House it had felt that way, but it didn't seem worth much tonight. What was the point of enchanting gentlemen if you couldn't help someone you loved in trouble, or even take a carriage where you wanted? It still rankled with Mary very much that Felix had been so cross about that carriage ride. She was a prisoner unless he deigned to let her out. He thought of himself as her master – not her friend or anything more.

"When did you say you'd meet her again?" Annie asked.

"Hattie? Tomorrow afternoon. Back at Covent Garden. I'll have to think of an errand to go on."

"That gives us time. I'll get Eddie on to it in the morning. He might know somewhere she could stay. You can go and pick up the master's watch from the menders for me. That's not far from Covent Garden. You can see her then and tell her what we've discovered. Unless another message from Lady Emmeline comes, of course."

"That won't happen. Felix is furious with me."

"For not posing for his precious painting?"

"For calling him a lapdog for not helping me."

"You called him a lapdog?" Annie's eyes were round. She burst out laughing.

Mary gave a small, sad smile. "I did."

"You're a brave girl, Mary Adams. Mad but brave. But you shouldn't have expected him to help you. Men don't, generally. You'll learn – babies are a woman's problem. That's just the way it is."

Chapter Twenty-five

It turned out that Annie was right. But the first lesson Mary learned was that the girl most willing to help Harriet was Annie herself.

Their animosity had melted into friendship the moment Annie shared her story. Mary thought of her quite differently now: as brave and clever in her own way, forging a life for herself in the biggest city in the world and leaving her past behind. As enemies they had made life difficult for each other but now that they were friends, everything was different. Annie didn't officially apologize for making Mary's life such a misery before, but everything about her manner now was an apology of sorts, and Mary gladly accepted it

Annie called for Eddie first thing in the morning. A network of coal boys and paper boys, stable boys and general ragamuffins turned out to be the most efficient way of finding and communicating with someone in London – far quicker than the telegraph. He came before breakfast and she set him off on his task of finding some sort of temporary shelter for Harriet, while they worked on a better plan.

He was back by lunchtime. It was Mary who opened the tradesman's door to him. He stood there, wiry and cocky, in his battered hat and better-days coat.

"Why, if it isn't Mary Adams."

"Eddie O'Bryan." She eyed him with what was intended to be fierce independence. She wasn't the girl he had caught by surprise all those weeks ago.

He didn't seem such a bruiser, either. She realized that despite his irregular face, with its broken nose and scarred cheek, he wasn't so bad to look at. In fact, she might have called him 'interesting'. His china-blue eyes seemed to dance with merriness and there was a certain flair to the jaunty angle of his hat and the attitude with which he wore his open coat.

"And how are you today?" he asked.

"The better for not being jumped on in the street," she said, looking at him squarely.

He had the decency to look embarrassed, slightly.

"No hard feelings?"

Under the circumstances, she decided to forgive him, though she was still wary. "Have you found anywhere?"

He nodded. "There is … a place. Not a good one. The last one on earth, really. It's where the ladybirds go."

"The who?"

"The ladies of the night – you know. It's damp. And dark. It's a warehouse by the docks and the wind comes in off the river. But at least the landlord owes me a favour. She mustn't expect luxuries like glass in the windows or running water. She mustn't mind the smell or the rats. But the door locks. The roof works. And it's not the workhouse. I can take her there if you want me to."

Mary nodded and gazed at the ground. "Thank you."

She tried not to look too downcast. He was right – it wasn't the workhouse. And surely they would find her something better soon?

"I'll meet you at Covent Garden in front of the church," he said. "Three o'clock sharp. Chin up, Mary."

She lifted her chin instinctively and he leaned in and kissed her firmly on the cheek. Before she could react, he was gone with another laugh. She was left to wonder how a brother and sister could be so different. And with the growing feeling that she could learn to like the boy as much as the girl.

❦

As good as her word, Annie found an excuse to send Mary instead of her to collect the master's watch, and so Mary was able to introduce Harriet to Eddie, who promised to take care of her as well as he could. Hattie's face was drawn. Her dress was splashed with mud and torn at the sleeve. She looked thinner, not fatter, since the last time Mary saw her, despite the growing child, and her hair hung limp and unkempt around her face. When Mary hugged her, she hardly had the strength to respond.

Mary gave her a little bread, cheese and fruitcake – stolen from the kitchen by Annie when Cook's back was turned – and promised to visit again soon, with better news. She felt the clock ticking the moment she left her. She thought of her namesake lying in the stream in Ireland, so real and dead and unlike *Ophelia*, and wondered how long she had before Hattie looked at the Thames and considered the same fate.

When she got back, an unexpected note arrived from

Lady Emmeline, requesting her services that evening. "At least she has the decency to require you once we are largely done with you today," Eliza observed.

Dressing up as Persephone seemed strange and dreamlike. Annie helped lace her into her new cream moire, made to her design by Kitty's seamstress.

"You look a wonder, so you do," Annie said, pulling the laces tightly.

Mary caught sight of her reflection in the skylight. The fabric seemed to glow against the dark evening sky – much like the *Persephone* dress. But even without the hoops and petticoats she couldn't afford, she decided it was a little *too* stylish. After seeing Lizzie Siddal she hankered for something timeless – or at least suggestive of a lost, romantic age. She caught herself thinking these thoughts and berated herself for being so frivolous.

"I'm a vain, self-centred fool," she told Annie, shaking her head.

"Any girl would be vain if she looked like you."

Mary tried to laugh. "What? With my cursed hair and all these freckles?"

"You look like an angel," Annie said simply. "You always did."

But Mary most certainly wasn't angelic, she knew, as she wrapped herself in Annie's cloak to hide the dress. She had vowed to think of nothing but Harriet and how to get help for her, but tonight she was no better than any other girl dressing up for a night with friends: instinctively wanting to please, hoping to impress.

⁂

This wasn't entirely selfish. As the Ballard carriage sped her away, she reflected that she was going to the right place. The Ballards were rich and could help her in ways Felix never could – if she appealed to them properly. And surely Balfour House must be where she was heading? It couldn't have been Felix who'd called for her. He wouldn't want to paint her at this time of night and, after their row, he wouldn't want to see her for any other reason she could think of. Even so, her heart contracted with disappointment when the carriage turned east, for Mayfair, not west, for Walton Street.

At the Ballards' grand home, Roly was taking advantage of his parents' absence on a trip to Russia to host a night of cards. When Mary arrived, he came out to meet her in the vestibule. He was jollier than she'd ever seen him, especially when he saw her dress.

"You're a vision!" he announced. "A pure delight! I couldn't have asked for anything better. Now, wait here while I... Martin! Bring me my opera cloak. We need something big to hide Miss Lavelle underneath. Are the musicians ready? I want her to make the entrance she deserves."

And so Mary found herself ushered into one of the reception rooms under the cover of a hot, dark cloak, to the sound of a dramatic drumroll, which climaxed when Roly whipped the cloak off her, revealing her like the star of a magic trick.

"Ladies and gentlemen. I give you ... Persephone Lavelle! The finest artists' model in London."

Disconcerted but smiling bravely, she surveyed the crowded room. The trick certainly seemed to have the effect Roly wanted. While the guests clapped, she quickly scanned the room for Felix's face and couldn't find it. Hiding her renewed disappointment, she forced a smile.

"Thank you, thank you. You are much too kind..."

Young men in tight evening clothes stepped forwards to kiss her hand. Older men nodded appreciatively.

Women gushed at her beauty and cast her jealous looks. Nearby, Kitty laughed delightedly and clapped her hands.

"My! What an entrance, Persephone! How lovely you look tonight."

Kitty did, too, as always. She was quite easily the prettiest person in the room, in tiers of sheer ivory gauze over rose silk taffeta, with a low-cut bertha neckline that revealed her swanlike neck and gracefully hugged her slender shoulders. Her hair was elaborately caught up with jewels and flowers. Every man should be looking at her, Mary thought, and told her so.

"Oh no! I'm very dull. You're all the fashion." Kitty didn't seem to mind, beaming at her friend's success. "Come and meet Lord Avebury. He's been dying to pay his respects since the Prinseps' party. Then you must tell me all about it. I've been longing to hear."

For a while, Mary indulged in being Persephone. She smiled graciously when her hand was kissed and coquettishly when complimented. When the conversation was dull – when it turned repeatedly to her 'charms' and 'the pleasure of regarding a beautiful woman', she smiled politely. When it was interesting, on the subject of painting or poetry, she joined in and watched as the men – they were always men – looked surprised at her knowledge and curiosity. Some liked it, she noticed, but most seemed to prefer it when she kept her full lips shut, so they could admire the curvature and not be distracted by her opinions.

All the time, the only thing she really wanted to do was get help for Harriet. But Kitty still needed to know about Sara Prinsep's party, so when she took Mary aside to a quiet spot by the window, she first had to answer a thousand queries about the dress, taste and hospitality at Little Holland House. Only when Kitty finally seemed to run out of things to ask could she finally ask a question of her own.

"Could you lend me some money?" She hadn't wished to be so bold about it but yet more guests were moving her way and she sensed there wasn't much time.

Kitty frowned at her. "How much?"

"I don't know. As much as you can afford."

Kitty's frown lines deepened. "That's not like you, Mary."

"It's not for me. It's for a friend of mine. She's in trouble."

"What kind of trouble?"

In this room, with its silk curtains and green baize tables, its champagne poured by the magnum and happy guests in evening dress, it seemed impossible to explain what kind of trouble. The gulf between the two worlds was too large to be bridged in a few simple words.

"A girl…" Mary faltered.

"Yes?"

"And a man. He left her. There's a baby. Or will be soon."

Kitty wrinkled her pretty nose in concentration. As Mary feared, she simply couldn't bring herself to understand.

"A baby? Isn't that good?"

Mary sighed impatiently. "No, it isn't. She has no home now. She needs my help."

Already a smiling gentleman was walking towards them from the other side of the room. Kitty frowned again and shook her head. She still didn't really follow the story but she could see Mary was distressed.

"I have no money. Well, a very little. If I want more I need to ask Papa. Would five pounds help?"

Mary suppressed a groan of frustration and

immediately felt ungrateful. What was she asking her friend for, anyway? To support Harriet indefinitely? How could she, possibly?

"Persephone. Enchanted. Richard Osmond at your service." The gentleman had crossed the room to greet them. The knowing, confident look he gave Mary made her shudder slightly. Not all of them did this, but the few that did were bad enough. A girl without a chaperone. An artists' model… They thought they knew the score and it was merely a question of price.

"Enchanted to meet you, too," she said curtseying. "I'm so sorry – Mr Ballard is calling me." Without a backwards glance, she left Mr Osmond to Kitty's mercy. It was time to appeal to someone with real access to funds.

❧⸭⸭❧

Roly Ballard loved the excitement of being asked, *sotto voce*, to meet Persephone alone in the little orangery in five minutes' time. He arrived rubbing his hands together.

"What ho! So, my dear – what adventures do you have in mind?"

He was less excited when Mary explained her real

reason for seeing him. Less still when he realized she wanted him to help her. His expression turned from cheerful curiosity to bafflement, to disdain.

"With the master's son? For months?"

Mary nodded. "He told her it wouldn't matter."

"Had she no morals at all?"

"She had no education, Roly! She was deeply in love with him."

"Ah. And there the road to perdition lies. I'd do anything for you, as you know, my dear Persephone. *You* are a paragon, as I've said before. But this Hetty – well, if I give to her, I'll be the calling point for every strumpet in London."

Mary bit back her retort. What was the point? He was worse than Felix. He patently *could* help but chose not to. Why help one girl, whose name he couldn't remember, when it would only lead to requests to help them all? Better to help none. Better not to think about it. Better to spend the money on a race between raindrops. At least then it wasn't *wasted*.

She said none of this aloud but her face did. The expressiveness that Felix loved to paint wasn't always a virtue.

"Don't stare at me so, dear paragon. It doesn't suit you," Roly said. "Let's talk of nicer things." His tone was light but the piercing look he gave Mary suggested hidden anger. He did not like to be made to feel ungenerous. As he offered her his stiffly crooked arm to guide her back to the card room, she felt a new hostility that matched her own. Neither spoke. They couldn't think of 'nicer things' to talk of.

Kitty, sensing trouble, came over and took her arm, guiding her back to their quiet spot by the window.

"What happened? I've never seen Roly look that way towards you."

Mary explained the whole conversation. Kitty understood at last and shook her head.

"Your mistake was to mention your cousin. You should have asked for money for a new dress for yourself and used it how you wish. That's how it's done. But it's too late now. He knows your secret." She spoke regretfully but lightly, as if this was a mere game of manners not a matter of life and death.

Looking around the room, Mary saw them in a new light: these dazzling women and their wealthy men. To get what they wanted, the women had to lie and cheat a little, so as not to upset their menfolk's feeling of superiority. It was expected and accepted. It made her feel quite ill. She had thought being as rich and cosseted as Kitty would bring a sense of freedom but it didn't. She began to understand the jealousy Kitty had expressed towards her in Cremorne Gardens. True, up to now Mary had lied on an epic scale – but not to people she loved. Not as a matter of course. Not as these women seemed to do without troubling their consciences.

Kitty talked on about the new Paris fashion but Mary wasn't listening. She felt stifled in the hot, stuffy room. She longed to get away from all the polite chatter, so she could think.

If Roly wouldn't help her – and Kitty couldn't – then who else could she ask? No other man, clearly. They all thought Edmond Harrington's seduction was Harriet's fault. Would Rupert Thornton have helped, perhaps, out of love for her? She'd hardly seen him since the Prinseps' party, though. She felt sure he was avoiding her and berated herself for being so rude to him. He was probably put off by the scandal, too. He must know about it: everybody did. He would see her as tainted by it, and he was right.

Who else? Who else?

Kitty was looking at her expectantly. She must have asked a question.

"I'm sorry," Mary said. "I don't feel well."

"Oh, dearest! Come with me."

Kitty led her to another room, as elaborately furnished as the last, but smaller, where a pair of hunting dogs looked up at her from the fireside.

"Don't mind them," Kitty said. "They're quite harmless unless you're a pheasant or a grouse! Sit here and rest. Can I get the servants to bring you anything?"

"No, no," Mary murmured, sinking into the nearest chair. "I'll be fine."

"Shall I stay with you?"

"No!" Mary realized she'd sounded rather harsh. "Please – do enjoy yourself with the others. I'm no company right now. I'll be better on my own."

Kitty left her, closing the door. Mary sat there for a long time, with only the ticking clock and snuffling dogs for company, wondering what to do. There had to be *somebody* who could help her…

The idea came to her then, perfectly formed.

Babies are a woman's problem.

She needed a woman who was rich, with access to her own money and no man who needed to be lied to. She already knew of one woman who had taken in a child. A woman who was strong and independent, who made up her own mind and led her own life. A woman Mary admired in many ways, despite her occasional pangs of jealousy. As Mary Adams, she was much too nervous and frightened to approach a grand lady and ask for such an almighty favour – but Persephone Lavelle could do such things and get away with them. After all, they had met on Piccadilly. They were acquaintances, almost. Persephone was enchanting and fearless. She would do whatever it took.

Mary got up and asked a servant to get her cloak. She slipped out of the house without disturbing Roly or Kitty to say goodbye. She would go to Mrs Lisle as soon as she could, with all the charm and loveliness that Persephone could muster. If Felix refused to use Mrs Lisle's money to save Harriet and her baby, then why not go straight to the woman herself?

Chapter Twenty-six

The grey brick house in Chelsea was set back slightly from the King's Road by a little garden shrouded in darkness. The clocks had struck eleven a while ago. It was so late that Mrs Lisle was probably asleep, but Mary didn't know when she'd next have the chance to visit. And besides, having had the idea to approach such a grand, fearsome lady, she wanted to do it before her courage failed her.

The door was answered by a butler in a stiff collar so high that it reached his ears. It was the front door, not the tradesman's entrance. Mary had never done this before, except in Walton Street, but Persephone Lavelle would not think to knock anywhere else. He looked at her severely.

"Yes?"

"I'm sorry it's late. I wondered … if she's here … could

I possibly ask to see your mistress?"

"And you are?"

"My name is Persephone Lavelle." Mary resisted the urge to curtsey.

"Wait here."

The butler gave her another look, more severe than the last, and closed the door on her. But he hadn't told her to go away. She waited nervously for quite some time, listening to the occasional carriage that drove fast down the road behind her. He returned again eventually and greeted her with a nod. "Come."

Mary felt a shiver of anticipation. She pinched her cheeks and bit her lips as she followed him through the hallway, trying to give Persephone her most beguiling glow. This was the Lady of the Tortoiseshell Comb she was about to meet. A woman of great taste and surprising kindness, too, for agreeing to see her at this hour. She tried not to feel too nervous. Persephone should not be nervous: she should simply be delightful and sincere. She put her shoulders back and forced her lips into a smile.

Given the widow's clothes, she had somehow expected dark walls and furniture, but the room the butler showed her into glowed with gold. Four large oil lamps cast a subtle light on walls whose paper was embossed with a gold-leaf design. Gilt edging picked out the carved shapes on the painted ceiling, panelling and the door frames. Pale green silk curtains hung in the windows, in fabulous swags edged with gold tassels. Even the small pianoforte in the corner was made of honey-coloured wood.

And there was a tiger, gold and black, as Kitty had promised. Not stuffed, but spread in a vast rug on the floor in front of the mantelpiece, which was dominated by a large pier glass in an old gold frame. Mrs Lisle stood with one of her feet on the tiger's shoulder. Her dark dress stood out against the glittering background. The effect, Mary reflected, was the exact opposite – but just as impressive – of *Persephone and Hades*. Here, however, Felix didn't lurk in the corners, watching. She tried to forget him. He had no relevance to what she had come to say.

Mrs Lisle looked at her for a long time without speaking. Mary stood Persephone-tall, Persephone-straight, smiling a gracious, grateful smile.

"It is very late for such a visit," Mrs Lisle observed eventually.

"I know. I'm sorry. I hardly expected to find you awake."

The other woman gave a little smile. "Oh, even old ladies like me do not always go to bed at sunset. We have our evening pleasures."

Embarrassed, Mary didn't know what to say. Was Mrs Lisle being ironic? She surely didn't think of herself as an 'old lady'. From a distance, she still looked quite young, with smooth fair skin and bright, enquiring eyes. Though her dress was as sober as ever, its wide skirts and sloping shoulders hinted at the latest Paris fashion.

"I-I'm glad to hear it," Mary faltered.

"I'm sure you have your evening pleasures, too." The slight smile grew a little wider but it didn't seem to reach the lady's eyes.

"Yes," Mary agreed, eager to make conversation and put herself more at ease. "I've just come from a little soirée at the Ballard house."

"Ah, have you? It was Roly Ballard's sister who introduced us, wasn't it?"

"Yes."

"Is she well?"

"She is, thank you."

The conversation faltered again. Mary wondered what on earth the other woman could be thinking. Such a strange expression played on her face – part quiet amusement, part curiosity, part surprise. Did she know about the picture? Had Felix told her anything?

At the thought of the portrait, Mary noticed more fully the four large paintings that hung around her. Even in such a room, they stood out for their luminosity and quality. Mary was becoming skilled at spotting good paintings now. One, she suspected, was a Turner. The others were Pre-Raphaelite: queens and princesses from ancient legends, alone or with their lovers. The familiar reds, golds and greens glowed with their own internal light. In each case, the model for the picture was ethereally beautiful, with long, flowing hair. One of the models looked much like Effie Gray. Her red hair dominated the painting, against a background of lilies and roses. Staring out of the fame with sky blue eyes, she looked as lovely as it was possible to imagine.

So this was the art that the lady loved? It gave Mary confidence. Not only did she agree – these were just the paintings she'd have chosen, too, had she the money –

but as Persephone, she was one of them, standing right here in this room. How strange it must seem to Mrs Lisle. No wonder she seemed curious.

"You must think it odd that I came here alone," she said, remembering that tonight she was a lady, too, and might be expected to have a chaperone.

"Not at all," the other woman said. "Though I wonder you came at all. Pray, do come and sit down. I'm sorry – I've been most unwelcoming."

They sat on silk-covered chairs, almost facing each other. Mary saw now the fine lines etched around Mrs Lisle's eyes and mouth. Her lips had lost the fullness of youth and her cheeks sagged a little, though the bones in her face were strong. She still carried herself like a woman worth looking at but Mary wondered how hard it must be to see your youth fade every day in the glass and watch the face of an old woman gradually appear where yours once was.

It would happen to her one day, she supposed. But right now she was Persephone Lavelle, the talk of artistic London. She widened her smile.

"I've heard so many wonderful things about you."

"Have you? From whom?"

"From Kitty, mostly. She talks of you with great awe."

"Awe…" The woman nodded gravely, still with the same unreadable expression. "I see."

"Oh yes. You're so assured and independent. We both admire you greatly." Mary spoke with some feeling now, because it was true. She felt so much better in this place than she had at the Ballard house, surrounded by all those self-regarding men and their jealous women.

Mrs Lisle's look shifted to one of pure surprise. "Oh?"

"You're an example to us."

A black eyebrow arched. "You wish for a dead husband?"

Mary risked a smile. "No! I wish for independence. And good taste. And the freedom to be kind."

Mrs Lisle shook her head. "I'm afraid I don't understand you."

"Kitty told me … you took someone to your heart."

The black eyebrows almost met in a frown. "I don't—?"

"A young girl…"

The frown resolved itself. "Ah! Juliette. You refer to my daughter."

Mary smiled. "You adopted her. Is that true?"

Mrs Lisle nodded slowly. "My sister's child. It was my duty when my sister died. And also my greatest joy."

"I have a ... friend," Mary said. "Soon she will have a child, too."

She explained the story, leaving the details somewhat vague but focusing on what she felt were the key elements: Harriet had been seduced and deceived; she had nowhere else to turn; without help her fate was hopeless. Throughout it, Mrs Lisle listened gravely, not interrupting. Though surprised at first she did not seem unduly shocked, Mary noticed, or dismissive. *At last*, she thought, *I've found someone who can help me.* Admittedly, Mrs Lisle's face became unreadable again, but then, she had much to think about.

"So. Your ... *friend* ... is a servant?"

"Yes."

Mary noticed the woman's eyes glance, just once, at her waistline and she blushed. For once, she was glad to be in a tightly laced dress, showing off her slim silhouette. No, it was not her own story she was telling.

"And she is quite far gone in the pregnancy?"

"She is." Though shameful beyond measure, it was a relief to be able to talk in such plain words about

Harriet's problem, with someone who did not want to forget it and talk about 'nicer things'.

Mrs Lisle stood up and paced around the room.

"And you cannot help her yourself, I take it … Persephone?"

Mary shook her head. "I wish I could."

"Tell me, where is it you come from? I forget."

Mary blushed again. She felt herself under scrutiny and was glad she had practised her story. "My parents are dead, sadly. I grew up in many places. I try not to speak of it."

"I'm sure you do. How kind of you to be such friends with a servant. How tragic for the girl." She looked at Mary for a long time, considering something deeply, then came to sit down again. "I am fascinated that you should come to me. And not a little flattered, too. I didn't know I had such a reputation for philanthropy."

"Will you help her?" Mary asked.

"What do you expect from me?"

"I don't know!" Mary exclaimed. "To find her a place in your household, perhaps, where she could stay with her baby? Harriet works very hard – and well."

"You ask a lot. She will be a young mother. They are

much distracted. And I have all the servants I need."

As herself, Mary felt desperation ready to engulf her, but as Persephone, she was made of sterner stuff. She stood up boldly. "I *do* ask it! I promise you wouldn't regret it." She felt the air reverberate with her passion.

But Mrs Lisle's eyes narrowed. Her lips pursed. "Only I decide what I do and don't regret," she said sharply. Mary felt stung and regretted her outburst. Mrs Lisle carried on, more quietly. "I run a little charity for foundling children. If the baby is born safely, you may bring it to me and I will ensure that it is housed and fed. Your friend may find new work then."

"But she has no references!"

One look from Mrs Lisle shut her up again, though the voice stayed calm. "That's all I can offer you."

Mary sensed the conversation was over. She bit her lip, stood up and curtseyed stiffly. "Thank you."

She knew it was the best she could hope for. It was already more than anyone else had offered. She had little idea what happened to foundling children in London, though she sensed it wasn't good. Even so, it meant food and shelter. Perhaps Harriet would somehow find another job. Without a baby she could go home and start again, as long as no one knew her story…

"My butler will see you to the door."

"Of course. Goodnight."

"Miss Lavelle? How lovely you look tonight. As pretty as a picture."

The unreadable expression seemed to be a horrid mixture of dark and light but the overall impression was of a smile. Mary bobbed and blushed and said nothing.

She knows about me and Felix! She must! Mary sensed she had made a huge mistake in coming here tonight, but she didn't know what else she could have done – and whatever Mrs Lisle thought of her, at least she had given Harriet faint hope. That was worth the risk. Nevertheless Mary vowed to herself never to speak to her or ask anything of her again.

Chapter Twenty-seven

Through Eddie O'Bryan, Mary told Harriet about the foundling charity and the chance of life beyond. But according to Eddie's report the following evening, Harriet had hardly listened. She sat in her room, listless and hopeless, waiting only for news of Edmond in Rome.

Mary wished for a brief second, on hearing this, that her cousin could do *something* to help herself. But what? Sometimes, in our darkest hours, we have to rely on the help of others and Mary knew it. Women in the village had helped Ma often enough. Pa had tried to beat it into Mary that she was a bad girl, but if she could save Harriet, that wasn't entirely true. She had made a promise and now she must keep it.

Mary felt listless herself in the days that followed. It pained her to feel so badly towards Roly Ballard, whom until now she had so much liked, as much because of his roguish nature as despite it. She missed Kitty, too, who had not been in touch and seemed to have forgotten the offer of the five pounds. Mary wished now that she had not seemed so ungrateful at the time. She had pushed away first Rupert Thornton and now Kitty. When Rupert had last come to dinner, with other student friends, he had studiously ignored her.

She thought about Felix every day, every hour. Sometimes it felt like every minute. She hated him and missed him, but missed him more than she hated him. She began to wonder if he would ever call for her again and sensed he wouldn't.

So when a note arrived from Lady Emmeline she was astonished and had no idea where the carriage would take her.

It was four on a Friday afternoon when the carriage drew up in Walton Street. Mary could have wept with relief but she still felt giddy with nerves. The last time they had met, they'd quarrelled. Since then she had recklessly visited his patroness – she knew it was reckless now. Would he forgive her, if he knew? Could she forgive *him* for being so heartless about Harriet?

Felix met her in the hallway, formal and reserved. Mary noticed the maid look from her to him and back again, and nod to herself. Maids notice things. She felt that this girl understood everything.

Straight-backed and silent in her peacock sateen, she followed him up the stairs. He was careful not even to brush past her clothes as he let her into the studio.

"And so – this time you came," he observed. His voice was strained.

"I usually do." She noticed that the portrait had been turned away from the door slightly, so she could not see it. "Am I to be painted?"

"What else?"

"Then I'll get ready."

Normally he had some new drawing to show her, or bread and cheese to offer, or a story to tell. Today Felix moved around in silence as she changed into the white dress. Mary could hear him rattling pots and jars, and wondered what he was up to. He seemed perturbed. Strangely enough, it relaxed her a little. He was behaving like Henry in a huff with his sister – more hurt than angry. Would he have called her back at all if he didn't want to see her?

"I'm done," she said at last, reappearing from behind the screen. "As much as I can be."

At the sight of her in the dress again he dropped a cup and it broke. He ignored the pieces.

"I'll help you."

She turned round. It took him an age to do up her buttons. He cursed under his breath.

"You're not yourself today," she said.

"I'm quite well, thank you."

Now his primness began to amuse her. She felt almost light-hearted. His brusqueness and clumsiness were the signs of an emotion he was struggling to control and she was glad to be the cause of it, whatever it was.

He gave her the crown to put on and she arranged it in her hair. As he led her towards her seat under the window, she briefly caught sight of the canvas at last, and noticed that it was nearly done. He'd been working hard. He had done a lot more work on the background and the face, dress and hair were almost finished. In fact, it seemed to Mary that they *were* finished. She couldn't see that there was a single brushstroke to add. They had the same clarity and luminosity of the paintings in Mrs Lisle's sitting room. She wished she could stop thinking of that room…

She noticed something else, as well – he had finished the other figure in the picture. Hades, dark and foreboding, lurked in the shadows, watching Persephone. He was only half-suggested – a figure in shades of black and green – but he was clearly a self-portrait. The longing with which Hades looked at Persephone made her smile. Felix had missed her, too. She was sure of it.

She sat down and noticed that he didn't specify exactly where she should look or how. *He really doesn't need me here*, she thought with growing confidence. She allowed herself a smile – for the first time his painting was the excuse, not the reason for seeing her.

At first they worked in silence – Mary on her pose, whether needed or not, and Felix with his brush. As always, she felt safe under the light of his window. She looked at the ornamental chaos on his trestle table, where today fresh dahlias, ruby red, sat among a fascinating array of pots and bowls, all dangerously piled. It took Felix a while longer to warm up but after a few minutes' painting he, too, relaxed a little.

"I heard you went to Roly's for a night of cards,"

he said. "Persephone was much admired."

"She was indeed. Even too much, sometimes."

"Oh?"

Mary thought of the man who had kissed her hand with such certainty in his eyes. "Not everyone respects her virtue."

Felix caught her eye and smiled. "Ha. Well, they should." Then his smile faded. "Roly told me what you asked him. He shouldn't have said anything. He gossips more than any woman. But I'm sorry he couldn't help you."

Mary shrugged. "His sister offered what help she could."

Felix heard the implied insult and merely nodded.

"I'm glad someone did."

At the mention of help, Mary thought of Mrs Lisle and sat up straighter, watching him for signs of pent-up anger that she had visited the woman he never talked about. Oh, how had she had the audacity to go there? She thought about things differently when she was Persephone.

But he seemed apologetic, not annoyed. His thoughts hadn't followed hers to the house in the King's Road.

It seemed Mrs Lisle hadn't said anything to him about her visit… Mary sat back gratefully, admiring the older woman once again. Perhaps, she even dared to hope, Mrs Lisle really didn't know of her connection with Felix, despite his artist friends talking of little else. Maybe he hadn't shown her the picture yet. Either way, she had behaved with great subtlety. Mary aspired to something like it herself in later life, though she didn't think she'd ever reach those heights of self-composure.

Felix dipped his brush in more paint. (Forest green. He wasn't painting her at all.) "Is your cousin … well?" he asked.

"She is, thank you."

"That's good."

He was trying to please her. He really was. Though the subject pained him infinitely and he clearly thought, like every other man, that Harriet's problems were her own, he wanted to make up after their quarrel last time. Mary had seen him as conceited from the beginning, which he was, and now she knew him to be more deeply flawed – but he was flawed in a common way, like Roly, and exceptional in so many uncommon ways. She didn't know what drew her to him most: his talent, his free living, his feeling for her or the sheer pleasure of watching him. She didn't care. Whatever it was, it made her want to make peace as much as he did.

She remarked on the beauty of the dahlias. It was a peace offering. Taking it, he told her about the trip to Oxford where he had stolen them from a college garden. It wasn't long before they were talking as easily as they ever had. By the time he put down his paints and she stood up to stretch, all the animosity between them had vanished like smoke in the summer air.

"May I see it?" she asked.

"Yes."

This time he didn't hesitate. Mary took it as tacit acknowledgement that the painting was done: as good as he could make it. He stood back, appraising it critically, and she came to stand beside him, her bare arm brushing his shirtsleeve.

She was right. *Persephone and Hades* was ready. She had known what to expect, of course, but still, it thrilled her. It was a painting alive with colour and emotion and swirling copper hair. What she saw was herself, but more than herself. It was the girl in the professor's story, caught between death and life. Pale skin, green eyes and a strong nose made beautiful because the painter willed them so.

"It's everything you said it would be," she murmured. If she had been testing his talent, he had passed the test.

"It is," he agreed. "Thanks to you. I told you it wouldn't be easy."

But it *had* been easy for her. It came naturally to arrange her limbs and look where he needed her to, to maintain her stillness, to catch the light with her eyes and keep it there. They worked beautifully together. An image came to her of the two of them growing old together, standing like this, admiring what they had made.

For a few moments they stood, arms touching, looking at the canvas. But Mary soon became aware only of the warmth of Felix's body through his shirtsleeve. Heat flooded through her at the thought of all their days of kissing and she knew that, despite everything, if she turned to him now, he would kiss her again.

As if he had the same thought, he started to turn towards her. She felt all her nerve endings tingle. Her body wanted one thing and so did his. No pretence now. He needed her as badly as he had ever done.

But she had too much to lose. Harriet had shown her

how much. With more self-possession than she thought possible, Mary slowly turned her back to him and bent her neck, sweeping her hair aside.

"Yes?" he murmured. He could hardly get the word out.

"My buttons, please."

He said nothing but his fingers shook. It took him an age to work on each hook. As he did so, to take his mind off what he was doing, he blurted out whatever he could think of, like the first time he had undone her.

"I ... um ... the painting... The *painting*. I've been in a rush to get it done... And there's good news. An exhibition happening in two weeks in a small gallery off Piccadilly. Some friends... Good pictures... They've begged me to include *Persephone* and now she's done. You're done. Oh God," he groaned, as the last button was released, finally.

Mary slipped behind the screen.

"Everyone wants you to be at the *vernissage*," he went on. "Millais. Gabriel. He says he met you. He still wants to paint you but don't let him. Turn down all offers. Promise me."

"Why?" she asked. She was standing in nothing

but her shift and feeling dizzy. It took an effort to concentrate on what he was saying.

"Because I have another idea. *Greensleeves*, from the song. Gabriel wants to do it, too, but I thought of it first. I've already designed the new dress in my head. You can suggest the seamstress this time."

"And what's a very-sarge?"

"A *vernissage*. A varnishing. It's the French word for the opening of an exhibition. A preview, for friends, when traditionally they put the layer of varnish on. Not that I can varnish *Persephone* yet. I'm afraid I won't be able to talk much that night. It might be a bit difficult..." He faltered slightly. Even in her dizzy state, Mary knew that tone. It meant the widow. "There may be other people I need to... You know how it is."

Behind the screen she nodded. "Of course." She understood. It was not forever.

"But you'll be busy being feted, don't worry," he assured her. "You'll have your portrait painted by half of London, Oxford and Paris. Just don't agree to sit for any of them yet."

"Until you've finished with me?"

His voice was low, full of emotion. "If I ever do."

Mary's dizziness turned to bubbles of expectation, like champagne in her blood. He sounded as addicted to her as she was to him. Hopelessly. Dangerously. Wonderfully.

She appeared at last and grinned.

"I promise."

Chapter Tweny-eight

Mrs Lisle must have resumed Felix's funding. He paid Mary well for the session – enough to buy good fabric for a dress for the *vernissage* and a shawl to match. More importantly, there was plenty for bread, cheese and beer for Harriet, without the need for stealing. Mary and Annie devised various errands that meant one or other of them could deliver a basket of provisions every few days to the warehouse where she was staying. Whenever she saw her, Harriet still looked sickly and despairing, but at least she was indoors and safe from fingersmiths and vagabonds.

In what few free moments she had left during the fortnight that followed, Mary made her outfit for the *vernissage*. Her fingers were delighted to take on the delicate work she loved and luckily, she didn't need much time because she had created a daringly simple, unboned design for the dress. Annie marvelled at it, hands over her mouth as Mary sewed.

"Lord! It looks like a nightgown."

"It doesn't, Annie! It's like a queen's dress, from the olden days."

"And it's green. That's unlucky."

"Only for weddings. This will hardly be that. It's in honour of another dress to come."

"And what dress would that be?"

Mary told her about *Greensleeves* and Annie's hands flew to her mouth in wonder again.

❦

With only an hour to go before the *vernissage,* she was putting the final touches to the hem when Annie called her from the stairs.

"Mary! You need to come! The mistress wants you!"

"Of course," Mary called back, laying the dress on the bed. She went to the door and looked down at Annie peering up from the landing below. "Is there a problem? What is it?"

Annie gave her the kind of look she gave Eliza Aitken when she had to explain that Alice or Henry had broken something precious. "It's Lady Emmeline DuLac."

"But I've already got the message. It arrived this morning."

Annie shook her head. "Not that," she said quietly. "The real one."

Mary's heart missed a beat. "Do-do you mean Roly Ballard?"

Annie shook her head again.

Oh no. Mary reached out and took a moment to steady herself against the doorframe. The children sometimes played a game where they built a tower out of blocks and amused themselves by pulling one out after another, until the whole thing tumbled to the ground. She felt like that teetering tower now.

"Come quickly!" Annie urged. "The mistress is all a-quiver."

"I'm coming, I'm coming."

Mary did the best she could to straighten her cap and smooth her dress. She clutched the banister, afraid she would fall. When she reached Annie, the other girl was equally pale.

"Mary – I promise…"

Mary raised her hand. "No need to say it." Annie was

her friend now. It didn't seem possible that she would have betrayed her.

They took the next staircase together. "And Eddie, too, I swear," Annie insisted.

"I believe you."

Eddie had his own code of conduct. He wasn't a gentleman but he was a man of his word, in his way.

Which left … who? Mary could only think of Rupert Thornton. She cursed herself again for being so rude to him at the Prinseps'. It shocked her that he would behave like this, but then she was starting to realize she would never understand his class and what they deemed acceptable.

Not that it mattered. Nothing did now. She and Annie had reached the grand landing that led to the first-floor reception rooms. Annie gave her hand a quick squeeze. Eliza Aitken stood waiting in the drawing room, in front of the mantelpiece.

One glance at her mistress told her not to retain any shred of hope.

"Mary," she said icily, "this is Lady Emmeline."

A regal old lady sat stiffly on a wing-backed chair, caught in a shaft of light. This person was small and thin and delicate, wearing a gossamer-fine lace cap, which was nothing like Roly in a coal scuttle bonnet at all.

She took one look at Mary and announced, "I've never seen that girl in my life."

Mary bobbed and said nothing. She was so scared she could hardly move, but not quite so frightened that she could not dislike the thin old busybody on sight. Would it have been so hard for her to stay in her grand, mysterious mansion?

"Not that you need to bother bringing her to me anyway," the lady continued to Eliza. "As I said, I have never had such an arrangement with any servant. The whole idea is preposterous."

For someone with a reputation as an invalid, Lady Emmeline sounded very loud and strident, Mary reflected. She looked suitably frail, though. Her skin was almost translucent in its whiteness and her wispy hair was white, too, under its elaborate confection of lace. Her hands were oddly large, stained with age and knobbly, folded over the handle of an ebony walking stick. But her eyes were the same bright, periwinkle blue as Kitty's, and looked at Mary with a mixture of sharpness and delight. She was clearly relishing the effect she was having and the destruction she was causing with this visit.

"Get the master, Annie," Eliza said faintly, at which Mary's heart plummeted to new depths. "Lady Emmeline – I don't know how to apologize enough. We were so convinced… I have no idea how this could have happened."

"Oh, *I* know," said the old lady indignantly. "It's why I'm here. My disreputable nephew impersonated me in one of my own carriages. The rumours are true. He doesn't deny it. He sees it as some sort of triumph."

"Your *nephew*?"

"Great-nephew. Though if he expects to feature in my will, he will be sorely disappointed after this."

"It was a *man*?"

"Please! The subject offends me. Roland is a disgrace to the family. He is dragging his sister into the gutter with him. And pray, don't apologize to me. You have been the dupe here, more than I. You must ask yourself what the girl was doing, if not called by me."

Eliza Aitken, whose thoughts and fears had focused purely on the great lady's inconvenience, now turned to

Mary with a sudden, awful realization in her eyes. Lady Emmeline followed her glance with grim satisfaction.

Why, thank you, Mary thought.

"What...? Where...? W-where were you?" Eliza stammered.

Silence.

"Answer me!"

What was there to say, except the worst she could imagine? Mary shook her head.

Eliza started to pace the floor. "All those evenings ... those afternoons ... those *days* when I needed you. The sacrifices we made. The things you said ... the gifts I gave..." She whipped round to stare at Mary. "The lies. The *lies*!"

Mary flushed. "I'm sorry, ma'am," she whispered.

Eliza tipped her head heavenwards. "Oh-oh-oh!" It started as a groan and became louder. "The scandal! In my own house!" She flashed a look of icy fire at Mary. "A man. A man! Are you...? Like your slut of a cousin?"

"No!" Mary cried out. That dreadful word felt like a wound. She didn't know if she was more offended for Harriet or herself. Where she had felt shocked and guilty, she now felt furious. "I've done nothing shameful!"

"Ha!" offered Lady Emmeline.

"Take her away from me!" Eliza screeched, flapping her hands. "Get her out!"

Mary didn't require assistance. She turned and fled, past Annie's white face at the doorway – and straight into Philip Aitken, who had been about to enter the room. She was going so fast she smacked right into his frock coat. Too shocked to speak, she stared at him like a cornered animal. He glowered at her for a moment, then caught her by the wrist. He was right: she had been about to bolt, though she didn't know where she was going.

Still holding her, he walked into the drawing room, where his wife gave a swift account of what had happened and Lady Emmeline nodded along.

"Leave her to me," he said darkly to his wife.

On the stairs below, Cook's astonished face was framed by those of two visiting servants, equally curious, in what Mary presumed was DuLac livery.

"Mary – my study," the professor instructed.

Turning reluctantly to go up the stairs, she noticed the heads of Henry and Alice poking through the banisters at the top. *I have an audience*, she thought, mortified to her bones. The professor led the way and she followed him.

When they reached his sanctum, she expected him to sit at his desk to scold her and dismiss her, but instead he went to his favourite chair by the window, where an oil lamp burned on a little table. She stood in the centre of the room, waiting, while he sat with his head in his hands for a while.

With the study door closed, all she could hear was the ticking of the clock on the mantel and the dim sound of distant carriages in the street outside. It was hard to stay standing. Her blood felt like cold treacle one minute and boiling coffee the next. Her emotions had swung between fear and anger in the drawing room but now she felt mostly shame. The professor's reaction confused her. She had never seen him like this.

When he finally looked up, it was almost as if he'd been crying.

"Mary, Mary … what did we do to deserve you?"

"I—"

"I thought…" He sighed. "I had thought you were unusual. I even dared to think I had found a fellow spirit. One I could educate."

"You had! You could!" she said, eager to reassure him. But he shook his head.

"Be quiet! The Good Lord has chosen to punish me for my hubris. We cannot elevate the lower classes. We shouldn't try. See what thanks we get."

"I'm so sorry," she said again, and she meant it this time. It mattered that she had let him down. He had trusted her and helped her. She had liked him very much, she realized. A single tear wended its way down her cheek.

A thought occurred to him. "Did Annie know?"

"No. No!" Mary assured him passionately. Lying again. Lying with every conversation they had.

"At least there's that. Annie is a decent girl. I'd hate to lose her. I feel that this is my fault. I have let down my wife and children by forming with you a certain understanding. I see it now: you were a siren on the rocks, sent to distract me..."

No! Mary thought. *That's not true!*

"I loved those books, sir," was all she dared to say, wiping the tear away.

He shook his head and held up a hand, as if to ward her off. "Don't pretend! Your interest was a ruse, to fool me. But I won't be fooled any more. Go and get them. Bring them here, then get out of my house."

"No, sir! Please!" Now that the moment was here, Mary suddenly felt the sickening truth of what she was losing. "I have nowhere to go!"

His face was granite. "You should have thought of that. My poor wife is distraught. Go to whichever den of iniquity you've been frequenting. May the Lord have mercy on you."

Even now, Mary couldn't help noticing the contrast between the fondness and amusement in his eyes when he talked of the irresponsible Greek gods and the flint in his soul when he invoked the unimpeachable Christian one.

She curtseyed deeply. "Goodbye, sir."

"The books! Then go!"

She went. He wasn't only thinking of God, she thought, as she ran up the back stairs to the attic. He was thinking of himself, too: not wanting his gifts to be found in her room. She gathered up the books he had found for her into a little pile and saw the green dress lying across the bed.

Her mind had been in a whirl. First panic, then anger, shame and dread at what was to come. She could hardly breathe with the shock of it all. But now the dress reminded her of something the professor had said and her breathing calmed.

He was quite right: she must go to the 'den of iniquity' she'd been frequenting. Not there exactly, but the place she'd been intending to go to anyway, where Felix and his friends would be. *I would not let this city destroy Harriet and I will not let it destroy me.*

⁓⊱⊰⁓

Downstairs, she could hear the sound of Eliza Aitken in hysterics and Lady Emmeline taking her leave. Mary struggled out of her black bodice and skirt as quickly as she could. As she stood in her stays, a small, blond head peeped round the door, with rags in her ringletted hair. Mary jumped. Alice Aitken's steady grey eyes stared at her.

"Is it true? You're going?"

Mary nodded, clutching the green dress to cover her modesty.

"Henry says you're a wicked fairy, like your cousin. Or a changeling."

Mary flushed. "I'm no such thing. I'm an ordinary person."

Alice grinned at her. "You're not ordinary. Nothing's been ordinary since you came here. We'll miss you."

Mary broke into a reluctant smile. "Thank you, Alice."

"You'd better go now, I expect."

Mary sighed. "I had."

Alice darted into the room and kissed her. A peck on the shoulder, which was as high as she could reach. "You were a good sort," she said from the door. "I'll tell Henry not to be such a dumb buffoon."

"You tell him that."

Mary gazed at the girl's departing nightgown. Not everyone would remember her as a wicked temptress. She wished she could have made a greater friend of Alice Aitken. But it was too late now.

She had finished dressing just as Annie came to find her.

"What's keeping you? The professor's after getting in another rage. You'd better make yourself scarce. Oh my!"

Mary was reaching for her shawl. The green dress shimmered in the moonlight.

"Wish me luck, Annie," she whispered.

"All the luck in the world. Don't worry about your things. Just send me word of where you go. I'll send them to you."

"Thank you."

Though heartfelt, those two words were not enough. Mary ran to Annie and hugged her for as long as she dared. But the professor was shouting for her. She grabbed the pile of books and took them with her, along with a new reticule she'd made, containing her remaining money and little else. It was a wrench to leave Little Miss Mouse behind but she would have to. Along with all her proper clothes...

What had she done?

On, down the stairs and along to the study, where she left the professor's books by the door. And then to the landing, where he stood, a figure of wrath, pointing ever downwards.

"Get out! Before I whip you out of here."

Down again, to the accompaniment of Eliza's wailing. Past Cook on the kitchen stairway, who stared and said nothing. Out of the tradesman's door and into the night.

❧❧❧

Outside in the deep, dark stairwell, Mary breathed again, standing with her back to the wall. She was lucky the professor hadn't taken a crop to her. Many would.

They were a kind family, despite Eliza's faults, and she had been lucky, especially once Annie became her friend. She only truly saw that now.

Her body shook as she ran up the stairs and on to Ecclestone Street. She would never come back. The disgraced servant. Her name would always be mentioned in hushed tones in Pimlico.

And yet … she had her honour, even if no one knew it. And seven shillings and sixpence of savings in her purse, and a beautiful new dress and a reputation as a model. And somewhere to go tonight.

By the time she reached the street corner, Mary felt almost optimistic. With perfect timing, an empty hackney carriage came by and she hailed it.

"Take me to Piccadilly!"

Her love of carriages was undimmed. They presaged adventures. In this one, she felt all her remaining fear and shame dissipate. *Now I have nothing*, she thought to herself. Her lips curled up at the corners. *So I have nothing to lose.*

As the carriage drew closer, her future grew clearer with every passing street. Felix would sell the painting soon and have money of his own. She would earn by posing for him, and then others, as soon as *Greensleeves* was done. He'd sell that painting and the next... He would be quite poor at first, but he'd have enough to be independent. She would live with him soon, if he'd let her. She sensed he would. From their flood of kisses, she sensed he'd welcome it. They didn't need a big house. If he didn't marry her at first, no matter: she would be one of those scandalous women like the Pre-Raphaelites' other stunners. Bold and beautiful and adored. Yes! He would paint and she would sew, and they would be uproariously happy, surrounded by the chaos of his art.

The carriage reached Hyde Park Corner, where the grand mansions of the super-rich and famous stood, like a series of temples to success. Mary pinched her lips and cheeks, and ran her fingers through her hair to arrange it in a thick, waist-length mane. They were close now. Mary Adams was no one. By the time they arrived, she would entirely be Persephone Lavelle, the toast of London.

Chapter Twenty-nine

The Berkeley Gallery was not large and took a little time to find, tucked away in one of the streets behind the Royal Academy. But when Mary got there, light spilled on to the street from the party inside, accompanied by the babble of excited voices. One or two gentlemen stood outside in top hats and opera capes, talking. A rich lady swept in with her male companion, her ruffled skirts swishing behind her. As Mary drew closer, a rose seller walked up to her and held out a white bloom.

"For a beautiful lady."

Mary smiled but shook her head. "I'm sorry. I can't—"

"No pennies required!" the woman assured her with a gap-toothed grin. "Take the pretty flower."

Mary held it by its stem. It was the only decoration she had. The men in opera capes bowed as she passed them. She nodded at them graciously and walked inside.

The room was full of people in evening clothes, drinking champagne. The walls were adorned with paintings hung in simple rows, so each one could be properly admired. Servants offered champagne from trays full of crystal glasses. Mary took a glass, holding it carefully. What did one do on a night like this? Who did one talk to? But she felt no need of Roly tonight. She was not so much afraid as excited. This was a new world, *her* world. She already felt the surreptitious glances. They caught her loose dress and abundant hair, and lingered on her, the way she had looked at Lizzie. Roly was right – it was Persephone's time now.

Soon one man introduced himself, then another. They offered to show her the paintings and asked if she was the model for the best one. She was whisked around the room and invited to admire the works for sale. All were in the naturalistic, bright-coloured style she knew so well, and none, she noticed, was even close to being as good as *Persephone and Hades*. Felix's contribution was hung in a plain gold frame on the furthest wall. She could just make out the pale glow of the white dress against the dark background in the distance, but the throng around it made it difficult to get much closer.

Felix himself was there, too, she saw, dressed to the nines in new evening clothes, the same as she, and wearing an emerald green neckerchief. *In honour of the next painting*, she thought. *Like mine.* Twin souls. She didn't have to talk to him to feel his presence. It was like an invisible shawl of comfort, wrapped around her.

When asked, Persephone pronounced every painting 'exquisite', though there were only one or two, aside from Felix's, that she really liked. After all, the room was largely made up of the artists and their friends tonight. The others were rich buyers, she assumed. Who would buy *Persephone and Hades*? How much would he pay? Or she, of course? Mrs Lisle had taught her that a woman could buy paintings, too.

And there was Mrs Lisle herself, at the far end of the room, near Felix. She looked up and gave a quick frown of recognition. Persephone smiled at her graciously.

To her surprise, the older woman said something to her companions and turned away from them, moving purposefully through the room. Mary had resolved never to speak to her ever again. She tried to move away, but the crowd of art enthusiasts around her made that impossible. Within a few moments, Mrs Lisle stood facing her. She gave her the same twisted smile as before, half dark, half light.

"Persephone. Good evening."

Mary curtseyed.

"I wasn't expecting to see you here this evening. Shall we go outside?"

"I-I'm quite happy here."

"But I am not."

Mrs Lisle swept towards the door. Mary hesitated to follow but the men around her stared at her with curiosity. She didn't feel she had a choice.

Outside the night was dark and chilly. Mrs Lisle wore sleeves to her wrists but Mary's arms were cold. She hugged them to her. The other woman briskly crossed the empty street and stood in front of a tailor's shop. Helplessly Mary followed her there.

Mrs Lisle's face was calm and composed. Her jewels glittered in the lamplight. As did her eyes. Mary thought she saw a hint of malice in them.

"I want you to go home now," she said.

Mary was too startled to reply.

"Don't be difficult. I'm astonished you had the effrontery to be here tonight. He knows I don't want to see you. I thought he had more taste."

Mary rocked on her feet. Every word was a shock. This was not the woman she had met before, who never mentioned her relationship with Felix. This one was harsh and condescending – and knew everything.

"It's my painting," she said, jutting her chin out. "Felix asked me to be here."

"It's not *your* painting." The words were breathed out in a low, measured voice. "It's his. If anything, it's mine. I paid for the materials. And if he unwisely invited you tonight, it was only out of pity. He won't see you again."

"He will! He has new plans!" Mary lashed out, stung by this last suggestion. Felix *had* to see her again. Everything depended on it.

"Oh, Felix's plans change by the minute. He's an artist. Quite unpredictable."

"No," Mary shook her head. "He isn't."

"I knew as soon as I saw you that you'd be trouble. Kitty Ballard, introducing you to me like some sort of social prize. I already knew about you, of course. I'd seen the drawings. It was a surprise to meet you in the flesh."

"So you took him away…" Mary murmured, thinking back to the sudden walking holiday and how she had dismissed the very idea of Mrs Lisle's jealousy as ridiculous. And she *was* jealous. Her calm voice dripped with it.

"I thought some time away from you would make him return to his senses."

"It didn't though," Mary countered. "He made me a crown of leaves from those walks."

Mrs Lisle pursed her lips. "Don't you dare flaunt yourself at me. He came willingly enough when I called. But he was still obsessed with the picture. There was nothing to be done. However, it's finished now." Mrs Lisle waved an arm dismissively towards the bright gallery entrance. "I have him back."

She seemed so certain. Mary felt a chink in her armour of confidence. She had completely underestimated the older woman as a rival.

"It's not just about the painting," she retaliated. "He kissed me."

"Aha! Of course he did. I'm sure he'd have done more, if you'd let him. Young men are all that way but it means nothing. They take what they can. You must get used to it."

Mary faltered. Was this true? She had often heard this

sentiment before. It hadn't felt like that at all when she was with Felix but he was the first man she'd kissed that way. How would she know? She'd been so sure of herself before and now she felt off balance. *Could* it have meant nothing? No. Mrs Lisle had sensed how deep his feelings ran. That's what she was jealous of.

"You've served your purpose," the older woman continued flatly. "You've given him a pretty face and pretty hair. I can give him so much more: the place, the materials, whatever his talents need. And the love to nourish him."

"I love him!" Mary said it with all the desperate truth she felt.

"You don't know what the word means. You're young. It's a game to you."

"How can you say that?"

"I can say what I like because it's true. Without daily sight of that lovely hair, he'll forget you in a week. There are other stunners to catch his eye. I'll help him find them."

Mary's mind raced. Why would this woman find him other stunners if she must be banished? The only answer was that he felt something deeper for her.

He loved her! The widow was lying.

"You can't make me stay away!"

"Oh yes, I can. I'm stronger than you can imagine, *Mary Adams*, and I have what you want." A look of dark, certain triumph spread across Mrs Lisle's face.

"What do you mean?"

The thin lips curled into a cruel smile. "You think I don't know who you are and where you come from? A few discreet enquiries... An unguarded remark... I know everything. You came to me, flashing your youth and beauty, so sure of yourself, calling yourself that ridiculous name, thinking I'd be impressed. You should have begged me on your knees."

"I would have, if you'd wanted!"

"Don't interrupt me!" Mrs Lisle growled the words. "You told me about your *friend* and assumed I'd step in and help you like some saintly virgin. Well, you got a surprise, didn't you? Why should I help Felix's lover? Why should I?"

"I'm not his—"

"Shut up! I know what you want. I know how badly you need it and I'm the only woman in London who'll give it to you. I'll take your cousin – yes, I know the truth – and her bastard child. I'll even be kind to them. She can work for me as a laundress. But on one condition."

The look of triumph filled her whole face now and soured it completely. Mary shrank inside to a point of darkness. The widow was right: it was over and she had won. In Harriet, she had found the perfect weapon.

"What condition?" Mary asked quietly.

Mrs Lisle raised her chin and enunciated each word clearly. "You will not see him again. You will not talk to him – not now, not ever. You will not take his messages. The painting is done – he has no need of you now. You will not tell him about our conversation or explain in any way."

Mary groaned. She could feel her heart break, then and there. It felt as though a heavy weight on her shoulders was pushing her down, down into the ground.

"Do you hear me? I *said*, do you hear me?"

"Yes," Mary whispered.

"If you ever break our bond, I'll turn your cousin out into the street without so much as a word. I'll keep the child and she will never see it."

Tears streamed down Mary's cheeks. She couldn't

move even to wipe them away. She knew of such cruelty but to hear it from the woman's mouth, in this place, with Felix so close, made her dizzy.

"Do we have a deal?"

"Yes."

"Good. Now go. Get out of his sight. Don't even look back."

Mary couldn't move. She could hardly breathe. Across the street, the gallery was full of the joyful sounds of guests marvelling at the new works on display. She pictured Felix looking around for her, wondering where she was. It was the world of light and she belonged in it.

But Mrs Lisle had created an uncrossable barrier: a River Styx between the living and the dead. She waited while Mary swayed with shock and found her balance, then watched implacably as she slowly turned and walked away.

The night was cold and dark. Without her shawl, Mary staggered along, blinded by tears. There was nowhere to go. Nothing left. After a few steps, she fell to her knees and wept. Harriet was safe and, after that, nothing mattered. But now she had nowhere to go. No one to help her. And even that didn't matter because without Felix, she couldn't see any future she wanted anyway.

I loved him so much. I didn't realize. I'll never see him again and he'll blame me or forget me. I don't know which is worse.

She truly had nothing at all. Mrs Lisle, rich, bitter and clever, had conquered her completely. Nothing would ever matter again.

Chapter Thirty

Dawn came, a dull, dusky pink through the London fog, promising a cloudy day. In their splendid palaces, the rich slept on. Roués and flâneurs returned to their beds after a long night's carousing. Stable boys and paper boys, milkmen and coalmen climbed into their dirty rags and set off, barefoot or in clattering carts, for their jobs around the city.

In her warehouse by the river, Harriet watched the sun rise through a grimy window, hugging a blanket round her shoulders. The old crones said there would be two months yet before the baby would be born but she ached already with the weight of carrying it. She had barely slept, lying uncomfortably on the cold, hard floor. She hardly ate these days, hoping that the baby would stop growing. She looked down and the sight of her stretched skin terrified her. It seemed alien and wrong. What was going on inside and how on earth would it come out of her?

At the knock on the door, she gave a startled scream.

"Who is it?"

"It's me."

Harriet didn't recognize the rasping voice but it was a woman. Nervously she opened the door. Mary half staggered, half fell into the room. Harriet cried out at the sight of her stained and ragged dress. She was freezing and shivering. The dark green eyes looked up at her for a moment.

"You're saved," Mary said. And fainted.

⁘

It was Eddie who found her there, later in the day, curled up on the floor in the corner of the room while Harriet sang to her and ran her fingers through her hair. Annie had sent him out, worried sick about her friend, with a parcel of food stolen from the kitchen in case he found her.

He and Harriet struggled to make her eat it. The light had gone out of her eyes. The spark that made her Persephone Lavelle was gone. They asked her what had happened but she wouldn't say. Mary was always hopeful, always fighting. Something terrible must have happened to shatter her like this.

It took a while before she could talk at all. When she did, it was to tell Harriet that she had a place to go to – somewhere safe and warm, where she would be looked after. Harriet choked and wailed so loudly at the news it brought the faintest smile to Mary's face.

"Anyone would think I'd condemned you to a prison hulk."

"You've saved me! You said you would," Harriet wept, covering her cheeks with kisses.

"I keep my promises," Mary said faintly, before closing her eyes.

Had she promised to see Felix again? Or simply assumed she would. She turned her face to the wall.

❧

Time passed. The room, and the day, felt unreal. Eddie came and went. Harriet begged for news of her benefactor and Mary managed to murmur a name and address, nothing more. Clouds gathered over the sun. The light faded. Night came.

At first light on the next day, Eddie returned. This time he was carrying her basket, with her working clothes and the remaining rags of her peacock dress. Little Miss Mouse was there, and Mary tucked the old threadbare creature against her cheek, with its familiar sacking smell. It gave her the energy to eat a little bread and cheese, and to drink some weak beer. Also, to think.

"Who gave you this?" she asked. "Annie?"

Eddie nodded. "She wants to know if you are well. I've told her you aren't."

"Don't frighten her!"

"She deserves the truth."

"I am well, please tell her that. Well enough. I'm alive."

He stooped down so his face was close to hers, and she saw the concern written all over it. "Alive is not enough, Mary."

"Yes, it is."

❦

After his visit, Harriet disappeared for a long time, came back and hugged Mary to her.

"It's true! It's all true! I hardly dared believe it!"

"What is?" Mary asked, sitting up. Her head hurt.

Her mouth was parched. The room stank of piss, and worse. How long had she been here?

"The house on the King's Road. I went there and it's paradise! Bigger than the Harringtons', even."

Mary's cracked lips smiled. "Not everything should be measured by the Harringtons, Hattie."

"I asked for the housekeeper and she was about to turn me away – she's a large woman with eyes like a rat and I was scared – but I mentioned Mrs Lisle's name and she came. She came, Mary! To me! She looked quite severe but she spoke to me kindly. She told the housekeeper that I can stay, even when the baby's born. She reserves the right to name him but I don't care. He will live, and so will I. I will work and work for her, and earn my shillings, and be good. He will eat and grow, and I'll watch him." Tears poured down her face. She pursed her lips and faltered. "I can't thank you enough, cousin. Whatever you did…"

"It was nothing."

"Whatever it cost…"

"Don't talk about it, Hattie, please. Don't ever mention it again."

"But I must!"

"Please! I mean it."

Hattie pulled back and dried her eyes, surprised by her cousin's firmness. "Y-yes. If you say so."

"I do." Mary wanted to turn to the wall again, but she knew it would hurt Hattie. Instead she asked about her plans.

"I'm going there tomorrow," she said. "I'll share a room with the other laundress. Her mother lives nearby and has given birth to seven children. She says she'll help me…"

Harriet chattered on and Mary pretended to listen. Knowing her cousin would be safe was enough. She felt as though she were underwater, cut off from the world by its weight and darkness. Or in Hades' realm, unable to find her way home…

❧❦

That night Eddie called to collect her. Mary bade Harriet a loving, fierce goodbye and promised to try and see her soon. Eddie had to support her to a waiting cab because she could barely walk. Mary let him take her and didn't care where they went. It was of the mildest of interest that the cab didn't take them to the docks or back to the countryside, but instead to the heart of London, not far from the square where the Ballards had their imposing home.

Eddie led her up three flights of stairs to a set of rooms. This building was nothing like the tenement. Doors were solid and no ragged beggars lurked on the stairs. It smelled of beeswax and beef stew, not human waste and vomit. Instead she saw high ceilings and tall windows, velvet-covered furniture and rugs on the floor.

"Who did you fight to get this place, Eddie?" she asked, half-teasing, half out of her mind with grief and exhaustion.

"I didn't fight. A friend of yours asked me to bring you. The only friend you've got. Be kind to him."

At this Mary's nerve-endings jangled. She was suddenly awake. Her body tensed with anticipation. "He gave me this? He brought me here?"

"Shh. Sleep now. You need it. There's food on the table. Eat when you can. I'll be back tomorrow. Take care of yourself now, Mary."

But she couldn't sleep.

Had Felix sold the painting so quickly? Had he paid for these rooms with the money?

She sat on a red velvet chair overlooking the street, wrapped in a cashmere shawl she found draped over it, waiting for a sign of him. She didn't stir or stop wondering how he had rescued her until she heard the sound of footsteps on the stairs outside the next morning.

But as the door opened, her heart broke once again.

"Rupert."

Rupert Thornton tiptoed towards her, the picture of concern. He looked the perfect gentleman – well-clipped hair, fresh from the barber, shining buttons on his coat, gleaming boots and polished, silver-topped cane.

"How are you, dearest? I've been so worried about you. I would have brought you here sooner but it took an age to find you."

Dearest?

Mary shrank back into the velvet chair. "I am better, thank you."

"You look terrible! I'm sorry – I didn't mean… You look magnificent, as always, but so thin. So pale. That witch of a DuLac woman tried to ruin you."

She stared at him. "You know about her?"

"That O'Bryan girl told me when I cornered her and demanded to know where you'd gone. My poor darling. And yet you found a place for your cousin, she said, and her baby. You're a marvel. I always knew it. No man could deserve you."

Mary closed her eyes. She'd thought for a moment that he'd discovered her pact with Mrs Lisle. But of course he couldn't have done – not the details. Nobody knew except the lady herself and Mary, and neither would ever tell.

"You're exhausted, darling." Rupert went down on one knee beside her, taking her limp hand in his. "I blame myself. I avoided you. I was hurt by our last proper meeting but I know it was your shyness and goodness that spoke, that's all."

Mary struggled to think. What was their last proper meeting? Then she remembered – the party. She had begged him not to buy the painting. Ha! She hadn't wanted him to own her. And now, here they were.

"Let me look after you," he was murmuring in her ear. "You're free now. I want to give you everything you deserve."

Free? Free of the Aitkens, perhaps, but what had she come to? She knew that any lady would run from this room, right now, and seek shelter from a chaperone. But she wasn't a lady. There was no safe place, no Aunt Violet. Mary forced herself to sit up properly and look at him.

"What things?" she asked.

He grinned. "Dresses and piano lessons. Books. Conversation. Your portrait on the wall. A dozen portraits. There can never be enough." He saw the way she stared and took it as an invitation to continue. "Jewels… When I have the money for good ones. I have a little of my own for now, but much more when I turn twenty-one, which is next year."

Next *year?* Mary tried to picture a year of living like this…

"I'm not a doll, Rupert!"

"I know! You're the most stunning girl in London."

An object. A thing of beauty. To be stuck in a dolls' house. He wouldn't be able to take her out in company – not if he was keeping her like this. And she wouldn't want him to.

"And how…?" Mary paused. It was an indelicate

question. But then, she was in an indelicate situation. "How should I pay you?"

Rupert frowned. He seemed shocked that she had even asked.

"I don't want you to pay."

A long silence followed. He was being obtusely innocent.

"A girl always pays," she said eventually, looking at him with a level gaze.

He recoiled. "I don't … I just…" He gestured around the room. "I just want you to be happy."

"That's all?"

"Truly. Whatever you want to give. Perhaps … in time … I might … appeal to you. You might come to love me."

Mary looked away. She liked Rupert, she always had, despite her reservations. But love…

"I don't think…"

"*Don't* think. Let me do this. Please. You need it and so do I. Be happy, that's all I ask."

She tried to imagine happiness. "I can't."

"I know you think that, with everything so fresh. I know the way you felt about … him. But you'll change.

You'll get better, Mary. There's more to life than painting. Let me show you."

More to life than painting... Yes, and she had just begun to discover that – but with someone else. Yet, without Rupert, there would be no life at all.

Could she do it? Live in these rooms, surrounded by gifts, with the world assuming she was Rupert's mistress? And the world, one day, not being wrong? If she didn't, what was her alternative?

"I'm sorry," she said, with a tear in her eye. "I can't … I'm so tired…"

"*I'm* sorry, dearest. I'm keeping you from your sleep. I'll come back later when you're feeling better. A woman will come this afternoon to see what you need. Ask her for anything – *anything.*"

His lips lingered lightly on her fingertips as he bade her goodbye and she tried to resist the urge to pull her hand away.

When he left her, she looked around the room again with new eyes. *So this is the Underworld.*

Then, at last, she slept.

❧⸙⸙☙

There is something about sleep, a warm room and beef stew. It makes even the most dire situation seem more bearable. Mary felt like a different person by the time she finished the last of the gravy in the bowl in front of her.

A rotund lady in dark blue wool and a fresh white apron gazed down at her with a smile.

"You needed that. I promised it would be good."

"It was," Mary assured her.

"There's more where it came from. Would you like some?"

"No, not yet."

"A chicken leg, perhaps? Some pie? A cake?"

"No, no!" Mary said with a weak laugh, waving the thought away. "I couldn't."

"We must feed you up. You're a slip of a thing. The master's worried about you."

"I know," Mary admitted. *I'm worried about myself.* But as the evening sun filled the room with warm light, filtered through the trees in the square outside, it was impossible to feel as low as she had this morning. *I deserve to be on the streets*, she thought. *Instead I'm here, with a servant of my own.*

"I've made up your bed and heated some water for

a bath. You're not to stir, the master says. You need to look after yourself."

"Do you know when he'll back?" Mary asked, flushing.

"Not for a few days. His father called for him today. Some business in France. He won't be long, though."

The woman smiled at her in what was meant to be a reassuring way. But, ungratefully, it was news of Rupert's absence that pleased Mary most.

"Thank you. I'm sorry, I don't know your name," she said.

"It's Mrs Howard. I'll be here when you need me. At breakfast and dinner certainly, and other times, if necessary. The master has taken care of everything."

Mary closed her eyes. *The master.* The shame would pass, she supposed, as her hunger had.

"Thank you, Mrs Howard. I have all I need for now."

༄༅

When Eddie arrived the next morning, she was bathed and rested, and her hair hung less limply around her shoulders. She sat straight-backed on the velvet chair, like a lady receiving visitors. There were still dark circles under her eyes and her cheeks were sunken, but she was recovering.

"You could look worse," he acknowledged.

"Thank you, kind sir."

"I like your … dress."

She glanced down at the highly fashionable tight-waisted gown that was one of several fresh from Paris, ordered by Rupert *en masse* and newly delivered. It was apple-green silk taffeta, as light as a feather and as wide as anything Kitty owned. Mary wore it because it was clean.

"How's Harriet?"

"Well. Happy. Grateful. More than grateful."

Mary nodded vaguely. "She needn't be. I wish she wouldn't be. Can you tell her I'm sorry, but I can't visit her there?"

Eddie raised one eyebrow. "I've done that already. She understands. She doesn't know what happened exactly but she senses there's no love lost between you and her new mistress. I told her there was a pact. Not the details."

"The details?"

Eddie crossed his arms and looked down at her like a teacher to a little child. "You're in love with an artist.

His patron grants you a favour. He asks for you, yet you don't go to him. Instead you come back looking like you're about to die. A man can put two and two together."

Mary stared at the floor.

"He asks for me?" she said eventually.

"So they say. According to my sources."

"Who?"

"Anyone that knows him."

She let a tear trace its way down her cheek. Eddie pretended not to notice.

"He thinks you're unwell. He knows you're in disgrace after the DuLac disaster. His friend Roly Ballard must have told him about that one. I saw his picture of you, by the way. Popped into that little gallery to take a look. Annie told me where to go."

Mary continued to stare at him, wet-cheeked. She wished he hadn't told her about Felix. She would rather not have known.

"It was beautiful," he was saying. "Everyone's talking about it. Shame it disappeared."

"What?" Mary started. "It *disappeared*? What happened?"

"It went a few days ago – halfway through the exhibition. Sold to a mystery devotee and taken off the wall. Not everyone thought it was so artistically brilliant, mind you, but there's some that say it's a masterpiece and Felix Dawson's the new Michelangelo. I like it when you smile. I should mention Michelangelo more often. Michelangelo. There, you see? I'm as cultured as an ambassador, not some boxer from County Cork. I brought you this, by the way." He handed her a newspaper cutting. She took it and, seeing Felix's name, folded it to read later.

"I…" His mention of being a boxer suddenly reminded her. "I owe you ten pounds. Or Annie, anyway, for you."

Eddie shrugged and smiled. "Did she say something like that? She's always trying things on, my sister. Don't you worry. I wouldn't take that kind of money off a woman. And certainly not a woman who'd be taking it off a man. If you get my meaning."

Mary instantly flushed the colour of the red velvet chair. "What was I supposed to do, exactly? Except go where you brought me?"

He held up a placatory hand. "I had no choice in the matter. Neither did you. And you must do what you have to do. Don't let me stop you."

"I won't."

"I pity you though, Mary."

At this she leaped up from the chair, adjusting her huge hooped skirts with a swish of apple green silk. Her eyes flashed fire as she brought her face close to his.

"Don't you pity me, Eddie O'Bryan. Don't you *dare*. I've saved my cousin's child. I'm not a drudge any more and I won't die in a garret with nobody knowing my name. I've got a life, a good life, because someone wants to care for me and what's wrong with that?"

Eddie smiled and backed away a little. "All right, all right! No pity!"

But she didn't stop. "He knows how I feel. I'll always be honest with him. It's not my fault if he wants me to have … all this. He'd only feel worse if I left him, and who'd win then? There's nobody to care about my *honour*." At the mention of the word, which had been everything to her before and now was nothing, she paused to catch her breath.

Eddie stepped in. "I care, for what it's worth. Which is very little. But like I said, I agree. Stop shouting at me!" He was still smiling. "Wear his dresses. Serve him tea. Play him the piano. I'm sure you'll be very happy together."

This shut Mary up more than any argument. She pointed at the door.

"Go!"

"I'm going!"

"Don't come back."

"You know you don't mean that."

"I do."

"Say you'll miss me."

Her arm shook with the strain of pointing. "Just leave, Eddie."

He went, with a sardonic tip of his cap. He didn't try to kiss her this time, so the slap she was ready to give him never came. She was oddly disappointed. A slap on Eddie's cheek would have relieved a multitude of frustrations. She waited until the door was firmly shut behind him before breathing deeply in the welcome silence.

Yes, it was possible she might miss him a little, if he truly stayed away – which she doubted. But she had other things to think about for now. She quickly opened the folded newsprint in her hand.

Chapter Thirty-one

SUCCESSFUL EXHIBITION FOR NEW YOUNG ARTISTS

STAR PAINTING DISAPPEARS

A Correspondent writes: The latest exhibition to be held at the Berkeley Gallery, in Mayfair, has caused something of a stir in the London art world. While the retrogressive style and questionable moral stance of the members of the now-defunct Pre-Raphaelite Brotherhood has often been cause for scorn among critics and established painters alike, the paintings themselves continue to sell for considerable sums. Now, previously unknown young men of talent are joining their starry ranks, not least Mr Felix Dawson, of Chelsea, whose 'Persephone and Hades' was the undisputed triumph of this show. But no longer. In mysterious and unprecedented circumstances, the large, luminous portrait of a girl with copper hair was removed from the gallery on the second day, not to be seen again.

It is understood by this Correspondent that the painting has been bought for an undisclosed amount by a private collector. Small daguerreotypes of the original are available, revealing a large scale painting of considerable skill and beauty, against which the other, more minor efforts pale by comparison. However, the gallery owners say they are very pleased with the response to the exhibition so far, and sales of the brightly coloured, emotionally charged works continue to exceed initial expectations...

She should be celebrating with him.

On the mezzanine above the studio, where she never dared go, with paint on her skin and champagne in a glass beside her.

Or touring the streets in a landau with Kitty, as Persephone. But Kitty had not been in touch and nor had Roly. It was only to be expected, perhaps, after what she had done to their friend.

Well, she would have to make another life. That's all there was to it. Persephone Lavelle was the 'girl with the copper hair'. She was the talk of London and she didn't need Kitty and her brother, or Felix, to be successful. She would tie up her broken heart in ribbon and put it at the bottom of her trunk, never to be unwrapped. She had survived the worst that could happen to her.

※

When Rupert came back from France, he was delighted to see her in satin and pearls, trying to pick out a tune on the piano.

"You look your old self at last!" he beamed, setting down the boxes of presents he'd bought for her.

"Oh no," she said. "I am someone entirely new."

"Well, I like her quite as much as the old one, if not better."

She let him kiss her hand. Even the new Persephone was not ready for anything more intimate and he sensed that.

"I'll wait," he said, over a quiet dinner for two. "Until you're ready. Until I can make you love me the way I'm in love with you."

Did he love her? Mary wondered. Or just love to look at her? She wasn't sure. But he was kind and interesting to talk to, and she had learned to appreciate that very much in a man – even if his sparkling good taste and his manner still occasionally infuriated her.

One thing she quickly discovered: despite his devotion, Rupert was not the mysterious purchaser of the painting. In fact, he was furious not to have procured it.

"Outbid!" he said, affronted, when she asked. "And I made a fine offer and upped it several times. But he would not be bested, whoever he was."

Mary sensed that 'he' was a she. *She* would not be bested. And she could guess which house the picture was in, if it still existed. And why it would never be seen.

The thought was like a knife in her stomach every time. The painting was the only witness to what she and Felix had become together. And it was so beautiful. Mrs Lisle would never have been able to live with the thought of it being on display.

"But there will be other paintings of you," Rupert said, cheerful again.

Mary smiled and nodded and gave him no hint at all of how she was feeling. He did not need to know.

As the trees turned to gold then brown in the square outside the window, she learned what to share and what not to share with him. She read to him when he came to visit and took lessons with the piano teachers he found for her. She visited Cremorne Gardens in fine dresses and let it be known among the artistic set that she was happy to sit for portraits. And they queued up to paint her, just as Felix had said they would.

She sat for Millais, who did several drawings of her, and for William Hunt and Julia Cameron, Sara Prinsep's sister, who took photographs of her with a huge camera, like a tent.

She looked sad in the photographs, whereas all the painters made her look inspired, the way she had in

Persephone and Hades. Mary liked the camera, because it told the truth.

Millais' pictures of her did not appeal the way she had expected. She found them syrupy – sweet-faced, innocent and smiling – which was not how she felt at all. Yet here she was, in his very studio, following *Ophelia*. That thought at least made her shiver. And better than that, to her great surprise, she found a new friend in his wife.

In Mary, Effie Millais saw an echo of her old self. They bonded over art. She recognized Mary's ambition, too. She herself loved high society and talked about how she longed to be received by the queen.

"We are both exiles, in a way. You because of … Rupert. And me because of my first marriage. Though I do think the queen might reconsider."

It amused Mary that Effie – who had been an artist's model and led such a fascinating life – should mind so much about the mores of society. Queen Victoria knew about her but refused to meet her because her first marriage had been annulled. Effie talked fondly, instead, of Italy, which she had visited with her first husband, Ruskin.

"In Venice I was received by *everyone*. Oh, the dukes and duchesses I befriended! The times we had. How I long to go back. You would love it, Persephone. The water, the palaces, the *people*. They're so cultured and so fascinating. The art. Why, you could see a different Titian every day. I would go with my dearest John, but of course, the children…"

Effie cradled her newest baby to her. The boy's red hair reminded Mary of Harriet's child, whom she had met at last. A girl, not a boy, as Harriet had imagined. The name she had been given by Mrs Lisle was Aileana, a Scottish name. Luckily Harriet loved it and her red-headed baby girl was her pride and joy. Mary was the fondest godmother and spoiled the baby every way she could.

❦

Red-gold autumn gave way to the first chill of winter. As usual now, Mary arranged to meet Harriet in Hyde Park on her cousin's day off. Mary was walking home towards Mayfair, thinking of the gurgle of her pretty niece and how well she looked in the baby bonnet she had embroidered for her, when her eye was caught by a flash of kingfisher blue in the distance. She looked towards it, heart pounding. She only knew one man who wore that colour. It couldn't be... It must be... It was.

He was helping a pretty girl out of a carriage. She had thick, loose hair – blonde, not red – and a striking face with a straight nose and large eyes. The new stunner – approved, presumably, by Mrs Lisle. Mary felt the hot bloom of a flush on her neck. She should turn away but she couldn't bear to. She hadn't seen him for four months. How was he? And who was this girl he had chosen to replace her?

Felix focused on making sure the girl kept her footing. He seemed well. He looked as Byronic as ever, with dark curls that were even longer than before, and an extravagant blue velvet coat. The girl was smiling. Giggling, even, Mary thought. She reached the ground with a neat step, glanced up and put a hand to her mouth. She had seen Mary. Before Mary could move, she was pointing and pulling at Felix's arm. She murmured something to him from behind her hand. He looked across and for the briefest instant he lit up with hope and their old connection. But a dark shadow of betrayal quickly fell across his face. His tortured look exhibited all the pain Mary felt. The stunner watched him awkwardly, ignored.

Mary longed to come forwards and explain herself but she couldn't. Certainly not here, with a dozen people watching. Any one of them could report her to Mrs Lisle. She dared not even curtsey from a distance.

Aileana. Aileana. This was all for her.

Mary turned her face and walked quickly in the opposite direction, knowing he would assume she was running to Rupert. He must have heard the rumours by now.

I need to disappear, she thought. *I don't have the strength to do this again.*

Mary arrived home in a fluster and asked Mrs Hudson to send word to Rupert that she couldn't see him today. She paced up and down, rethinking her plans. She had to get out of the city, at least for a while. *Only artistic circles will receive me and I can't spend my life avoiding Felix Dawson. I don't know who would go mad first: him or me.*

But where to go? Where could she persuade Rupert to take her?

It was only as daylight fell that she spotted a letter on the table. It was Kitty's writing. Unfolding it, she saw that the paper was crammed with news in her old friend's neat hand. It took three reads through on the red velvet chair by the window to understand it all.

She wasn't avoiding me! She hasn't changed!

Kitty wrote in detail about the trip she had taken with her parents to St Petersburg, to meet the man they wanted her to marry. But another place name leaped out of the pages at Mary: Venice. This was where Kitty was headed next.

How I long for you to join me there! Oh, the larks we could have! Think how much more enjoyable your company would be than that of dear old Aunt Violet, or Mama, who gets seasick and won't even ride in a gondola! If only you weren't so busy in London…

Kitty had heard the news of her artistic success. Mary noticed that she was much too polite to mention Felix or Rupert in the letter. Above all, her constant friendship sang from every line. And she was soon to be married, it seemed. Mary longed to know more.

The idea came quickly and would not leave. By nightfall, she was certain. She sat at her dressing table, where Kitty's letter lay in front of her, and dreamed by candlelight as she ran a brush a hundred times through her hair. She would go and see Titian's paintings in their true surroundings and spend time with her friend again. She would ride on a gondola and mix with duchesses, just as Effie Millais had. It would mean abandoning Harriet and Aileana, and Annie and Eddie, and poor Rupert. But this was not the first time she had abandoned people who were kind to her. Such are the sacrifices you make for love.

Mary put her hairbrush on the table and stared at herself in the mirror. The girl who stared back was ready to take what life could give her, and life was still like salt spray on her skin. It glimmered in her eyes.

Right. It is time. She tried not to think of Felix watching and smiling to himself as he tried to capture her. Instead she took up her pen and started to compose her reply.

Acknowledgements

This story was very much a work of collaboration – my favourite kind. First of all, thanks to Jenny at ANA, for making the introductions. Then to all the team at Stripes. You've been fabulous! To Paul for his work on the standout cover, and Lauren and Charlie for telling people about it, and everyone behind the scenes. Above all to Katie Jennings, who had the original idea for Mary/Persephone, for being a brilliant editor through some interesting times.

To Alex, Emily, Sophie, Freddie and Tom. For all the times you got with your lives while I was lost in Victorian London. To the Sisterhood, the Manatees and all my writing friends, the Moore Street Masterminds, the team at Authors Aloud and everyone who's made writing possible over the last year. To the teams at the Tate and the V&A, for everything you do to bring art and design to the people. And to anyone who's shared info online about fashions and daily life details of England in the 1850s. I probably came across your work at some stage, so thank you.

Art has been an essential part of my life since I was a teen. Making it, appreciating it, learning about it, being inspired by it. I was so grateful to get this chance to write about it.

Above all, I hope it inspires readers to get out their pencils or watercolours, to have a go at something new, to visit a gallery or even just to look up at the sky and appreciate its depth of blue. Art is a chance to see the world through someone else's eyes, and that is a great gift. Of course, so is a book…

Places to go and see the Pre-Raphaelites and their world:
Birmingham Museum and Art Gallery
Tate Britain, London (which is where you'll find Millais' painting of Ophelia)
Manchester Art Gallery
The Walker Art Gallery, Liverpool
Leighton House Museum, London
The Victoria and Albert Museum, London
Kelmscott Manor, Kelmscott, Gloucestershire
Red House, London
Buscot Park, Faringdon, Oxfordshire
The Oxford Union, Oxford

Sophia Bennett

Sophia Bennett always wanted to be a writer. Her first book, *Threads*, was published in 2009 and sold around the world. Since then she has written several acclaimed books for teens, including *The Look* and *Love Song*. Her favourite subjects are art, music, fashion, travel and adventure, all of which make it into her stories. Sophia lives with her family in London and escapes from them to write in a shed at the bottom of her garden. When she isn't there, you can generally find her in a gallery somewhere, soaking up the art. You can also find her at her website: sophiabennett.com.

Look out for the sequel, coming soon...

Secrets. Temptation. Treachery.

Hoping to get over her first love, Mary follows her friend Kitty to Venice. There she meets a charismatic, masked young man who seems willing to offer her the world. But when she discovers his true identity, Mary finds herself faced with a terrible dilemma...